PATRIMONY

Jane Thynne is a media journalist and the former media correspondent of the *Daily Telegraph*. She is a frequent guest on Radio 4's *Start the Week* and *The News Quiz* and has made many TV appearances as a newspaper reviewer and commentator on BBC Breakfast News. She is married to the novelist Philip Kerr, with two young children. She is at work on a second novel.

D1102221

'Thynne writes confidently in a number of voices and historical periods.' *Daily Telegraph*

'Excellent researched and movingly told. Thynne has the ability to paint a landscape and explore a character, and her skills are well deployed in the poignant descriptions of a countryside and men destroyed by war. Elsa, the modern heroine, speaks from the heart when she says that to make a romantic and rosy picture of such a past is to betray the dead who were forced to their deaths in a war that was neither rosy nor romantic. Thynne has been true to her heroine's standards. She has not written a "dreadful sepia-tinted love story", but a thoughtful and powerful account of a war which still casts a shadow today.' Philippa Gregory, *Independent*

'A haunting paradox explored with grace and intelligence.' Elizabeth Buchan, *The Times*

'Jane Thynne's first novel captures beautifully the atmosphere of the period's literary gatherings, steamy salons and decadent house parties. Even more impressive is her evocation of the horrors of that war, the realities of the slaughter and the wilful unawareness of those left back home.' *Good Housekeeping*

'An enjoyable literary mystery which shifts between London in both the present day and in the years leading to the First World War.' *Sunday Times*

'Past and present are elegantly interwoven, period detail is impressive as is the ambition of the theme.' *Harpers & Queen*

PATRIMONY

a novel

JANE THYNNE

FOURTH ESTATE • *London*

This paperback edition first published in 1998

First published in Great Britain in 1997 by
Fourth Estate Limited
6 Salem Road
London W2 4BU

1 3 5 7 9 10 8 6 4 2

A catalogue record for this book is available from
the British Library.

ISBN 1-85702-764-7

Typeset by Avon Dataset Ltd, Bidford on Avon,
B50 4JH
Printed in Great Britain by Clays Ltd, St. Ives plc,
Bungay, Suffolk.

For Philip

Chapter One

'FIRST RAT DESERTS the sinking ship,' said Simon Pardoe bitterly, emerging from his office with an opened letter in his hand.

Elsa Meyers felt the usual rush of panic which she had come to associate with the arrival of the morning mail.

'What is it now?'

'Bloody Alan Evans. Feels he is "unable to continue in the post of researcher". Gives notice henceforth. Don't know why he's bothering with the legalistic language. We never gave him a contract, thank God. Otherwise we'd probably be paying out three months' money. Well, that's one mouth less to feed, I suppose.'

Elsa grimaced and tucked her straight hair behind her ear, in the way she did when she could think of nothing to say. Simon stalked over to the kettle and helped himself to a cup of instant coffee, before turning to face her. 'The annoying thing is, you know, he really was rather good. I was frankly quite surprised when he agreed to do the job for the money we were offering.'

Both looked over to the empty desk which had been occupied by Alan Evans, the huge American graduate student they had hired to work for their company, Durban Films. His silent shape, bowed over a pile of books, had become quite a fixture over the last few months. He certainly gave no indication that he was unhappy. With some people, it was just so hard to tell what was going on in their minds.

'Where's he gone?'

'Doesn't say. But it can't have been the money that made him go, because he's still owed about a hundred quid if you remember, and there's no mention of that in the letter. Unless he's made off with the company silver, that is.'

Elsa and Simon gave a quick, unconscious glance round the premises. It was not a sight to warm the heart of any petty thief. It started all right. Durban Films had a good

1

location, a top-floor office right in the middle of Bloomsbury in Little Russell Street, a stone's throw from the British Museum. The office itself had a smart glass door with a jaunty little logo painted on it, and as you came through you saw the receptionist's pristine desk, enhanced by her own specially purchased office accessories, sharpened pencils, smart black Rolodex and flowers. After that it went downhill rapidly. The plush carpet ran out, untidily, just beyond the reception area, to be replaced by wormy cord matting. Aged, plastic ribbons of venetian blind sagged at the window, drooping with decades of dust. The walls were covered in a dingy, nicotined wallpaper and their only valuables, a virtually obsolete fax machine and photocopier, huddled in one corner almost invisible beneath an excrescence of yellowing newspapers. Elsa had fondly imagined that being so close to the British Museum would be intellectually in-spiring, but any radiating atmosphere of ancient books and priceless treasures was masked by the penetrating smell of chips floating up from the Italian restaurant two floors below.

She sighed. 'Well he is American. Maybe he got homesick.'

'Maybe he got a call from the Inland Revenue,' said Simon, taking a dour slurp of his coffee. 'Maybe he's being held in a cell at this moment while they calculate just how much National Insurance we haven't paid on him.'

It was only ten past ten but suddenly Elsa felt the last vestiges of her early morning well-being vanish like the dew. She had left home that day burdened with nothing more than a bag of books and a rather heavy bank loan. Indeed she felt almost jaunty as she walked down Tottenham Court Road and crossed left into Bedford Square, feeling the weak prickle of sunshine on her skin. Though the London sky was its usual cardboard grey, there was an optimistic note in the air and the wind, like a true believer in pathetic fallacy, was pushing friskily through the delicate, lime green bud leaves poking out of the fingers of the chestnut trees. But as soon as she clambered the stairs to the offices of Durban Films, the familiar cocktail of anxiety and unease descended.

The first thing Elsa registered, with a *frisson* of alarm, was that the desk belonging to Michelle, the receptionist, had acquired another arrangement of astronomically expensive cut flowers. That day it was purple and white mottled freesias already unfurling their pungent, invisible scent around the room. Michelle herself was nowhere to be seen.

Fortunately there had been no sign of Simon either. Draping her coat over the hat stand, Elsa had crossed to the tiny kitchenette and switched on the kettle for a cup of coffee, emptying the brackish water out of the least filthy cup in the sink. She rejected the milk floating lumpily in a clear plastic carton without a top, and stood there, drinking her coffee black and bitter, thinking of all the other things to do on a day so sunny and ripe with possibilities. It was only when the fax machine started to stutter and a phone began ringing that Simon had emerged from his office, brandishing the letter, complaining about rats.

'Well it looks like he's gone for good so unless you've got any bright ideas for a replacement,' continued Simon accusingly, as though the whole thing was Elsa's fault, 'it's just you and me from here on.'

He did not sound delighted by the prospect. To be fair, the last thing he had expected when he purchased Durban Films seven months ago was that he was acquiring a twenty-nine-year-old research assistant with it. Simon had bought the company from Alex Durban, the film producer, who was off to Hollywood with a fifty-two-part spaceship series for cable TV. Alex had forgotten to mention until after they signed all the paperwork that he had promised a job to Elsa, developing an idea for a film about the first world war. But it was no problem, he assured Simon casually. When she turned up for work the following Monday Simon should just tell her to get lost. He owed her nothing. Just for God's sake would Simon not pass on his address in LA.

Simon really had intended to take this advice. He'd known enough starry-eyed girls in film production to know he didn't need some old flame of Alex's hanging like a millstone on his balance sheet. Some clueless *ingénue* incapable of earning her keep. Unfortunately, when he turned up to his new company the following week, this girl was already there, sitting on her desk with her long skinny legs kicking carelessly and her briefcase unpacked, looking like she owned the place.

At the sight of her, brimming with enthusiasm for the new job and for Durban Films, Simon froze. Like most Englishmen he abhorred confrontation. What if she argued about being sacked on her first day? What if she demanded compensation? Worse, what if she cried? So he gave her his coldest greeting possible, a glacially half-raised hand, and put off the evil hour.

Despite Simon's stony demeanour, Elsa tried hard at Durban Films. She had every reason to. Five years ago she'd had a promising television career. She'd been told she would go far. But somehow her dreams of directing cutting-edge documentaries turned into an overlong stint on a dismal daytime chat show. It was a hopeless cul-de-sac and the only consolation was a fellow producer, an erratic, tangle-haired woman called Alison Joliffe, who hated the whole thing even more than Elsa. Alison stalked the studio brandishing a clipboard like a loaded gun. Her chief responsibility was frightening the disparate elements of the show – guests, host, audience and production staff – into the simultaneous compliance needed for live transmission. This was easy for Alison because she had equal contempt for them all. But together she and Elsa began to lay plans to escape and set up their own company in partnership. They had been pleasant times, sitting together in the canteen, looking out on the jagged concrete horizon of west London and talking for hours about production budgets, creative adventure and artistic freedom. Until suddenly, without warning, the station gave Alison her own show to host. It was a dazzling opportunity. Double the salary and significant exposure presenting an afternoon chat series called *Good Relations*. It would have been criminal to turn it down. So Elsa was left to resign alone and settle for this new job, where she floundered along unwanted, beside a man who treated her with as much enthusiasm as a case of flu.

Elsa hunched her narrow shoulders and heard in her head her father's flat Germanic voice: 'The trouble with you is, you want to be liked. Forget it. No one ever got anywhere wanting to be liked.' Well thank God he was hundreds of miles away now, dissecting other people's problems. And in many ways, she consoled herself, Simon Pardoe had turned out to be the ideal partner. He was calm where she was excitable, downbeat where she was up, with a mind as meticulous as one of his own filing cabinets and just as hard to prise open. He would stash away their mail – that dismal collection of disappointments and threats which trickled through the door each day – and retrieve papers when necessary like a dog unearthing its bones. He worked ridiculous hours and did not believe in sparing his criticism. In a strange way they complemented each other. Unfortunately, Simon did not seem to appreciate this yin and yang factor in their relationship. Somehow, she doubted that he would consider her the ideal partner in any way at all.

Perhaps it was asking too much that he should display a positive outlook on life. As they spent their days worrying about obtaining script development funds and making costly, fruitless long-distance phone calls to Los Angeles, one by one all the projects left to Simon by Alex Durban fell through. It was then that Elsa suggested resurrecting her original brief, to adapt the true story of a group of artists and writers thrown together in the trenches during a few desperate days in the battle of third Ypres. After the war the group had met up again to mark the valiant death of a friend, Valentine Siddons, the only one to die at Passchendaele. Some relationships survived, others perished under the weight of what they had all been through.

It would be a wonderful film, Elsa argued. There were locations in London and Oxfordshire, and Essex could double as Flanders. It would be another of those small-scale British films with exquisite attention to period detail which seemed to take Hollywood by storm. Unfortunately, 'Passchendaele the Movie' had evoked about as much enthusiasm on the other side of the Atlantic as Britain's original declaration of war.

There had been some encouraging signs. Daniel Eckstein, a small, hyperactive producer from Pluto Films, a young subsidiary of one of Hollywood's biggest studios, had taken them out to lunch to discuss the project and said, with a show of interest that enthralled Elsa, that he loved it. He said the first world war was 'both resonant and contemporary'. The treatment had 'legs'. It would have to fight it out for funds with a TV mini-series about Nazi Germany, but he felt confident that if he took their idea back to Hollywood, there could be some talk about co-production.

That, anyway, was what he had said. Now Eckstein could reliably be found in a meeting when telephoned. Durban Films teetered on the brink of bankruptcy like an alcoholic on a cliff edge. Each bank statement read like the latest instalment in a horror story. Elsa felt faint every time she paid Michelle her breathtakingly large weekly salary. The money situation was not just bad, it was taboo. Even Simon's habitual calm had become a kind of tense, surly brooding. His lean frame seemed even thinner as he skulked around monosyllabically, dangerous as a wounded wild animal.

The fact that Simon had actually mentioned money for the first time in ages, seemed to make things worse.

'Things are really going badly, aren't they?' ventured Elsa. 'Should we sack Michelle too?'

She wondered how he would react to this. Michelle, a pretty south London blonde with extravagant habits picked up from her last job in an American bank, was vastly over-qualified for the desultory tasks Elsa and Simon had in mind. Though she acknowledged this by the perfunctory way in which she answered the telephone, and the bored, precision-tidying of her desk, Michelle's contempt for their small set-up was tempered by her fondness for Simon. Her steely glare softened in his direction. She preferred coffee cups to him as though suggesting sexual favours. For all Elsa knew, she was. There was no accounting for taste.

Simon dismissed the idea of sacking Michelle with a low grunt. 'Well,' Elsa hurried on brightly, 'at least we don't have to replace Alan. I've finished fixing most of the locations now, so I can take over the research before we start the next draft of the script.'

Michelle came up the stairs, rustling importantly, set a couple of paper bags on her desk and proceeded to unwrap some tissue-covered crockery. There were cups, saucers and plates painted with childish green leaves and garish fruit. As Simon and Elsa looked on wordlessly, she drew four glisten-ing, sugar-crusted cakes from the bags and plonked them on the plates.

'Just the thing to cheer us all up,' she said, offering them up. 'I got four of everything, for you two, Alan and me.'

'Bit of a superfluity, actually,' muttered Simon darkly, disappearing back into his office with an almond croissant.

It really wasn't constructive the way Simon was always looking on the bad side, thought Elsa, who had read a book on business dynamics and attempted herself to project a 'can do' attitude. She told Michelle about Alan Evans' defection but Michelle, who had never warmed to the hulking American with his thick glasses and worn sports jacket, was still bridling at the idea that her crockery was an unnecessary use of company funds.

'I think it's money well spent, if it cheers people up,' she complained defiantly.

Elsa sighed. As no one appeared even remotely cheered up, she went over to her desk to begin to work where Alan Evans had left off.

She decided to start with Valentine Siddons, whose death marked the focal point for the film's storyline. Siddons, a minor figure in the extraordinary flowering of poets produced by the first world war, died on the western front in 1917, heroically trying to rescue another, badly wounded officer. His bravery won him a posthumous VC. Barely out of public school when the war began, he was one of the thousands of youthful idealists who joined up almost as soon as they could, swept up in a national fever of patriotic excitement. Unlike many of the other war poets, he had been taken up and fêted in artistic circles even before his death. But the distance between his aristocratic admirers and his own middle-class origins only emphasised the subtle sense of isolation which underlay his single, slender collection, *Stanzas from Battle and Beyond.*

At least Valentine Siddons was topical, thought Elsa, her spirits lifting a little. Interest in his poetry was fast gathering pace. The centenary of his birth meant that according to the fickle dictates of literary fashion he was coming back into vogue. To mark the occasion, some of his best work had been reissued in *Between the Lines*, an anthology which also contained the work of his more famous contemporaries, Owen, Brooke, Blunden and Sassoon. Siddons' poems, though there weren't many of them, were celebrated for their realism, compassion and bleak disillusion, a stark contrast to Brooke's more ecstatically received war sonnets, even though some were written contemporaneously. *Between the Lines* also contained some reproductions of watercolour landscapes which Siddons, a talented amateur painter, had sent home from the front. Ironically, they revealed a lyricism and gentleness that was mostly absent from his poetry.

Rupert Brooke died of a mosquito bite and Wilfred Owen was pointlessly cut down just days before the Armistice, but the heroism of Siddons' death had become an integral part of the mythology of his life. His last, fatal dash into the darkness of No Man's Land had been foolhardy, but glorious. His body was recovered days later, so shattered with shrapnel it was almost unrecognisable, but for the identity disc which every soldier carried for just such an eventuality. It was hard to read his work without remembering his death, perhaps because so many of the poems seemed to prefigure it in their preoccupation with the Flanders mud and floods, which enveloped all and obliterated all.

Siddons of course was far from obliterated in death. Indeed to coincide with the new anthology, a biography was also being published. The biography was already attracting the interest of film makers, colour supplement editors and TV shows because it was written by the poet's own grandson, Dr Oliver Eastway. Eastway, now of Christ's College Oxford, was the son of Siddons' daughter, the daughter the poet never saw. In one of the manifold small sadnesses of the Great War, the baby was born to the young Emily Siddons just months after she received the telegram informing her that she had become a widow. Eastway's work, *Valentine Siddons: A Life*, was due out that autumn and by sheer good luck, or more likely dogged persistence on Alan Evans' part, the author had agreed to act as an unpaid consultant on the film.

As well as the poems and the proof copy of Eastway's biography, Alan Evans had been supplementing his research into the poet's life with the help of his notebooks. The Siddons notebooks, which he had kept intermittently and illicitly at the front, were not well known but students of his poetry would occasionally make time for them. The last little black leather book had been discovered, sodden but intact, in the inside pocket of his jacket after the poet's death. Dating from 1913 when Siddons was still an undergraduate at Oxford, the notebooks provided an invaluable insight into the illusions and the horrors of a first world war officer. There the journey from youthful enthusiasm to weary experience was telescoped into a few brief years. At times there were glimpses of a cynicism, a readiness to carp and cavil, which almost belied Siddons' potential for heroism. But all that was redeemed by the manner of his death.

Idly, Elsa flipped open the Eastway biography quoting from the early part of the notebooks, written before he sustained the shell shock that was to keep him out of the fighting for many months in the middle of the war.

JOURNAL. JUNE 1915
This morning, before we came up into line again, I took a short walk round the village where our billets were, thinking I might snatch a moment sketching. The sound of the guns beyond, booming like lions, always seems to give everything an added sharpness. The cloud was lying in gauzy stripes across an azure sky, the plane trees in the square were peeling in leprous patches and the larks were shrilling over the fields as they always do, but it was as though I was seeing them for the first time. Standing in an abandoned garden where peonies and pinks were opening up to the sun, I thought of Gray's 'flower that's born to blush unseen'. But having to rack my brains for the rest of the quote just reminded me again of the total lack of books out here and the moment was ruined.

Despite the fact that they're a few miles away from a living hell, the people in this village seem prepared to extract the maximum profit from their situation. Most of them are selling eggs and coffee and beer and those whose houses have not been blown to smithereens collect a generous billeting allowance. There's not an iota of love lost between the locals and the troops, but fortunately the people at our farm have been quite civilised. They barely raised a murmur when they were obliged to vacate their front room for our mess and crowd into the kitchen at the back.

The farmer's wife, who seems a decent woman, even proffered a large jug of frothing milk as we went off.

Most of the houses on the north side of the village are blasted to rubble. Even the church is only half there. The squat tower and front are still standing, like a theatrical set, but the back is all blown away and its innards quite exposed. When it was shelled the priest here scurried in and collected up everything, all the hangings and the statues of the Virgin and even the font, which, like a good papist, he buried in the churchyard in case it was put to any sacrilegious use. God knows why. Perhaps he was worried some soldier would try to use it for a basin. As if the squalor of this war would ever wash off.

It's just possible, I suppose, that the priest might have been trying to prevent troops taking souvenirs, as the most extra-ordinary things are taken. One lad was showing off a silver photograph frame, complete with a picture of a lovely, dark-eyed girl smiling out. But of course it wasn't his girl and the woman in the picture might have been dead for all he knew. It was dreadfully pathetic to see this boy, who God knows probably will not see his own sweetheart again, parading this imaginary girl around. I thought again of the picture in my own breast pocket and couldn't make him put the photograph back.

Late morning we moved on up the line to the reserve and I am now sitting in a damp, vile, miserable little dugout as I write this, with a candle spluttering on the shell box by my elbow, the gas blanket blowing in the breeze, and the odd shell and distant flare to remind us what delights the next few dismal days hold.

The extract ended there but Elsa knew just what the next few days held for Siddons and his men. In July a German mustard gas attack brought shells marked with yellow crosses raining down on the men at Ypres. The gas induced vomiting, red and blistered skin, and finally blindness. There were fourteen thousand casualties in just three weeks. That time at least, Valentine Siddons had escaped unharmed.

It occurred to Elsa that Alan Evans had been using her own, out-of-print copy of the complete Siddons notebooks. It was an old, brown-backed book with flaking corners and its pages slightly foxed. She scoured the top and drawers of the desk.

'Simon, you haven't seen my copy of Siddons' notebooks?'

Simon came to the door of his office and grimaced. 'Only in the possession of laughing boy.'

Considering he often used this sobriquet within the hearing of Alan Evans, Elsa wasn't that surprised the taciturn researcher had left them.

'I've got a horrible feeling he's walked off with it.'

Simon ran his fingers through his hair until it stood up like a stiff little halo round his head. He gave her a look of infinite weariness.

'Shall we sue?'

'There's no need to be difficult. I need it. If he's got it, I'm going to get it back. What's his phone number?'

Michelle cut in, witheringly. 'He wasn't even on the phone.' Then snapping open her Rolodex she continued: 'I've kept his address though. Flat 4, Lansdown Mansions, Bayswater, London W2.'

CHAPTER TWO

As ADDRESSES GO, Lansdown Mansions read better than it looked. Perhaps the tall, redbrick block, tucked one street behind the heaving, Middle Eastern bustle of Queensway, had once rejoiced in its grandiose title. But now it seemed to shrink back from the road, its face hidden under a veil of dilapidation. Decades of perching pigeons had left chalky streaks beneath the broken, central balcony, almost obscuring a small brick shield which read BUILT 1902. Trails of ivy wept from neglected windowboxes. A rusty pushchair was suspended bizarrely on the flaking railings, secured by a bicycle chain. Even to Elsa, who would have moved to virtually anywhere in Bayswater from her cramped basement with its damning Shepherd's Bush post code, this was hardly a desirable residence. As she stood before it, two corpulent Arabs in grey suits shouldered past her and went up the steps. Elsa, uncertain of the etiquette of confronting a colleague on his home territory and accusing him of book theft, hesitated for a few seconds before following the Arabs in.

Inside the dingy stone hall she found Flat 4, up one unlit flight of stairs. It had a distinctly abandoned feel about it. There was no answer to Elsa's knocking and when she pressed her ear to the letterbox, she could detect no sounds within. Peering through, she saw that the room was bathed in sunshine, but the air seemed to hang stagnant, its microscopic motes twirling gently in the light, undisturbed by occupancy. Alan Evans was clearly out.

She was considering scrawling a note and pushing it through, demanding the return of the book. But though she was half relieved that he was out, she felt too impatient to wait for the return of her property. Backing down the hallway, she found a placard promising 'Service' nailed to a closed door, and knocked.

A small hatch in the door slid upwards and a scaly face poked tortoise-like towards her.

Its owner was an old man with an Einstein haircut and beady wandering eyes.

'He's out,' the man said shortly.

'You mean Mr Evans?'

'The caretaker. So if you've got any complaints you'll have to wait until tomorrow.'

'I haven't got a complaint. I need to get hold of Mr Evans in Flat 4. It's urgent.'

'Can't do anything about that,' said the man with satisfaction. 'Wait till tomorrow. Or Monday.'

Though she had been feeling nervous, Elsa now sensed her impatience rising, the way it did when speaking to obstructive receptionists or the menders of domestic appliances. Very slowly she enunciated:

'Do you know where Mr Evans is?'

'He's gone. Without paying his service charge too. Owes us fifty quid for the year and he vanishes.'

'Do you know where he's gone to?'

'Vanished, as I said. Owing fifty quid besides.'

The old man was evidently enjoying himself. Anticipating a prolonged opportunity to thwart Elsa's wishes, he emerged from his grubby cabin and gazed up the stairs distrustfully. 'Might have to enter the flat and reclaim goods to the value of,' he ruminated.

'Does that mean you could get me in?'

'Couldn't do that. It's against the rules. You'll have to wait for the caretaker. He'll be back on Monday.'

'But you have got a key?'

'Oh yes. I've got the keys, all right. But I can't let you in. Not my job.'

Suddenly something about the exquisitely irritating pensioner reminded Elsa of an airport official in Nigeria, who had repeatedly told her that her bags were lost, despite the fact that they were plainly visible, behind his enormous, uniformed bulk. Elsa's energetic hopping and pointing had no effect until an English ex-pat had come over to help and said: 'Chap wants his bride, I'm afraid.' A handful of crumpled notes had instantly done the trick, and with a toothy grin, the loathsome official had helped her load her bags on to a trolley.

It occurred to Elsa that she had brought with her an envelope containing the money Alan Evans was owed, just in case the meeting became uncongenial.

'How much did you say he owed? Fifty, was it?' She took five tens from the envelope and held them folded in her hand. 'If you can just let me into the flat, to collect some of my possessions . . .'

With surprising speed the old man's greasy fingers closed over her notes and transferred them to a pocket in his cardigan. 'I suppose that would be all right,' he said gruffly, as he unhooked the key, climbed up the stairs, and opened the door.

Once inside the flat there was no problem confirming that Alan Evans was gone. The place could be surveyed entirely at one glance. Even an estate agent would have been forced to call it compact. It was really no more than a bedsitter and bathroom, with a little cupboardy kitchen at one end, and an opened sofa bed facing the back window. The window itself looked out on to a weed-infested yard, where a few boys were scuffing around with a dog.

The place looked lived in, but as her friend Alison might have said, By what? It had the feral, glandular odour of male habitation and was spread with a bachelor jumble of pull-overs, discarded beer cans and magazines. A rickety card table at the window bore some papers and books. The bed, with rumpled grimy sheet and blanket, seemed to have been recently slept in. Yet as was often the case with men, it was hard to tell from the state of the flat whether Evans had departed for a trek in the Himalayas, or simply popped out to the shops.

Elsa began to explore with the forensic ease of one quite used to snooping amongst other people's belongings. She had grown up as one of five children, cooped together in too few rooms, forced to preserve their privacy and secret spots with unusual ingenuity. The family house, a teetering north London terrace, squashed narrowly between its more substantial neighbours, was all her father could afford on an NHS surgeon's salary with a non-working wife. But the tight squeeze at number 7 Kempton Street had cramped the teenage Elsa's style. She loved her siblings, but privately wondered why her parents, constrained neither by religion or ideology, had not confined themselves to the more modern-sized families of their friends. When asked, Elsa's mother would say dreamily: 'Your father always wanted a big family' – a mystifying notion when you encountered the paterfamilias, prone to prolonged sulks and bursts of irritable rage.

Alan Evans' possessions gave little away. One of the few interesting items was a walnut photograph frame on the bedside table. The girl in the picture looked like she had stepped out of a Californian country club. She was lean as a greyhound, with skin as smooth and sheeny as a Ferrari Testarossa. She had glistening white teeth and a crown of glossy chestnut hair. Her long brown body was sheathed in a brief tennis outfit and she leaned forward on her racquet with a devastating, all-American confidence. So he's not gay after all, thought Elsa. It was Michelle who had diagnosed the UCLA graduate's sexual orientation from his simple failure to speak except when addressed.

Having seen no sign of her book on the table, she finished her patrol at the bookcase, where she bent over, examining spines. Harold Bloom, Richard Ellmann, Frank Kermode. Alan Evans' thesis had been on 'The influence of the psycho-biographical school of criticism on the study of early twentieth-century English literature'. She remembered this because before they employed him she had read it out to Simon from his CV, remarking that it was an interesting, if rather diffuse approach. Simon, who had done a history of art degree, was less impressed.

'Some people are fascinated by all that stuff, aren't they? Was Keats sexually abused as a child? Was Shakespeare a cross-dresser? Did John Donne hate his mum? Who cares? What's it got to do with the literature?'

He paused and smiled. 'That rhymes actually, doesn't it? There once was a poet called Donne, Who decided he hated his mum. If only his father Had hated her rather, Then John Donne would not have begun.'

'Terrible ending,' Elsa had said. 'And I totally disagree with you about his thesis. If you want to understand a writer better, it stands to reason you should understand the life.'

Simon had peered at her sardonically over the rim of his glasses.

'Ah, but if knowledge of the life can affect the appreciation of the work, does it affect the value of the work itself? Is a text's integrity dependent on the conditions under which it was written? If Shakespeare was homosexual, do his hetero-sexual love poems count? Does it matter whether when Coleridge wrote "Kubla Khan" he was under the influence of drugs, or just pretending to be?'

This little dissertation left Elsa rather surprised. 'I thought you weren't interested in this subject?'

Simon returned to his work. 'I'm not. But that's the kind of claptrap all the Eng. Lit. girls I knew at university used to come out with. The kind of thing you get if you spend half your life in therapy.'

So they had hired Alan Evans, and however interesting or worthless his thesis had been, it had not mattered because he had barely spoken a word in the few months he had been with them, except to relay information about Passchendaele, or check with them on the limits of his duties.

After a quarter of an hour looking, Elsa's hope of finding her book was fading. She had found Evans' own, glossy copy of *Between the Lines*, the new war poets anthology, but nothing resembling the notebooks. Then, just as her eyes were cruising idly along the top shelf of the bookcase, her gaze was drawn to one volume. It was tucked strangely into a corner, back to front, with only its spotted yellow pages showing, almost as if it had been concealed. She pulled it out. *The Notebooks of Valentine Siddons. 1913 to 1917.*

'Bingo.'

Swiftly she stashed the book in her bag, slammed the door behind her, and marched out into the mild spring air.

* * *

On the way back to her office Elsa paused to buy a cheese roll and a can of Coke for lunch and took it with her into the gardens of a small City church. She found a bench in a warm pool of sunshine, where pigeons patrolled like traffic wardens, keeping a beady eye on her food. She sat down to eat and pulled out the notebooks but as she did so a flurry of paper dropped to the ground. The fluttering cascade of sheets, jaundiced with age, floated to rest round her ankles and glided out of sight under the bench.

At first she thought, with a surge of irritation, that Alan Evans had mistreated her book and broken the spine, causing its pages to come loose. But as she began to collect them up, she saw that the sheets were in fact quite separate, bigger folded pieces of paper. They might have been Evans' annotations or notes, but on closer inspection they were just too old. The paper was a delicate parchment colour, like the skin of fresh mushrooms, in places faded to a dull beige with darker, sepia borders. What were they? wondered Elsa, shovelling them up. Letters, perhaps? Part of a diary?

She knew how terrible it was to read other people's diaries. Terrible, usually, because they were so dull, so full of parties and agonised office politics and in the worst case she could recall, actual accounts of meals eaten in restaurants, course by course. Besides which, one had to flip through so much mundane chronicling to find any reference to oneself. But as she crouched there in the churchyard, collecting up the sheets of paper, Elsa felt guilty of more than the usual invasion of privacy. She had the strange shivery sensation of being watched. Looking at the curls and spikes of words unfolding across the pages was like observing a bodily nakedness. These were poems, she realised. Their short little stanzas jumped out at her. One of the sheets, different from the rest, looked like writing paper and in the top right-hand corner, in faded brown italics, were the letters 'V.S.'. Beneath it was typed a short piece.

> When memory fails it's final as the heart.
> The ash of its dim files obscures
> Specific detail of the fatal hurt,
> What we were saying and how your
> Face looked, pondering, just before
> You told me. When I go back to the start
> Those slipping seconds still evade my grasp.
> And only isolate the moment, stark.
> The clouding wine suspended in the glass
> The fading blaze of roses and your eyes

Whose blue at one time froze me, fast
Unfocusing, with pain of being past.

As she read it, a strange excitement rose within Elsa. It was
nothing to do with the odd little poem. It was the initials
which provoked in her such a confusion of emotions. The
poem she had read was certainly unlike Valentine Siddons'
other writing, but the presence of these sheets in his notebooks could mean only one thing. Alan Evans had made a
considerable literary discovery. He had unearthed some of
the war poet's unpublished work. It was a possibility she
hardly dared articulate even to herself. This poem and the
others with it did not appear in any anthology of Valentine
Siddons' work. They were a new find.

And now Alan Evans was gone. But did he realise what
he had discovered? Certainly the poems had not been inside
Elsa's book when she lent it to him, yet the fact that he had
placed them there suggested that he saw the connection. And
what did he intend to do with them? Perhaps he planned to
publish them in the *TLS* or some other literary journal. In
which case Elsa should by rights return to his flat straight
away and leave the papers there with a short, congratulatory
note explaining her visit and her removal of the Siddons
notebooks and hoping he would get in touch when he
returned. Except that Alan had disappeared without trace.
There was really no way of telling if he planned to return at
all. Perhaps, she argued to herself, he was not even aware of
the importance of the find.

Elsa realised that this was something of an ethical cross-
roads. But she also knew that she was alone, and that no one
could possibly witness how carefully she had looked down
the paths to left and right, before deciding to press ahead. If
Evans wanted the poems back, let him come and collect
them. She could always plead a legitimate mistake. Other
people's motives are notoriously difficult to judge.

CHAPTER THREE

SIMON PARDOE FLICKED breadcrumbs off the starched linen tablecloth with an individual savagery, as though every one of them was an executive vice-president of a major Hollywood studio. Daniel Eckstein, the particular executive vice-president who was his lunch date, was now in the lavatory. Eckstein, whose Californian tan had not yet palled under England's leaden skies, had insisted on consuming his bread roll the French way, messily with no plate, despite the fact that they were dining in the heart of London in a restaurant famed for its exquisitely English cuisine, not to mention its hundred-year history as a meeting place of thespians and scribes. Or that was what the proclamation painted on the oak panelled walls said – the one slightly tasteless touch amid the otherwise understated elegance. The walls bore original paintings by artists who had eaten there and paid in kind, people like Wyndham Lewis, Duncan Grant and even Picasso, if the signature beneath the simple line drawing hung unobtrusively in an alcove was to be believed. On the tables silver cutlery gleamed in the jewelled light of stained-glass windows, and the conversation dropped softly, like the hush of tall corn harvested, when a well known actor or television executive swished through the room.

But then not being able to tell the difference between French and English dining habits was in line with Eckstein's general cultural ignorance, Simon mused resentfully. Simon himself had seen Europe in yearly instalments during his aspirant middle-class upbringing, squashed between brothers in the back of an old Rover, scratching mosquito-bitten legs as he traipsed round châteaux and palazzi and Schlosses. The holidays were orchestrated by Norman Pardoe, Simon's widower father, a small-time manager in a printing firm, in a half-hearted attempt to give his three boys the kind of education he had never had. The more glamorous trips, usually undertaken to impress Norman's girlfriends, invariably involved his father's lofty observation that small things, like how the French broke their bread straight on to the tablecloth, should be noted just as much as the big things, such as the way Rembrandt used light, or the history of the blue glass in Chartres Cathedral.

Eckstein, who pronounced Cannes in the plural, had been discussing the Bloomsbury group. Or rather the Blooms-berry group. Either way, his feeling about the Bloomsbury group was that they were dead.

'Well certainly, the main protagonists are by and large dead, but there are plenty of peripheral survivors,' Simon volunteered. 'Lettice de Beer, for example, who's ninety if she's a day and knew all of them – the Woolfs, the Bells, Duncan Grant, Lytton Strachey and everyone. She's agreed to be interviewed for background.'

'No, I mean they're kaput, passay, over,' explained Eckstein patiently. 'They're not interesting any more. The American public love all that English country house stuff, but they can get too much of it. And they have had these Bloomsberry types up to their ears in the past few years. Too many beards and suicides. Too many, y'know, friends of Dorothy.'

Though in general, Simon cared as much for the pre-occupations of the American public as he did for those of the pigeons in Trafalgar Square, he was uncomfortably aware that as a film producer, the tastes, thoughts and feelings of people in Des Moines and North Dakota were now among his primary concerns. In Simon's mind a cultural chasm yawned dauntingly before him, a sheer, barely bridgeable divide between the film that he wanted to make and the movie whose gestation Eckstein might, just possibly, agree to assist. The whole enterprise was proving exhausting. Already he was weary from constructing an edifice of euphemism about the research that had gone into this Passchendaele idea, plus a sprinkling of lies about the British appetite for films about poets and artists. Equally it was plain Eckstein had been less than frank himself about his ability to secure even a paltry development budget for Durban Films from his Hollywood masters.

'What I'm really after, Simon, is the high concept,' he had

repeated, in his curiously irritating nasal whine. 'I know you've given me the synopsis, but I need to sum up the whole film in one sentence. Y'see if I can call up my people in LA and say hey, we're talking *Four Weddings* meets *Platoon*, then it's so much easier to visualise. They're like, "Are we talking about a shooting movie or a kissing movie here?" If I just tell them it's about the war they may think action adventure, but if we go into this whole Bloomsberry thing, it looks like kinda fringe art-house, which doesn't play too well in Lincoln, Nebraska.'

Simon wondered what Elsa was up to. It had to be admitted, these meetings always went better when she was there. Not only did she thrust ahead with the central, defining question, like 'Are you seriously intending to fund our film?' – the only piece of information which Simon actually wanted to elicit from this encounter – but her optimism and sheer enthusiasm always managed to put the executives in a good mood too. Whereas Simon had only managed to bumble around the issue for two hours as Eckstein consumed a bottle and a half of heartbreakingly expensive claret and moodily discussed his marriage break-up, his kids, his alimony payments and his dislike of English weather, food, culture and television. He was bored by Glyndebourne, despised Ascot and had not seen the point of the Test Match. But if Elsa had been there, Simon knew, he would have been all smiles.

Perhaps that was what had persuaded him to carry on with Elsa rather than heeding Alex Durban's brutal advice. Because frankly, she was scarcely a good bet any other way. She had absolutely no idea of how to handle a budget. She had never worked in films. She had no money or contacts. On a purely practical level she was horrifically untidy. Sharing an office with her was purgatory and Simon had taken to keeping valuable documents at home, rather than risking them being stamped with coffee stains on Elsa's desk or chucked away with her parking tickets.

A waitress approached with the bill and Simon told her to wait till Eckstein returned. He tried to concentrate his mind again on Elsa's faults. No one could call her classically good looking. Her figure was like something by Giacometti. Her hair was dark and glossy, but it hid her fine eyebrows and she had to keep brushing it untidily out of her face. Her deep, chocolatey eyes only emphasised the pallor of her complexion, and she had a little bump halfway down her nose. Definitely not Simon's type at all. But she did have a certain, confident way about her as she gesticulated, swinging her arms in excited, theatrical circles. And just sometimes, when an idea or inspiration hit, a pleasing, spontaneous smile of delight enveloped her face. Tersely, Simon halted his train of thought. Considering Elsa had these few attributes, they might have been far better employed in attending a hopeless meeting with an evasive producer than disappearing heaven knows where looking for some ancient book.

'Where's your colleague Miss Meyers today, then?' Eckstein had returned, having glad-handed a variety of minor actors and writers on his way back to the table.

'Working on something rather hush-hush,' lied Simon, wearily.

* * *

When he got back to Little Russell Street Elsa was sitting in the faded light of late afternoon, feet on a discarded TV set, reading, her chair tilted perilously on its back legs. She looked completely absorbed, shrouded in a baggy red jumper far too big for her, with a little frown of concentration on her face. For a moment, the way the mellow sun fell on her face, creating little pools of shadow beneath the cheekbones, lighting up her complexion from within like a gentlewoman in a Vermeer interior, made him want to paint her. He had studied art for a while, but his creations never managed to reproduce the pictures he held in his mind's eye. He was a perfectionist, he supposed. One day he had wrapped up his brushes and oils and stashed them away like a guilty secret. But the urge to paint was not so easy to suppress.

As he came in she pushed her book down hastily, jumped up and came over to him.

'Any joy?'

Generally, and he didn't really know why, Simon found

himself wanting to keep bad news from Elsa. It wasn't that he wanted to give a Panglossian view of the world. Perhaps it was to do with his own vanity, or his superior status in the company. Anyway, he was always editing in his head, blacking out the scenes of utter hopelessness, jump-cutting to the parts of conversations where people said, 'Well there's nothing architecturally wrong with the script,' or, 'With a bit of work, this idea could turn into a concept.' Today, however, the news was not so much bad, as absent.

'No news is good news, I suppose.'

Elsa did not look as disappointed as he had feared and instantly he resented her for it.

'Did you get the book back? Was Evans there?'

'Yes, I got the book but he wasn't there. They had to let me in. And the people at the building had absolutely no idea where he could be. You know, I think he may have upped sticks altogether. It's very peculiar.'

To Elsa's relief, Simon did not want to pursue the subject of her visit to the flat.

'He's got some post here.' He was shuffling through a handful of letters on what had been Alan Evans' desk and picked out one, with a small black crest on the reverse of the envelope. The handwriting was angular, but dashing at the same time, signifying a kind of thoughtful spontaneity on the part of its author. He skimmed the letter.

'Christ's College. Oh it's Dr Eastway. Could Evans come and see him as soon as possible. Great. The first thing we have to tell our distinguished consultant is that our re-searcher has gone AWOL. Very impressive. Very professional. I suppose I'll have to go.'

Elsa took the letter from him.

'No. I'll go. I'd like to meet him anyway. I'm reading his Siddons biography and there's a lot I'd like to ask him.'

In particular she wanted to know what it was like to be the grandson of a famous poet. To inherit a literary legend and to invest in it with such diligence, such application. For Oliver Eastway there had first been his thesis, then the years of teaching and lecturing and now the biography. When your grandfather's life was your work, what did that do to your life? Was it a blessing or a burden to have the past always perched on your shoulder? To be bound to your subject by unbreakable chains of DNA?

She also wondered whether Valentine Siddons, however vital and appealing he appeared, was in reality like other academic subjects – those writers, poets and historical figures who came alive in the fusty atmosphere of the library, but who faded like wraiths in the harsh, corporeal world of waiting for buses and doing the washing. When the person you spent your days writing about was your mother's father, even if your mother never met him, how could you ever feel truly, academically, objective about him?

Admittedly, if this had been a quandary for Oliver Eastway, it didn't really show from the biography. He guided his reader through the short life of Valentine Siddons with sympathetic confidence, placing him fairly in his larger context without making unjustified claims, underlining the idealism of the young undergraduate poet faced with a war which would change everything, but which everyone believed would be over by Christmas.

And now there was one other, more burning question Elsa wanted to ask. Oliver Eastway would be bound to know whether his famous grandfather had written much before the war, and if so what had become of his earlier work. The difficulty would come in asking that question, without letting on that she had a particular interest in the answer.

When she volunteered for the task of tackling Eastway, Simon was dubious.

'Well if you're sure you can spare the time, you go,' he said, trying to interpret this sudden burst of enthusiasm. Why was she so keen? Was it just the chance to have a day out of the office and away from his lowering presence? Oh probably. Well let her go, then. He had a lot to get on with himself.

* * *

Having resolved to take the train up to Oxford next morning, Elsa went home early and let herself into her flat. The first thing she saw was that there was a call registered on her answerphone, but when she switched it on there was nothing. Elsa turned away from the phone with an irritated sigh. It had been the same for the past two nights. After her own voice, a disembodied cheerleader twang, had coaxed callers to leave their message, there would be five or ten seconds of breath and then a click. A drop of silence in the pool of urban noise. A heartstopping hiatus. It was silly to read anything into it. Lots of people disliked talking to machines. But it made her nervous and she wished they would just not ring in the first place. Thankfully the non-message was followed by one from Alison. In contrast to the mystery caller, her friend positively relished talking to answerphones, possibly because they didn't interrupt.

'Elsa? I know you're screening. Would you please pick up?' That wouldn't stop Alison. One-sided conversations were her favourite. 'I have just had the Day From Hell. Remember that radio programme I was invited on? *Morality and the Modern Woman?*' Alison's job as a pseudo agony aunt on *Good Relations* frequently led journalists to assume she possessed some psychological expertise. 'You cannot believe how tacky it was. They put me on with a priest and I made some light remark about the Catholic Church's famous tradition of oppressing women, right, and he called on all Catholics to stop watching the show. Really! Live on national radio. My executive producer is going to go through the roof. Now I know what a *fatwa* feels like. Hold on, that's my other line going.' She paused breathily. 'It could be the press. Call you later.'

Elsa smiled and curled up on her sofa with a bag of crisps and the Valentine Siddons biography in preparation for her meeting the next day. Its short introduction dealt with the legacy of his heroism, his role in Great War heritage and the impact of soldier poets on following generations. She felt she had Valentine Siddons by heart now, but she would flip through the book again all the same. Dr Oliver Eastway was known for asking particularly searching questions.

CHAPTER FOUR

EXTRACT FROM *VALENTINE SIDDONS: A LIFE*

In June 1914, Siddons came down from Oxford to spend the summer with his parents at their new home in Putney. It was a particularly happy reunion for the family, enlivened by the good news that Siddons' first poems had been accepted for publication.

* * *

VALENTINE'S FIRST THOUGHT, as he stepped off the platform at Putney station, and made his way through the unfamiliar suburban streets, was that nothing could be as bad as the last vac. He didn't know if he could bear any more of that terrible atmosphere in Edwardes Square, with his mother and father not speaking and the maids creeping around in that cowed, yet conspiratorial way they had. He was not looking forward to the sight of the 'awful little suburban vicarage', as Mother had acidly dismissed their new home, but as soon as he saw it he felt pleasantly surprised. It was a solid, redbrick affair, with a friendly ivy twined round its white painted portico and large wide windows giving an unexpectedly rustic view across the common, complete with grazing cows and a distant churchyard. And despite all Mother's railing at the idea of moving from central London, she seemed perfectly cheerful as she greeted him in the new drawing room, gushing about the move and her plans and the friends who had already made the journey to visit.

He noticed immediately that she was a little flushed and excitable in her pale lilac linen dress, and there was a pungent fragrance of eau-de-Cologne, which signified she was suffering from a headache, but it was accompanied by none of the usual melodrama. Instead she took his hand and began dashing around, showing off a gleaming rosewood piano and the conservatory, sweet with the scent of creamy yellow gardenias thrusting out of shiny abundant foliage, and a new set of card tables she had acquired for bridge and canasta parties. For Valentine there was a small but adequate study where she had carefully laid out all his books. He was relieved she seemed happy, especially as his father had insisted on cancelling their annual break in Marienbad, due to the mounting rumours of war on the continent.

Throughout the last month, reports of the atrocities by Serbians against Albanian Muslims and by the Bulgarians against the Serbians had spread like a stain across the newspaper front pages. Most people, it had to be said, were more interested in the possibility of civil war in Ireland over the Home Rule issue. And from what his father said it seemed the men at his bank reserved their most passionate outrage for the suffragettes, whose assaults on the establishment now included slashing the Rokeby Venus in the National Gallery and attempting to break down the gates of Buckingham Palace.

Valentine himself had managed only a fleeting interest in the reports of hostilities in Europe. A lot of the men at Oxford believed that war was inevitable and spent evenings in the common room arguing over the build-up of arms. Some said the attitude of Winston Churchill, who was hell bent on boosting the numbers of battleships and aircraft, was a danger to world security, and others claimed it was simply good judgement, considering the way the German navy was growing and that Germany was undoubtedly preparing for war. It had of course occurred to Valentine to wonder what might happen to his studies if war broke out. He had given the problem several minutes' respectful reflection, the way one dealt with all hypothetical questions in Oxford's ageless academic tranquillity.

Anyhow, the day after his arrival, a far more pressing piece of news arose as he was sitting with his father, discussing the possibility of a visit to their fantastically dreary cousins in Sidmouth. The idea of seeing the cousins, who lived in a poky house miles from the sea, let alone staying with them for several weeks, was almost more than he could contemplate. Was it really only last year that the shy flirting of chubby fifteen-year-old Helen, plainly overawed by her tall, blond cousin, had seemed appealing to him? Now the thought of that rough, loud family, endlessly arguing and careless of privacy, made him shudder like the only child he was. So when the housemaid brought in the mail, Valentine, grateful for any diversion, seized on it.

To his great surprise it contained a letter from Ronald Foxley. Foxley was the editor of the *Journal*, a literary magazine run by members of the Georgian school, to whom he had sent off a batch of poems. His letter brought more than Valentine dared hope for – the magazine wanted to publish at least three poems straight away, his pastoral pastiche, 'The Wood Pigeon', and two of the Oxford poems, 'On Tom Quad' and 'Vanished Spires'. Could they meet to discuss 'further commissions'? If so, would he attend their offices in Doughty Street? Mr Foxley awaited his reply.

Valentine had sent his reply within the hour. He suggested a visit the following week, when he would, by prior arrangement, be passing that part of town. The last bit was not strictly true, but he was keen not to appear too enthusiastic; a professional, published poet would, he felt, maintain a certain natural reserve.

Yet the waiting was far from easy. His mother's constant interruptions, combined with the hot weather, did not make the time pass any faster, let alone allow him to abandon himself to work. His Anglo-Saxon primer loitered unread on the desk, its pages ageing in the sunlight. On the garden wall cats dozed, their fur dusty, eyes narrowed to green slits, dismissing insects with an irritable flick of their tails and stretching their mouths in sharp, pink yawns. Beneath them the gardener toiled and beyond the wall children shrilled on the brown grass. In the oppressive lethargy of heat, life dragged by in slow motion. Sweltering blue days followed each other without a break. The common was scorched and the cattle roamed around restlessly, uprooting the last tendrils of green. From time to time came the soft explosion of pears and plums dropping in the orchard.

Within the house, shrouded by blinds, the torpid air hung heavy and still. Though she remained outwardly cheerful, his mother did not look well. Her eyes were unnaturally bright, pink spots burned in her cheeks and she fluttered her hands nervously, maintaining an absurd preoccupation with the news from abroad. She wanted to exchange the family's banknotes for gold because of worries about inflation. She bottled jam frenetically, as though whatever was happening in the Balkans and beyond would stop the sun shining, or the bees pollinating, or the fruit trees slowly ripening their load.

She was also annoyingly curious about the letter that arrived for Valentine one morning with an Oxford postmark. Though he had taken the slender white package from the maid as inconspicuously as possible, the round, curving hand, so obviously a woman's, caught his mother's eye. She wanted him to speak, but he said nothing. The friendship which had developed between himself and Emily Torrence, the daughter of his college bursar, was too embryonic to be straitjacketed in words. They had met at a dance in Oxford and had passed the next few months in an flurry of stolen walks through the parks and surreptitious meetings in the tea-rooms by the Bodleian Library. Her apparent infatuation was flattering but the relationship, still in its unfolding early stages, was far too delicate to offer up for dissection by Mother, to be picked over and filleted with her brittle enquiries like some tawdry society scandal. She hated his silence and brooded visibly, buttering her toast and drinking her tea with precise, injured dignity, as though demonstrating an ordinary English breakfast to foreigners. His father, not notoriously sensitive to emotional nuance, did not intervene.

By the time Tuesday arrived, the day that he had arranged to visit the Doughty Street offices of the *Journal*, Valentine was almost enervated with mingled excitement and apprehension. He left the house at nine o'clock sharp, his hair, which was naturally curly, plastered down across his scalp, and his collar, overstarched by the new laundry woman, uncomfortably rigid. The heat was already rising and as he made his way to the station the hollyhocks and roses in the gardens seemed to wilt in anticipation of the blazing sun to come. In his pocket he carried a letter to Emily, written behind closed doors in the study his mother had so carefully furnished. It contained his first tentative declaration of affection. His tiny recent achievement, the three soon to be published poems, was nothing to anyone, of course. But the insignificant name of Valentine Siddons seemed more substantial when it was about to appear in print. That little inky gang of printed characters, which would be stamped by the printing press, what? at least five hundred times, felt at once so personal and so gloriously official. Somehow his forthcoming byline seemed to lend his feelings for Emily, which hovered somewhere between novelty and idle flirtation, more authenticity and depth. Besides, he wanted someone to tell.

The offices of the *Journal* in Doughty Street were slightly less impressive than they had loomed in his imagination. The dark, soot-blackened building was dignified enough, but it took repeated ringing on the bell for anyone to answer. Eventually, the door was opened by a young woman, her pasty complexion transversed by a bright gash of crimson lipstick, her shapeless body draped in a loose, unflattering orange gown which hung dejectedly around her. She was wearing spectacles and a slightly distracted air and seemed neither to expect his appearance, nor in the least surprised by it.

'You want Ronald, I suppose,' she said rather absently, motioning him up a dark stairway.

Her approach threw him and for an instant he looked hastily around the cluttered hallway for signs that this was indeed the right place. 'Mr Foxley, is . . . that is to say, I hope you received my letter saying I was coming? I think I am expected.'

'Oh yes, Ronald expects everything. Nothing surprises him,' the girl replied, a little flippantly he thought, preceding him up the gloomy stairs and knocking perfunctorily on a first-floor door before entering.

Inside the room a man he took to be Ronald Foxley was sitting with his feet propped on the most untidy desk Valentine had seen in his life. Overheated by a large gas fire, the office was lined from floor to ceiling with books, which were also piled on almost all the available chairs and the windowseat. A *mille-feuille* of papers obtruded precariously from the bookshelves. Although the sun was almost wholly banished by a pair of long green velvet curtains, the dim light was enlivened by splashes of colour from a throng of paintings on the wall, most of them, he could not help noticing, depicting fat naked ladies in obscene contortions. Foxley himself had dark, centre-parted hair threaded with grey and hanging untidily long down either side of his face, pale slate-coloured eyes and a monocle, through which he was squinting at a newspaper. When Valentine came in he flung it down and opened his arms as if to embrace him.

'My dear fellow, welcome, welcome. Do sit down.'

Valentine moved towards an empty leather armchair only to find as he sat down that what he had taken for a small brown cushion let out a yowl and streaked out of the room in a flash of fur. Flustered, he stood up again.

'Mr Foxley, I'm Valentine Siddons. I do hope you received my letter. About the poems?'

As though he had not heard him, Foxley seized the news-paper and waved it in front of him. 'What do you think of it all, Mr Siddons, eh? The Pope has fainted! The Emperor Josef has been seen to weep! The assassination of the Archduke Franz Ferdinand sounds like a clap of thunder over Europe! What are we to make of it, eh? Do you think there will be war, Mr Siddons? Are you girding your loins to fight the German threat?'

Though his father, reading *The Times* over breakfast, had relayed some information about a foreign archduke's assassination, Valentine had not given it his full attention. All the talk about a secret Serbian society called the Black Hand, supposedly complicit in the killing, and of Austrians dancing in the street as they burned the Serbian flag, seemed so distant on that quiet Putney day. Besides which, Father was only partway through reading the report when Mother had intervened brightly, as though quelling some nonsensical story.

'Frederick please, please, don't go on. I simply cannot bear to hear any more. All this terrible talk of war is bad for everyone's nerves. And when you think of what it could mean . . .'

Here she fell silent and although she remained smiling, as she cast him a sidelong look he saw a twitchy anxiety in her eyes. It occurred to Valentine that she was already imagining what might happen to her only son should war break out. As so often with his mother's anxieties, it was entirely baseless.

If Britain became mixed up in war, which hardly seemed possible, he would most certainly not be joining up. He had not the slightest intention of dying in some sordid continental battle about which he cared little. How could his mother expect that of him? It was not the sort of thing he felt like saying, as it could be taken the wrong way, but he was far more interested in what Ronald Foxley would say about his poems that morning than the distant prospect of European war.

Now, however, the notion that Valentine was about to receive some kind of glowing literary criticism of the sort his tutor was prone to deliver about the poems of Keats or Wordsworth as he strode up and down his Oxford rooms, seemed increasingly remote. Mr Foxley was more like an embarrassing stranger in a public house, aggressively soliciting one's views while underneath it all he was really spoiling for a fight. Valentine tried to be diplomatic.

'I haven't given it much thought. But I don't really think there'll be a war,' he said cautiously.

'He hasn't given it much thought,' said Foxley in a rather sarcastic voice to the girl, who was loitering by the door.

'I don't blame him,' she said shortly, before turning and shutting the door behind her.

The meeting did not seem to be getting off on the right footing, but Valentine was determined to bring the conversation back to poetry.

'I was delighted that you've accepted my work. You said that perhaps you, er, might like to discuss more commissions?'

Foxley's wild face creased into a kind of manic grin. 'Quite right, quite right. A man who has his priorities in the correct order. Why talk about war when we can talk about poetry. Tell me, have you heard of the Vorticists? What do you think of them, hmm?' He thrust into Valentine's hands a large book, with the word 'Blast' on the cover. 'Out last week. A new school of poetry dedicated to the overthrow of the middle classes. What should be done with the middle classes, Mr Siddons? Is violent revolution too good for them?'

Valentine felt he was getting out of his depth. But the

book looked interesting. He flicked through it for a moment and then said carefully:

'I don't believe violent revolution is the right answer to any social problem.'

'Ah ha! A pacifist! A man after my own heart.'

So saying, Foxley stood up, strode round the desk and clapped his shoulder, before calling down the stairs: 'Margaret, it's all right. We have a pacifist in our midst. Bring up the tea!'

Though he gave a pretty intolerable first impression, Foxley was nowhere near as bad as he appeared. When he got on to the subject of the *Journal*, and how he had kept it going despite lack of funds, Valentine came to like him a little better. They admired the same poets, and he knew Professor Herbert Kelly, his Oxford tutor. But it was Foxley's thoughts about the prospect of war which impressed Valentine. He kept counselling him against contracting 'war fever', as though it was some kind of disease one could guard against. He said Valentine was just the kind of person who would be sucked into a futile, imperialist bloodbath played out by proud old men who had no conception of the modern European order. His attitude seemed so much more reasonable than the passionate diatribes Valentine was used to hearing at the college bar, or his father's complacent proclamations over the marmalade. After a while the girl Margaret reappeared with chocolate cake and a pot of tea, and sat drinking it with them while she looked him up and down in an appraising way. Then she said:

'If Valentine is a pacifist, perhaps he should come to Bedford Square with us. I'm sure Lady Ottoline would love to meet him. He's just her type.'

'I say, that's a good idea. There are bound to be some of our other contributors there. How about it, Siddons? Would you like to meet the cutting edge of the London artistic scene? Or perhaps something rather blunter? Either way, there's a party this Thursday evening.'

Chapter Five

Extract from *Valentine Siddons: A Life*

Soon after war was declared, through his acquaintances at the
Journal *Siddons came to know a circle of artists and writers at
the centre of literary London, revolving round the Bedford Square
salon of Lady Ottoline Morrell. But while he found them a
stimulating distraction, he had already made up his mind to
obtain a commission and join his university colleagues, already
on their way to France. At the same time the most momentous
meeting of his life, with Emily Torrence, the daughter of Dean
Torrence, his college bursar, had led to thoughts of marriage.*

* * *

'To me, Nijinsky is more than a man. When he dances he
transcends humanity and becomes . . . pure idea.'

There seemed no point quarrelling with this. Hester
Moriaty, dressed as a Turk with purple turban and golden
striped harem pants, seemed to have adopted Valentine from
the moment he walked through the door. She was not the
ideal companion, he was forced to admit. For a start she was
at least sixty, with a tanned little simian face and a neck
rouching generously down into a low neckline, where two
dimply breasts struggled for supremacy in a space too small
for them. She was also hard to interrupt, but it didn't seem
to matter because at that moment she ended their conversation, glided down the stairs past Valentine and blew
cigarette smoke in his face as she passed. Valentine grimaced,
but followed her obediently into the first-floor drawing room.

He was only just beginning to learn the signs and signals
of this new world, from where he stood on the far horizon
like a conquistador, all too often frozen in silent wonderment.
Mostly he tried, very hard, to look neither shocked nor
impressed. But he certainly would not have managed that
had he been there the previous week, when according to

Foxley, one of the guests, a female painter, stripped off her blouse and chemise to reveal her naked breasts and then took a partner for a waltz round the room.

Tonight though, there had been no nakedness. Instead most people seemed to have adopted fancy dress, generally dazzling and exotic robes with a vaguely Eastern theme. A high excitement ran through the party when the celebrated dancer, who was in London with the new Russian ballet, had performed with sinuous and astonishing skill a short demonstration before the admiring guests. Large muscles bulged softly through his swarthy skin, yet he flipped round the room as lightly as a fish and his dark eyes when you looked at them were inscrutable and foreign.

Now that Nijinsky had left, Russian ballet music was still being thumped out at the pianola, with more enjoyment than talent, and people had cleared space for another pair of dancers. They were an odd couple. The man, thin-faced with long auburn beard, brown velveteen jacket and gold-rimmed glasses, seemed the more ludicrous through his choice of partner, a striking tawny-haired woman, at least a head taller than himself, with a long gold brocade train fluttering behind her. Round they whirled, with little rhythm and a lot of stumbling, until the music stopped abruptly and they both sank on to a sofa laughing hysterically. Around them the guests broke into indulgent laughter and applause.

'Lady O's on magnificent form tonight, isn't she?'

Foxley had come up beside him and offered him a Turkish cigarette, which Valentine hastily accepted. As he bent to light it, Foxley murmured: 'I've got someone who rather wants to meet you. Interested?'

This was the third time that Valentine had attended one of the Thursday evening parties in Bedford Square and he was only just beginning to lose his social unease. The mixture of aristocrats, writers, politicians and unconventional artists had been daunting at first, but Valentine soon discovered that Foxley's recommendation had travelled before him. Most of them seemed to accept he was a young poet of precocious talent and others, who had perhaps more experience of Foxley's introductions, nevertheless seemed friendly enough, asking who he knew at Oxford, and expressing polite enthusiasm to read his work. No one seemed to think he should not be there. The only hint of rudeness came from the gaggle of Slade art school girls, with their severe bobs and blackened eyes and their hobble dresses which showed clear above the ankle. Among them were a couple of suffragettes who had just been released from prison after the Prime Minister's amnesty.

'Who is it? Not one of the cropheads, I hope.' His eyes travelled over the other guests. Across the room Hester had fixed on a fat man with a cigar, who was trapped next to the pianola, nodding disconsolately. Then Valentine lit on a lone figure standing beside the long windows giving out on to Bedford Square, looking out into the still night. Foxley followed his gaze.

'Right first time. Constance Emberley. You know who she is, of course?' There was an arch, almost lascivious note in Foxley's voice as he looked at the dark-haired woman, despite his own leanings, which Valentine had already discerned were quite the other way.

'No. Should I?'

'You might have heard of her as Connie Fanshaw. The actress. Did extremely well for herself in getting Viscount Emberley to marry her, though his family almost disowned him in the process. But she's managed beautifully. Quite grown into the role, as they say in Drury Lane.'

As if sensing she was being discussed, Constance Emberley turned. The movement brought her out of the shadow and a splash of candlelight fell on the opalescent skin of her shoulders and well-rounded arms emerging from a dress of rich, raspberry red. A few sleek curls had escaped from the coils piled on her head, secured with a sparkling jewelled clasp. Heavy pearls were slung against her neck and her eyes, large and round beneath a high white forehead, were surmounted by arched eyebrows that gave her a slightly surprised aspect. She looked down again, but not before catching Valentine's eye.

'Come on. I'll do my introduction.' Foxley took Valentine's elbow and steered him firmly across the room. 'Lady Constance, may I present Valentine Siddons. One of our most promising young poets, and one of my own discoveries, I may add.'

'How clever of you, Ronald, I don't know how you do it,' she said in a slow, clear voice with, Valentine realised, perceptible irony.

'Connie is an important patron of the arts. All the finest talents of our times prostrate themselves before her,' added Foxley grandly.

She held out her hand to Valentine with a lazy smile, and as he took it he thought, with a slight shock, how like his mother's it felt, slight and bony with no residual plumpness. The hand of a woman past her youth. How subtle a chronicler of age were the hands, accumulating rings like a tree. Yet even while he wondered how old she was, he was desperate to dispel any idea of him as yet another begging artist or worse, one of Foxley's fey young men.

He blurted: 'Is your husband Viscount Emberley the minister?'

'The warmonger,' chimed in Foxley, melodramatically. 'The man who urged Asquith against all reasonable voices to go ahead with the show.'

If Constance Emberley was offended, she didn't betray it, only arched her eyebrows higher, smiled and said: 'Now run along Ronald, I want to forget all about the war and discuss Mr Siddons' poetry with him.'

'Oh, call me Valentine.'

'Well then, Valentine I must tell you how much I enjoyed your pieces in the *Journal*.'

For a panicky moment, Valentine felt the heat rising up his neck and threatening to creep beyond his collar and spread a flush across his face. He was unused to compliments on his poetry. The probing scrutiny with which Constance Emberley fixed him seemed to discern in an instant, both that he had never been published before, and how much those three pages in a small-circulation magazine had meant to him. He turned to open the window, so that his boyish blush should be hidden in the shadow and his face cool in the night air. As he did, he accidentally brushed her bosom with his arm. He pulled away from the soft, lace-covered swell as though he had been stung and said hurriedly: 'It must be hard for you to forget the war, though. With your husband, I mean.'

Accepting a glass of champagne from a waiter's tray, she moved to join him at the window.

'Not really. Religion and politics are the two things that shouldn't be discussed among decent people, my husband always says. There's a third thing, isn't there, that you shouldn't discuss?' She raised her dark-lashed eyes at him innocently. 'What's the third thing?'

'Gambling?' Valentine's awareness of these niceties of etiquette was dim.

'No. Not gambling. Oh I remember. Sex. Decent people don't discuss sex.'

She took a sip of her champagne. 'Besides, my husband's views and mine on the war don't coincide.'

For Valentine it was unusual to hear a woman publicly disagreeing with her husband on matters of state. His own mother, though she was only too forthright on the question of where and in what sort of house they should live, whether three maids and a cook were enough and why they had to attend Ascot and Goodwood that year, rarely disagreed with his father on politics. On top of this, the mention of sex astounded him.

'And where is your husband now? Unless, that is, he's here, of course . . .' Valentine looked round hastily. For some reason this prospect had not occurred to him.

'He's shooting,' she said flatly. 'In Scotland, that is, not France.'

They stood together, looking out at the horse chestnut trees in the square. It was only September, but already an autumnal tinge edged the air and its sharpness mingled with the musk of Constance's perfume to stir a sudden tremor of expectation within Valentine. The anticipation was heavy as an impending thunderstorm. The touch of her elbow against his was electric.

In the street below a group of youths passed, chattering excitedly. There was no doubting the subject of their discussion. Though the new Russian ballet may have been the talk of the Bedford Square party, in the nation beyond there was only one topic of conversation.

When war had been declared on Bank Holiday weekend the crowds had surged like a dark flood up the length of Whitehall to Downing Street, cheering Asquith with their hats in the air and singing the National Anthem. In the universal mood of righteousness and optimism, it was almost impossible to remain unaffected. Even Valentine's mother had taken out her knitting needles and set about personally responding to Queen Mary's appeal for 300,000 pairs of socks and mufflers to equip the troops. His father, who worked at a Belgian-owned bank, announced with satisfaction that all the 'Germs', with whom he had co-operated quite amicably for many years, had been cleared out of the company and had gone back to their own country. Then, less than a month into the war, the blow of the forced British retreat from Mons had brought a redoubled frenzy, so that the recruiting stations were packed with volunteers: bank clerks and accountants and labourers, so many that the army ordnance department could not cope with the demand for khaki and gave out the old blue-grey jackets instead. There were pictures in the newspapers of the lines of hopeful volunteers stretching round the block, and stories of men who committed suicide, worried they might not be accepted for service. Several of Valentine's Oxford contemporaries were already holed up in training camps around the country. Everyone was anxious to teach the Hun a lesson.

This anxiety did not, of course, extend to Bedford Square, where Lady Ottoline had pronounced the war the end of civilisation and a cultural catastrophe liable to render the rest of their lives a worthless sham. In Doughty Street Foxley and Margaret announced their pacifism with a mixture of pride and despair. They even considered, as a short-term measure, renaming the *Journal* the *Pacifist*, but as one of their chief financial backers was an assistant to Winston Churchill, this was deemed unwise. Valentine had taken to dropping in on Doughty Street, at first ostensibly on small formalities, and then overtly, like many others, for the pleasure of their company and the rowdy discussions they carried on, sustained by unending quantities of tea.

Their company was a relief to Valentine. Temporarily at least it helped him forget the problem of Emily. If he had stopped to think about it he might have worried that a woman should pass from being a pleasure to a problem within so few months. Indeed with her unflinching adoration and doll-like prettiness it was hard to see precisely what the problem could be with Emily. He did not discern the steeliness behind the sharp blue eyes or the firmness in the grip that belied her eighteen years.

When he first expressed his admiration for her, he had meant it in a general, artistic way, as poets did, but Emily had taken it as so much more. She had arranged a series of piano lessons in the town centre so that when he was in Oxford they could meet covertly several times a week. He could not deny these were enjoyable times. They would walk through the gathering afternoon light, talking earnestly of Valentine's plans for a literary life. Sometimes he would catch a reflection of them in a shop window and the image of his slim figure looming above her tiny frame stirred a dull protective flicker in him.

Though she had not said as much, he guessed that she loved him. There was no doubting, behind the soft words and the endearments, that Emily knew what she wanted and it was him. He supposed there was something admirable about someone who knew their own mind. She said she was 'proud' of him. She longed to meet the exciting friends he had made in London. Momentarily he had tried to imagine a meeting between Emily and Foxley and flinched.

But the real problem with Emily was not the love thing but the assumption, repeatedly expressed in her letters, that he would take the honourable course and seek a commission. Her voice was an unwelcome echo of the mounting chorus inside him predicting that he would soon have to forget about Oxford and poetry, just as things were becoming so much fun, and sign up for France.

At that moment, as if to echo the shouting in the street, the sound of raised voices in the drawing room caused the guests to turn round, intrigued. A little foreign-looking man, with sallow skin, close-cropped, curly hair and burning eyes, was engaged in an argument. His opponent was a good friend of Lady Ottoline's, a Cambridge don who had shown an especially kind interest in Valentine's plans and urged him not to neglect his studies for the excitement of a short-lived war. Now his benign, friendly face was flushed pink and his moustache seemed to bristle with indignation. The foreigner was shouting at him in a thick Belgian accent.

'You fat hedonists have no idea what you are talking about,' he shrieked. 'Haven't you read about it in the papers? The agony of Belgium? How can you close your eyes to the atrocities which are being inflicted on my countrymen? When Antwerp fell priests were hung upside down in their own steeples and tied as live clappers to their bells. They should shock you, these tales, because they are the truth. Little babies have had their tiny hands cut off along with the breasts of the mothers who fed them! Nuns, virgin nuns, raped and defiled for their barbaric pleasure! The Germans must be stopped! It is not just your duty, it is the duty of any civilised human being to fight them. What do you mean by talking of peace?'

The conversation in the rest of the room fell into an uneasy lull. One young man, in a flowery cravat and bottle-green velvet smoking jacket, sniggered as he lit a cigarette but was hushed angrily by his neighbours. The don was answering, arguing that war always brought with it sensational tales. That even the reports in the newspapers about Russian soldiers landing at Leith and coming down by train from Scotland were optimistic nonsense. The story had only got about because some Cameron Highlanders, asked where they came from, had replied Ross-shire, which in their broad Scottish accents sounded like Russia. And what about the angel who appeared in the sky to the British troops retreating from Mons. Did the Belgian believe in that too?

At this point, Lady Ottoline rose from a chair to her full height, resembling with her beaky nose and her vast gold dress a huge, slightly moth-eaten eagle.

'Ernst,' she said gently, laying a hand on the Belgian's shoulder. 'I think our guests have listened to enough of this. We are agreed that this war is a horror, and a horror which we must oppose? Hmm?'

Firmly she steered the quivering man from the room. Someone sat down at the pianola again and started up a Hungarian dance. A woman in a feathered turban and green silk trousers took centre stage, whirling around like a dervish in some strange invention of her own. Beside Valentine, Constance Emberley stirred.

'What a bore. I like a good row. Were you here for the dinner?'

'No, just the party afterwards,' Valentine replied, instantly aware how the timing of his invitation categorised him. But she said:

'So you haven't eaten either. Would you like to come out to dinner with me?'

Valentine tried hard not to register the shock of being asked to dinner alone, and by a married woman. Would he be expected to pay? Did he have enough money? 'Ah yes . . . that would be nice,' he faltered.

At the door she wrapped herself in a wine red cape, donned her hat, and they made their way through the shadowy Bloomsbury streets to Covent Garden. As they walked, Constance asked about his poetry, and his aspirations. Whether or not it was deliberate he could not tell, but she did not press him on his feelings about the war, nor ask him whether he intended joining up. For that, he felt grateful.

As they approached the restaurant, gusts of loud laughter and conversation billowed from the door. It was a theatre restaurant, and the management there evidently knew Constance Emberley from her former life. Some of the other diners, whom Valentine took to be actors by their raucous laughs and open displays of affection, stopped her as she passed, with cries of recognition and very little deference to her present rank. They eyed Valentine, hovering inconspicuously behind her, with frank interest, but did not ask about him. Nor indeed did they mention Viscount Emberley. Nevertheless he was glad when they were shown to a corner table, curtained off by velvet drapes, where Constance ordered more champagne. Outside the wind sounded against the windows like a sigh, but inside this plush cocoon, supplied with soup and fish, champagne, fruit and a dessert wine like nectar, Valentine felt the constraints of his ordinary life falling away.

Constance, too, in her old milieu, seemed to undergo a metamorphosis. Her stiffness melted, her manner became less arch and calculating. Suddenly he could see the Connie Fanshaw who had defied all the conventions of a girl of her class and gone on the stage. She had made up her mind after seeing Mrs Patrick Campbell as Lady Macbeth while still a pupil at her respectable private girls' school in Hampstead. She told him how she had withstood the slights of a society that equated acting with easy morals, and how even when she had become well known, with her name on the bill outside Drury Lane, her mother had still refused to watch her daughter perform. Her father had come, however, a little embarrassed, sending roses to her dressing room with a little note not to let her mother know. The mother had, of course, agreed to attend the grandest performance of Connie's life – the high society wedding at St Margaret's Westminster, at which Connie had become Lady Emberley several years ago.

At the mention of that, the corners of her small rose mouth turned down, and she exaggerated the gesture in mockery. Laughing about it emboldened him to ask: 'Was it a difficult decision? To marry him, I mean.' Astonishingly, she did not seem to mind such directness.

'Oh no. He was large and rich and he dazzled me. He took me out to his country estate and there were acres upon acres of woodlands and fields and marvellous gardens, and a hundred staff to run three homes. Then there were these fabulous jewels, family treasures inherited from his ancestor Jane Seymour, who was of course the only wife to give Henry VIII a son, which is more than I can manage for my husband, it seems. And he thrust all these wonderful possessions towards me and I was impressed. And before I knew it I had become one of them. I think I also enjoyed annoying his family, who of course were most put out.'

She laughed lightly, recalling such entrenched enmities.

'But you never really became one of them, did you? I mean with the difference in backgrounds and all that.' Valentine reached over to fill her glass, so he did not notice the hardening of her features, or the infinitesimal chill in her voice when she said: 'Well I've been married a long time now. Let's talk about you instead.'

Then Valentine, garrulous with wine, took up the

conversation, and felt less inhibited than usual at discussing his own parents and his mother's horror at moving from Edwardes Square to the suburbs, and her covert disappointment that Father had not risen further in the bank. He confided his excitement at being at Oxford, and the poets he admired. He did not mention Emily. He thought he detected a slight envy in Constance: at his freedom, perhaps, or his education. She was certainly well read, and when at one point he likened the Germans to the Merchant of Venice, in the way they had called in the money owed to them by other countries, while leaving their own debts outstanding as they prepared for war, she quoted Portia and Shylock by heart.

As he talked he tried to conceal his shock at the way she had described herself as a 'possession', the expression raw as a gaping wound. After a while she leaned over and said: 'You don't know how good it is to have someone young to talk to. Someone whose blood hasn't congealed in their veins. And who doesn't talk forever about the war. Everyone seems to have been carried away by this dreadful false emotion. They don't seem to see the horror of it all. Such a ghastly thing for civilised nations to do.'

When they left the restaurant it was drizzling slightly, and as they got into a taxi, she said: 'I'm not going back to Eaton Square. I'm going to our house in Chelsea.'

Was it a proposition? Valentine was agonisingly unsure. He felt as if he had stepped into an alien land, whose customs were unknown to him. Sitting in the back of the four-wheeler cab, heavy with the smell of damp polish and old leather, he seemed to see London for the first time. Past them loomed the great, blackened honeycomb of the Houses of Parliament, the place where this woman's husband had argued for the prosecution of the war, and helped decree that thousands of young men should leave their homes and sink into the mud of Flanders. He saw the round smudgy globes of the Embankment lights, half muffled in blue, and the beautiful iron cobweb of the Albert Bridge slip by. Beyond them the lazy Thames lapped, glinting and still. All the while Constance talked, Valentine felt his heart beat against his ribcage so hard that it seemed audible. Desire shot through his body so that his legs were weak with it. As the cab jolted, one of her heavy pearl earrings fell on to the seat behind him. Picking it up Valentine reached to replace it and suddenly the bare, curled flesh of the ear, so vulnerable and undecorated, seemed irresistible, as though promising what yet remained covered. As she turned her face to him to help, their mouths collided in a clumsy kiss.

Valentine still said nothing when, as the cab arrived at the house in a Chelsea side street and he paid it off, she took his hand, opened the door and led him up the steps. Inside, the house was in darkness but in the bedroom the moon broke through the clouds and streamed in through the long, un-shuttered windows, bathing everything in a lambent milky gleam. With his hand on the doorknob he hovered, paralysed by virginity, watching as she pulled down her red dress over her shoulders, slipped out of it like a snake shedding its skin, and freed her body from its corset so that her small breasts stood exposed. Beneath them he saw a plump stomach and round stockinged thighs, before she crossed the room, placed her arms round his waist and pulled his groin towards her. Only then did he lose control. Her vulnerability roused a strange aggression in him. With angry kisses, he pushed her on to the soft down of the bed, fumbled off his own clothing and fell roughly on her, as though already fighting some perverse and violent war of his own.

CHAPTER SIX

ELSA GOT UP early the next day, went to Paddington and caught the Oxford train. Finding a carriage without children or lone men, she leaned back, letting the sun shine a livid tapestry against her closed eyelids. The train pulled away through the dingy suburbs, where houses clung drably to the railway line as if the glamour of travel might rub off. The untidy yards and gardens were strewn negligently with washing and old furniture, putting on no airs for the people on the train. Before long the houses tapered out and they entered the construction-free zone that Elsa classed the countryside proper.

Like most town dwellers, Elsa was suspicious of the countryside. It looked all right. The fields, with their brown, corduroy folds peppered with rooks, the neat woods sliced up like cake by tidy fences, the miniature villages, each with its regulation spire. But when you actually entered it, the countryside became a much more alien and threatening place than traditional pastoral idylls might suggest. Its thorny hedges bristled horribly with barbed wire, its turf was pitted and sodden and cows wandered the fields aimlessly, like long-stay hospital patients. The inhabitants, mistakenly famed for their friendliness, spent their time in deadening rural pursuits, such as watching satellite television or drifting round barn-sized hypermarkets.

Turning away from the window, she opened her book and relaxed. It was a relief to get away from the office. Simon had taken on some arduous freelance work, producing commercials to keep things ticking over and, as she was uncomfortably aware, to pay her salary. It kept him chained to the desk, head down, with an ear to the telephone, radiating a moody silence. The silence was different in quality and texture from his usual wordless state. This was no mere absence of conversation, but an active, oppressive thing, which expanded to fill every corner of the office. Elsa shuddered. It would be wonderful to exchange the dismal atmosphere of Little Russell Street for the mellow serenity of Oxford's cobbles and churches and quads.

She was also excited at the prospect of meeting Dr Oliver Eastway for the first time. In the photograph of him on the inside jacket of the biography, he even resembled his celebrated grandfather a little in the strong straight nose, the wry, cruel curl of the lip suggesting some private joke, the generous mouth. His voice on the telephone had sounded smooth and slightly amused, but not at all put out, at her garbled explanation that it would be she, and not Alan Evans, who would be coming to see him. He was, of course, famously accommodating. When he appeared on TV shows and radio programmes he always managed to be gracious in his criticism. He would never merely select his victim and unleash a cascade of withering sarcasm. He was constructive, inspiring almost.

In her time as an undergraduate Elsa, along with most of her contemporaries, had envied those taught by him. She recalled his bulky, thickset frame and wavy, leonine hair and she could see that in his youth he might have been attractive. Behind his hornrimmed spectacles, his green eyes had a light in them, like a little laugh. He wore well-cut European jackets, but then spoilt the effect by rolling up the sleeves when distracted. He smoked French cigarettes. He was unmarried, but not, judging by his string of girlfriends, averse to female company.

The proof copy of Eastway's biography lay on her lap. But Elsa had something far more important in her inside jacket pocket. For the tenth time that morning, she could not resist pulling out the small sheaf of poems and shuffling them gently in her hands. She had already read them several times, and the thought that she, or rather Alan Evans, had uncovered some unpublished Siddons was increasingly exciting. Yet the more she read them, the more possessive she felt about them and the problem of publicising the discovery, without knowing where Evans had found them, or incurring his fury, seemed insoluble.

It was inconceivable that once he realised the poems had gone missing, Evans would not try to get them back. The only question was, would he discover who had taken them? If Evans stayed away from his flat until the usual caretaker returned, he would have no way of knowing about the girl who had gained entry. But what if he had come back already, and had recognised Elsa from a description? Would he not come to find her and retrieve them? The very thought had made Elsa jumpy all morning. She consoled herself with hoping that Alan Evans really had gone abroad or disappeared for good. In the meantime, if he did track her down before she had decided what to do with the poems, she could always deny having found anything between the pages of the Siddons notebooks.

Before her the flimsy little sheets lay, innocent of their explosive potential. They gave off a fusty fragrance mixed with something like soap, or was it lavender? Who knew where they had mouldered away all these years. Delicately, she laid them out on the table in front of her and tried, once again, to decipher them. There were six poems. All about short meetings, love – which to Elsa's eye looked pretty unconsummated – and loss. She wondered how old he was when he wrote them. They were not exactly juvenilia, but they certainly pre-dated his well-known poems, the bleak, anguished pieces he wrote at the western front with their fresh, colloquial style.

He had moved into Lower Binding when he was twenty, after his marriage to Emily, while he was still mostly away at war. The cottage was a wedding gift from her father and, according to the biography, Siddons had been delighted to accept it. He had apparently been keen to get away from the trivial excitements of the London social scene during his leave and find somewhere solitary to write. Later, as the war wore on, the image of the peaceful cottage seemed to obsess him, so that he itched with a kind of desperation to get back there.

Reading the poems again, Elsa felt a strange, unexpected prickling of envy. She asked herself what she had to be envious of, but she knew the answer. She had never adored anyone enough to write them even the gauchest love poetry. Now that she was nearing thirty, Elsa mulled over this fact with growing alarm. In her student days, when the great, expected passion usually arrived, she had lived with other girls and watched the carnage of hearts shattering around her with curiosity. She looked at the callow men who precipitated these feelings with disbelief. Determined to cure what she considered a kind of emotional frigidity, she went out with some of them, slept with them, enjoyed their devotion, but failed to feel more than sadness, mingled with relief, when the relationships ended as they always did. It was not that she had not had fun. Among the set she went around with, there were several fey, sophisticated men always bombing down to London in sports cars bought by their fathers, holding extravagant parties in other people's country houses, drinking, laughing, staging plays, and getting sent down for ludicrous stunts. Later they had become merchant bankers or accountants or television producers, and now they were getting fat and married to the same girls whose hearts had been broken by others. But not to Elsa.

Alison Joliffe, always a keen student of pop psychology, had spent many happy hours analysing the shortcomings of Elsa's private life. She told Elsa that she had deliberately cultivated spiritual isolation and had symbolically demonstrated it by choosing to stay in Britain when at the age of seventeen the rest of her large family moved to Germany. Alison assured Elsa she was suffering from a deep-seated fear of the male gender, primally represented by her father with his surgeon's knife, and would never be able to sustain an intimate relationship. Elsa did not actually believe all this, but it made her uneasy, even though Alison's outrageous diagnoses invariably collapsed in gusts of raucous laughter.

Out of the window, the grape-grey domes and spires of Oxford materialised suddenly, as they always did on this journey, like something imagined, unreal. Elsa put the sheets back in her bag and thought what fun she might have had with the undiscovered Siddons poems if she had stayed on for research work. She would have been the envy of the English faculty. But lingering beyond her first degree had never appealed to her. She had wanted to get away and into television as quickly as possible, she remembered ruefully.

On Oxford station platform the familiar rush of nostalgia

enveloped her like nausea. It was a feeling that could be cleared by fixing on something new and strange. The shopping centre, for example. That hadn't been there. Even new shopping centres managed not to look like monstrosities in Oxford. She walked the well-remembered route to the ancient part of the city, down the High and into the door of Christ's. The porter showed her across the quad to a doorway, where a board painted with scrolled Gothic writing proclaimed that Dr Eastwood was in.

He was on the telephone when she entered and waved her to a sofa with a smile.

'My next student isn't coming, so I'm all yours.'

'Can't be too often your students cancel on you,' said Elsa, politely.

He shot her a surprised look and, putting the phone down, came over to shake hands. He was older than she remembered, the blond hair at the sides flecked with grey, but much taller than she had thought.

'I can't say I'm too cut up about it. I'd rather not think about Lord Rochester before lunch anyway. Can I offer you coffee, Miss Meyers?'

'Call me Elsa.'

'In which case you must call me Oliver.'

How pleasant the academic life must be. The sun streamed into Oliver Eastway's study through leaded mullioned windows, lighting on thousands of books, piled floor to ceiling, ranked along the windowsill and mantelpiece and balanced, in narrow precarious towers on every available surface. Dust danced minutely in the beams like angels on the head of a pin. Beyond the striped lawn of the tranquil quad, the bells of several churches began, with a carefree lack of synchronicity, to ring the quarter-hour.

Eastway returned with steaming cups of coffee.

She said: 'I'm sorry it's me and not Alan Evans.'

'I think I'll survive the disappointment.' He smiled. 'Did he brief you at all on what we'd discussed already about Siddons?'

It was interesting that Eastway said 'Siddons' and not 'my grandfather'. Academic distance, she supposed.

'I'm afraid he didn't. He took his notes with him too, so

we're starting from scratch, I'm sorry to say.'

'Oh well. Best place to start.'

He sat down opposite her and fixed her with his briny green eyes in a way that was somehow intensely flattering, suggesting the subject had his undivided attention. Elsa knew all about this mannerism. She had heard about it from friends who had been taught by him. Among the generality of dons, who liked to drink while they listened to essays, or mutter irrelevantly, or stare vacantly into the middle distance, it stood out rather. But it made Elsa uncomfortable, so she took her notebook and went through a broad outline of the film and the areas of Siddons' life that would feature. There was not much. A short scene after he joined up, at the OTC, perhaps a meeting with friends at the Continental in Calais, then a scene at the front, just before his death. When she had finished she sat back and said: 'I liked the biography. Can I ask why you decided to write it?'

He laughed. 'Oh the usual noble motives. Fear and loathing, petty academic rivalry. I'd been thinking of it for some time and then Scotts, my publishers, came to me and said someone else had approached them with the idea and was I interested? And that sort of spurred me on. I had a lot of private photographs and letters, you see. They said if I knocked him on the head with the definitive version, just in time for the centenary, that would fob off the others. Publishing's like that, apparently. Humankind cannot bear very much biography, it seems.'

'But it must have been so interesting to write about your own grandfather. And presumably you had all those anecdotes from your mother which no one else would really have been able to unearth.'

Even as she said this, Elsa squirmed with embarrassment. Why was she so tactless? Eastway's mother, to whose memory the biography was dedicated, had died last year. But if he was distressed at the mention, he did not betray it.

'Yes it was. Funnily enough, I've been studying Siddons' poetry for thirty years now, evaluating his place among the other war poets. Lobbying for him, polishing up his little niche in posterity, if you like. But it wasn't until I started thinking about this book and got my mother and other people to talk properly about him, that I really felt I had the measure of the man. It's as though if I really wanted to know you, I'd have to write your biography.'

'I don't expect that would be very exciting,' muttered Elsa, concentrating on her coffee cup.

His eyes glinted. 'Oh I don't know. Even younger lives have their interesting evasions and culs-de-sac. All those dark little corners passed over in the official version. I'm sure you've had failures and achievements which never get mentioned on your CV but are far more important than exam grades.'

'Well no biography of me would ever be an authorised one.'

'Good. I prefer it that way.'

He sprang up and started putting his jacket on. For a moment Elsa took this as an eccentric, abrupt signal to leave, until he said:

'If you really want to get a feel of Valentine Siddons, you should see his home. I'll show you, if you like.'

'Lower Binding?'

'The Poplars, yes, it's mine now. Since my mother died. I don't live there of course. In fact I keep intending to rent it out to students but we still get the occasional fan who's travelled all the way from Ohio or wherever wanting to visit, and it seems a shame to disappoint them. Besides, when the book comes out there's a TV company wanting to film there, so it's just as well I haven't got any tenants in. I've told Christ's they can use it meanwhile for visiting lecturers, so I suppose it's OK for the moment. I'd be delighted to show you round and we can deal with all your questions on the way. That's if you've got the time, of course?' he added with elaborate courtesy.

Elsa had the time. They drove out to Lower Binding in his dark green two-seater, and as it was nearly one o'clock he stopped on the way to pick up a French loaf, cheese and a bottle of wine. It was shaping up to be a glorious spring day and the countryside looked quite a different proposition from the seat of this shiny, glamorous car. Reflected in the gleaming bonnet, clouds wandered across the high blue sky and the wind bent and flattened the sleek pelt of grass in the passing fields. As they drove along the brow of a hill, the country below them undulated in swells and hollows, the ploughed earth speckled with chalk, the receding grey hills languid and relaxed.

Oliver took her on what he called his favourite long cut, flashing through villages which apart from the odd satellite dish and climbing frame seemed unvisited by the twentieth century. He said how difficult he still found it to live in the town, even though by most people's standards it was not a particularly distant migration.

'You have the choice. I mean you're not married, are you?'

He glanced at her from the driving seat. 'No. But I've had some lucky escapes.'

Elsa wished she could say the same. Still, he must be − what? − nearly fifty. Certainly very middle-aged. It was unusual.

'Here at last.'

At the tail end of a village they drove up a short lane, narrowed by overgrown hedges on either side which scraped their tendrils against the car. It led to a cottage, in standard honey-coloured Cotswold stone, its tiny front garden studded by spring flowers. There were primroses in the grass and clumps of snagged daffodils. The sides were bounded by fruit trees, apple, pear and cherry, tipped with a spume of blossom.

Behind the house was open country with fields rolling away into the smudgy distance, and the view was bisected by a line of poplars, a windbreak straight as a die, reaching down the hill into the valley. The silver-backed leaves buckled and bowed as one beneath a sharp wind, as they stretched down into the Oxfordshire countryside, stooped like a line of soldiers home from war.

'Oh it's wonderful,' said Elsa. 'And now I understand the name.'

'What?' He followed her gaze. 'Oh, the poplars. They're rather fine, aren't they? My grandmother planted them right after the war. They're along the boundaries of what used to be our land. They reminded her of northern France. She said every time she looked out of her bedroom window, she'd remember the ranks of men cut down.'

They stood for a moment and watched the poplars ripple

and sway. They were old trees now, though their height and slender shape made them look deceptively young.

The paint on the front door was hot from the sun. Oliver pushed it open and they entered the cool, dark interior, its floor bare stone flags, the walls brilliant with William Morris wallpaper, writhing with emerald leaves and red roses. Oliver had been right when he said the house would give a feel of Siddons. There was a powerful sense of the dead man. Even the air seemed freighted with his memory. The fireplace, where he used to sit with his pipe, the scored pine desk at the window where he wrote most of the poems, and everywhere the fusty, leathery smell of past learning.

Beside the desk was an oak chest. Dropping to his knees Oliver unlocked it, bringing out a small notebook, covered in black leather, cracked and worn.

'First versions of "Forgotten" and "Winter 1915",' he murmured, turning the faded pages. He fished out a file. 'I could let you have some photostats of these. They're the letters he wrote to my grandmother from the front, right up to the last one before he died, in which he talks about the forthcoming birth of his first child. That was Violet, my mother, of course. He never saw her.'

He handed her a sliver of paper, across which a blue, angular hand marched erratically. She took in snatches of it: '. . . glad to hear your news,' she read. 'Forgive me if it all seems rather distant here . . . Quiet time at the moment, behind the lines, at least the men are getting what rest they can . . . Could you send a copy of *Stanzas* to the names and addresses below?'

Oliver was looking up at her, another sheaf of papers in his hand. 'There's a bit of detail you might find useful about the trenches, and some of the men he was out with. Foxley, MacPherson, Hughes, Stewart.'

Elsa handled the frail pages so carefully she scarcely read them, as if the mere act of passing her eyes across the page might cause some damage. Oliver, head deep in the chest, passed more papers out to her.

'His will, in which he leaves everything to Emily – what there was to leave of course – except some of his water colours, which he left to a young corporal in his company.'

'Aren't these a bit precious to leave in here? I mean, they do have burglars in Oxfordshire, don't they?'

Oliver sighed and closed up the chest again.

'I know. I lock the place but anyone could get in, really. My mother insisted all his things stay here. She specifically asked me just before she died. It's so hard to know how far you should honour the wishes of the dead. It's so impractical. In the end I compromised and left these but donated various other bits, like the diary notebook he had on him when he died, to the Normandy Foundation. Come and see his room.'

In the bedroom, the sense of being in a shrine, or rather a mausoleum, intensified. Oliver gave her a conducted tour, taking in the framed version of Siddons' first published poem, 'On Tom Quad', his leather-bound volumes of Tennyson, Kipling and Shakespeare, ranged neatly on a shelf, the certificate for a school poetry prize. But as well as these, someone, Emily perhaps, had imported other childish leavings. A pair of small, scuffed boots. A sepia-tinted photograph of a rumpled, sailor-suited little boy, staring soberly at the camera. The boy was clutching a boat awkwardly, as if well aware that no one played with sailing boats in the drab, curtained studio of E. H. Brown, Kensington High Street. Around the walls hung landscape watercolours, Siddons' own work she presumed.

At the other side of the stairs, Oliver flung open another door.

'And my old room.'

'More museum pieces here?' Elsa joked.

Oliver, who was standing beside her, smiled wryly. 'You're right. I suppose I'm old enough to be your father.'

Silence widened between them. Elsa instantly regretted her flippancy, but he had already moved away and she looked curiously round the room. It was bare, except for a narrow bed and a couple of old trunks. The leaves of the fruit trees, crowding against the window, gave the room a strange underwater feeling, allowing only a dim, emerald light to filter through.

So this was where the young Dr Eastway had grown up. Like a strange facsimile of his grandfather's room, there was also a single photograph on the windowsill, but this was of a sweet-faced grinning boy, wearing a grey school blazer, resting on his elbows, head cupped in his hands. Oliver as a boy. It was hard to imagine him young, somehow. One front milk tooth was missing, which made him, what? Six or seven. Elsa was no good on childhood detail.

Oliver had bounded downstairs and into the kitchen.

'Fancy a spot of lunch?' he called

Thankfully, Elsa thought, the kitchen was distinctly post-war. It ran to wineglasses, plates, washing-up liquid and an electric kettle. Evidently someone did the housekeeping too. The kitchen garden outside looked well tended. There were pots of red geraniums casting a bloody spatter of petals beneath the heavy lace of clematis climbing the fence. Young honeysuckle curled round the door frame. The garden was still, the quiet so deep they could almost hear the sap surging through stems and leaves. Even the sudden roar of a low-flying jet which tore the air apart as it rose from a nearby airbase only intensified the silence.

Lunch, a hunk of bread and Brie with glasses of good burgundy, was relaxed and expansive. Oliver had an easy, intimate way which invited confidences. Curling his hand round his glass he leaned back in his chair and said lightly:

'I want to know everything about you. For the un-authorised biography, that is.'

'And what have you gathered about your subject so far?'

'Well you're not English for sure. Not with a name like Meyers and those flashing continental eyes.'

'I am English. Half. I mean my mother's family can trace themselves back to the Norman invasion and I've always lived here. But my father's German. He comes from Munich.'

'And is this father still with us?'

'Yes and no. My parents and brothers and sister went to live in Berlin twelve years ago. My dad's a surgeon and he got a job there. I chose to stay here.'

'Why?'

The question Elsa had so often asked herself.

'Oh I'm the independent type.'

'Nonetheless you must miss them.'

'I do. It's silly when they're only a plane journey away, but when they left I did feel rather as though I'd been orphaned.'

It was hard to explain just how estranged she had felt since first making that life-changing decision and refusing to climb down. Why had she done it? A teenage thing, perhaps. There had been a boy, a social life, a chance of an Oxford place. Her aunt had been happy to give her a home and Elsa had implored and assured her parents that she was happier in London. She still saw them, of course, a couple of times a year, and from the cheerful letters she received it was clear her family loved their new life and were glad to have exchanged Camden's litter-strewn, crime-ridden streets for Germany's affluence. The older brothers had left home, taking up jobs in banking and translating. With a German wife and girlfriend respectively, they had woven themselves deep into the fabric of their new country. They were solid, metropolitan citizens with expensive haircuts and stylish European clothing who spoke, thought and probably dreamed in German now; if they still had dreams, that was.

Her younger brother and sister had been closer, and so were harder to lose. A few years ago her sister, hoping to entice Elsa to migrate to Berlin, had made a video record of her daily life there, the shops and night-clubs, the cafés along the Ku'damm, the rubbly remains of the Wall, garishly painted with butterflies and CND symbols, her school, her friends, and Wolfy, her mongrel dog. The video was on the wrong standard for Elsa's equipment, and had to be converted before she could view it. Afterwards she wished she had not bothered. Nothing was so alienating as to have seen those familiar faces living everyday lives in their new setting. Only her mother's face bore a worn, wistful expression, only her washed-out English eyes looked as though they still remembered, let alone regretted, the London buses and department stores, the fields and the commons and parks they had left behind.

Her aunt had done her best to become close and they had even spent last Christmas together in Wales, a very cold, wet Christmas playing cards and drinking home-brewed cider.

Elsa was aware the synopsis of her life had a maudlin ring to it. Hastily she said: 'But it's you we should be talking about. This is your family home, after all. Do you prefer your academic life, or all the TV and radio stuff?'

'Whenever I'm doing one, I'm glad I've got the other. A lot of the university people don't like it, you see, the journalistic side. Having a career outside academia. They call people like me "telly dons". Going on Radio 3 they can just about cope with, but Channel 4 really distresses them. Though the media types are just as bad.'

'Sorry.'

'Present company excepted, of course. But journalists crave sensation. The people on these arts programmes are far more interested in the trivial scandals that punctuate the lives of novelists and playwrights than in their work. And usually there's precious little scandal to tell. Most writers live very dull lives. Feed the cat, go to the study, work all day, kiss the wife goodnight.'

'You don't have a dull life, I bet,' Elsa said.

'What do you think?'

'I imagine you have some very glamorous academic girl-friend, a lecturer probably, specialising in sub-textual feminism in Shakespeare's later comedies, late thirties with gold-rimmed spectacles, frighteningly intelligent with a passionate nature.'

'Sounds awful. What about you?'

'Oh a multimillionaire art collector with houses on three continents, a Ferrari and six lovely cats.'

'I suppose it would be almost worth it for the cats.'

They smiled at each other for a moment then Elsa broke off and got up to wash the glasses. She was wondering if this was the right point to raise the subject of the writings of Valentine Siddons, and whether any unpublished poetry remained. But just as she was about to ask, swilling the glinting dregs pensively under the tap, Oliver rose noiselessly and came to stand behind her. He leaned forward and curled a loop of her dark hair behind her ear. She smelt his hot, masculine scent mingled with the wine they had just drunk.

'You really are a gorgeous little girl, you know.'

He looked down at her testingly, and Elsa, shocked, could not meet his eyes. She knew she should feel patronised and affronted but instead his words unleashed in her an unaccustomed rush of excitement. Behind her she could sense the hard chest, the large arms, and she felt a strong desire to let herself turn and step into them. In the breathless solitude of the warm afternoon, so far from anywhere, she almost did.

But this man was a virtual stranger. It was beyond the pale for him to take her here and make a sort of pass at her, if that's what it was. It was unforgivable, when she had come here in a professional context. Inside her head these strident protests rang, cold, hollow and imperative.

Flustered, she put down the dishcloth and picked up her bag. She forgot to ask about the photostats he had promised.

'I really should be getting back if I'm not going to miss my train.'

He did not apologise. And although on the way back Elsa was almost mute through nervousness and embarrassment, he acted as if nothing had happened between them, talking of quite other things, the film, and his next television assignment. But when they reached Oxford station, and he parked to let her out, he leaned over and said:

'I think you and I should talk some more.'

CHAPTER SEVEN

EXTRACT FROM *VALENTINE SIDDONS: A LIFE*

By October 1914, Siddons' desire to join the army and fight had become irresistible. Unlike many of the early volunteers, he found himself processed through training camp and commissioned very swiftly so that by the end of December, the battalion he had joined had been sent out to France. At the same time he succumbed to a mounting desire of a very different kind. He proposed marriage to Emily Torrence, and was accepted.

★   ★   ★

'IF I HADN'T seen it, I wouldn't believe it,' said Captain Hudson, with a disbelieving laugh. 'I mean it. There's a Boche out there giving a haircut to one of the Scots Guards. Sitting down in a chair, sweet as you like, smack in the middle of No Man's Land. It's unreal.'

Hudson manoeuvred his large bulk through the narrow entrance to the dugout and sat down precariously on an orange box which was doubling as a chair. Inside the cramped, freezing space his hot breath rose in clouds. Through the mud-spattered veneer of his face he looked more cheerful than Valentine could remember having seen him in their entire acquaintance, all two weeks of it. He beamed round at them.

'Fritz started it, apparently. One madman stood up and waved at our men and they all came out in droves, swapping whisky and cigarettes with the Hun. I mean it's not as if they're playing football or anything, but it's pretty bloody friendly. I suppose somebody had better put a stop to it, but it's not going to be me.'

'Why should someone put a stop to it?' Robert Fleming's quiet voice cut in acidly. He had been a schoolmaster in Harrow, and had taught German culture and language to the few boys who wanted it. It was a bitter irony to him that this love of Goethe and Wagner and Beethoven should have propelled him into fighting against the nation that bred them. Yet since the terrible developments of last summer, the sly innuendo and the crude looks which followed him down the corridors, the whispers of 'Hun lover', the Kaiser moustache with which someone had decorated his face in the year's school photograph, had left him with little choice. He had put down his pen after the end of school one October afternoon and gone out to the local recruiting office. Then he had returned to his lodgings in town and informed Mrs Annersley his landlady, who for the first time in all their years together had wiped away a small tear with the corner of her apron and said she was proud of him.

After all, he had no wife or children to miss him, only a few of the older boys, known at school as Fleming's Lads, who would now lose their evenings listening to Bach, or reading German poetry round his study fire. A number of his lads had been commissioned too, but so far, thank God, he had not had to serve alongside any of those whose intelligence and youthful enthusiasm had been his life's pride. Since reaching France Fleming found himself faced with a situation that could not be controlled, like a classroom, through a mixture of sarcasm and heavy irony. He reacted by speaking very little. Now he said:

'They're burying the dead out there, for God's sake, and singing carols together. It's about the most constructive thing anyone has done for the past six months. Let them get on with it.'

Valentine filled his pipe with the last of the tobacco sent in his Christmas parcel from home. But after the slight physical disruption needed to accomplish this, he remained horizontal and immobile on his rudimentary bunk, shrouded in his British Warm. It was a method he had evolved to combat the penetrating cold. It meant that his legs were numb, and would be painful when he tried to shake the circulation back into them, but on the whole he reckoned it was more successful than trying to keep warm by puffing and slapping his arms the way the others did. Also in the Christmas box, and now mostly gone, had been a Fortnum's fruit cake – got by the rats – a jar of stem ginger, almonds, chocolate and several packets of Woodbines. But his bad cold meant he could hardly taste them. In an unusually thoughtful gesture of his mother's, tucked along the top was the December edition of the *Journal*, which Valentine had not been able to bring himself to read. It rested there among his belongings, a mocking reminder that two such starkly different worlds could exist just miles apart. That a reader of the *Journal*, reclining say on the Sussex downs, could on a still day hear the distant booming of the guns, yet have no idea what went on at that place where the earth shook beneath them.

If anyone had told him last Christmas that at the same time the next year he would be sheltering in a support trench in northern France, sleeping in a bunk where the rats sometimes ran across his face, wearing clothes encrusted with mud and crawling with lice, he would have looked at them with blank incomprehension. As it was, he felt pretty blank anyway. The shock seemed to have subdued his reactions, as though he was living in a state of suspended animation.

It had rained almost continually since he got off the train from the coast exactly a fortnight ago. That was bad enough back in the village where they had been briefly billeted, but in the narrow trenches the water sloshed down the walls, drenching the earth on the sides and turning it to slime, causing the grey-green viscous soil to slide down between the duckboards to a deep channel beneath. Sometimes, if he were not careful, a man could step through a hole in the boards and slip down, trapped up to his chest in the freezing mud. In other places the trench was already waist high in sludge, which meant that rifles were clogged and incapacitated, boots and even clothes were pulled off by the clinging earth. Stumbling heavily, blind and exhausted along the zigzagging, submerged path, a man would sometimes feel the terrible soft give of a corpse beneath his foot. When that happened, you had to hope the dead man was facing down, because all too often bloated stomachs ruptured beneath the tread.

Fortunately the trench they currently occupied, which had been captured and occupied by the Germans and then recaptured, was not flooded. But all along its length a soldier was apt to come across stark reminders of the previous inhabitants. A birdcage of ribs breaking jagged out of the ground, the white curve of a skull mushrooming from the dark earth, and in one case a dropped pocket New Testament, inscribed JOHANN VII. X. 1913.

In some places it seemed to Valentine that the dead were the only landscape left. Everything else which might have gone by that name, houses, trees, animals or roads, had been ravaged by artillery fire. Some trees still stood, but their branches were blackened and twisted by fire. Just behind the front line, a few straggling villages were left, but elsewhere heaps of rubble and masonry were all that remained of farmhouses and of barns that had stood for centuries. The roads were pitted with shells and their banks marked by the rough graves of men.

On the way up the line, it was quite common to see engineers filling the shell craters in the road with blackened bodies, the flesh swollen and oozing gas. Until then Valentine had never seen a dead person. Now that he was so near to becoming one himself, the state of annihilation seemed appallingly familiar. Puffed, erupting flesh scarcely made him gag. The yellow stare of killed men barely gave him a jolt. The cries of pain from the mangled, mutilated bodies being brought down to the casualty station must have evoked a horror in him, but it was a horror which anaesthetised. Sometimes he was still caught out by the wide-eyed babyish faces of the younger dead, the sixteen-year-olds who had lied about their years and so fatally forfeited them. But generally shock had formed into a hard, sheeny carapace, protecting him as the thick ice on the ground around them shielded murky pools of water beneath.

A leaden enervation prevented Valentine from exploring his feelings more than superficially. But anyway he had no desire to. The images which had sparked and flickered through his brain in his other existence, his poetry-writing life, had vanished. In their place everything appeared in monochrome. Above the grey scarred earth the cloud-clotted sky hung, a great oppressive weight of nothingness, shrinking horizons and contracting the world to smaller margins. His past and his future were both out of sight. And whenever Valentine did find the energy to consider his situation in any depth, the problem of women arose.

It had been his mother who first signalled the complexities of this war business. He had gone to his parents' house in Putney, to tell them he had joined up. He was expecting them, of course, to be proud and pleased. They were in the drawing room when he arrived, she fiddling with a vase of tawny autumn chrysanthemums, his father with his back to the fire, absorbing all the warmth in his habitual way. His mother looked up joyfully at his entrance, but as soon as he had broken his news her blue eyes filled with water, spilling over in silent tears down her pillowy cheeks.

'I wish you wouldn't go,' she sobbed quietly.

His father laid a hard hand on her shoulder and squeezed, cruelly.

'That's enough. I'm proud of you, son. You're doing the right thing.' He couldn't resist showing off his up-to-the-minute knowledge of the war situation. 'Sir John French says it will be over in a few months. And it has to be only a matter of time before the States come in.'

Valentine was dismayed. His father was behaving predictably, but why was Mother crying, blast her? God, it wasn't as though he really wanted to enlist.

Since the Constance Emberley episode, everything about the Michaelmas term at Oxford had been frightful. Even two months after war was declared, the place had changed virtually beyond recognition. The parks were full of men marching and drilling and a persistent queue formed outside the city recruiting office. To make matters worse, most of Valentine's friends had already joined up and those who remained in college were diffident and subdued. Valentine's tutor did not attempt to hide his opinion of them.

'Only wish I was young enough to serve,' he said menacingly, comfortable in his fat, tweedy complacency that he would never be called upon to fulfil this yearning. On every letterbox posters declared that due to national emergency Lord Kitchener needed another 100,000 men. Valentine had tried not to look at them whenever he passed. Then a detachment of women from Somerville, which was being taken over for an infirmary, flocked chattering and twittering into Christ's like so many hatted and high-collared birds, thronging their segregated section of the dining hall and some of them staring with accusatory interest at the motley male undergraduates who remained.

The sensation of almost universal disapproval was not pleasant. Once or twice he had been down to London to escape into the uncensorious company of Foxley and Margaret and the unaccustomed feeling of being proclaimed a pacifist hero for his reluctance to enlist. Foxley himself affected not to understand Valentine's discomfort. He even attempted to enjoin him to hand out anti-war leaflets which he had obtained from a new group aiming to stop the fighting. Valentine had refused to attend their meetings.

'I can't say I blame you,' Foxley sighed. 'They hold very admirable sentiments, but my dear. They meet in a sordid little hall and bleat on and on about the new world order when it's plain no one of any importance is going to take the slightest notice of them.'

That didn't prevent Foxley's attempts at unilateral action, though. There had been one horrible time when walking down High Holborn together, Foxley had been handed a white feather by a patriotic young woman, brimming with the righteousness of her gesture. Valentine flinched but Foxley had not minded a bit and called her back, arguing that the war was merely a struggle between the ancient ruling classes of Europe, not the workers who should rise up and condemn it, and commending her to read a piece on that subject in the latest edition of the *Journal*.

Then, of course, there had been Emily. She and Valentine were meeting almost every day but the practicalities remained difficult. For an unchaperoned girl to enter a man's rooms was not unheard of in Oxford, but the ranks of those who braved scandal and flaunted convention were never likely to include Emily Torrence. The most secluded place they found was a café in Oriel Square, near to the flat of her music teacher. There they would eat toasted teacakes and drink steaming tea as Valentine contemplated the admiring, passionate attachment that Emily appeared to have formed for him.

One teatime, as the warmth and light of the café's interior glowed out against the wet October dusk, they met for a hurried session between Valentine's Latin and Anglo-Saxon tutorials. Emily's smooth blonde hair, tucked demurely under her hat, framed her eager white face, which became tinged with pink when excited. She was wearing a smart navy jacket with a fur collar, but with her clear, delicate features and innocent, china-blue eyes he might have been sitting there with a sixteen-year-old relative, rather than holding a secret liaison with an eighteen-year-old sweetheart. The idea raised a faint revulsion in him. She was telling him about her brother George, a second-year who had not even bothered to return to the university after the outbreak of war but had gone up to join the Cameron Highlanders, their uncle's old regiment, and had just been sent to France. Emily's usual excitement at seeing Valentine seemed dampened by apprehension at what might lie in wait for George.

'We had no idea he would be sent to the front so soon.'

Valentine reached over to caress one small, gloved hand. 'Don't worry. I'm sure he will be all right.'

Sharply, she withdrew her hand, as if from an assault. 'And what would you know about it?'

This was so unexpected that Valentine recoiled as if he had been slapped. Until now, Emily's adoration had not allowed for a single cross word to pass between them. Not even Emily's persistent belief that he should enlist had marred her shy expressions of affection. It was hard to avoid the posters plastered round the city. They were not subtle. One of the most prevalent read: 'If your young man neglects his King and country, the time may come when he neglects you. Think it over.' And Emily had. But her scruples seemed tempered by an overriding desire to believe that whatever Valentine did was right. Talking to her was like looking into a mirror which would reflect only the most flattering view.

After her hasty words over George, Emily's face showed a momentary confusion, but with a little effort she resumed the old, admiring expression and stretched out her hand again.

'I'm sorry, Valentine. I didn't mean that. Tell me about your Latin tutorial. Was it as terrible as you thought?'

Suddenly, the image of his Latin class, the translations he had slogged his way through, and the wheezing professor, who had appraised him with wandering rheumy eyes, sickened him. The passion which had flared from Emily's earnest face sparked an answering urge within him. He heard himself say: 'Don't talk about that. Emily, I've been thinking of enlisting. What do you say?'

She looked away, beyond the windows trickling with condensation, into the gaslit square.

'Don't ask me that. It has to be your decision. Of course, I don't want you to go away. I hate to think of you coming to harm. It's just . . .'

Almost as soon as he'd spoken, Valentine cursed himself. What on earth had made him say something so rash? And now he seemed to be placing the responsibility for his decision on her shoulders. Ambition, obligation and desire churned painfully in him, confusing every move and motivation.

* * *

If his judgement was badly clouded, there was no mistaking the reason for it. The next day, after a meagre breakfast of tea and toast brought to his rooms by his asthmatic, resentful scout, he took the train down to London. Since the night four weeks ago that he had met Constance Emberley, the memory of her was continually before him. A hot mingling of excitement and self-disgust burned in him. Questions he would not allow himself to ask collected unspoken in his mind. Why had she wanted him, and would she want him again? Of course he had betrayed Emily, in a far graver way then by his simple failure to join up. He wanted to write to Constance, but could not think how best to cast the letter. Yet the urge to see her again was irresistible. He had obtained her address from Foxley, under the pretext of thanking her for dinner. Leaving the train at Paddington, he took a taxi to Eaton Square and stood outside the creamy, imposing terrace, trembling slightly with anticipation.

The butler listened to his request with a reptilian flicker of curiosity. Then he left Valentine waiting while he disappeared into the drawing room. When he returned, his leathery face was closed, inscrutable.

'Lady Emberley is otherwise engaged. Do you wish to leave your card, sir?'

Valentine had no card to leave. He hesitated.

'Could you . . . Just tell her Mr Siddons called, and wished her good-day?'

The heavy black door closed on him and he made his way down the immaculate steps, trailing humiliation and anger like a ball and chain. He felt her laughing eyes burning into his back. That moment decided him. He had seen his parents, then returned to Oxford, gone to the OTC and sworn his allegiance to King and country.

★   ★   ★

Precisely two nights after the Christmas fraternisation, the crump of guns and the whine of shells began again. At standdown, as the dawn mist silvered the ground, preparations started for a move up to the front. Valentine strode up ahead of the company with Fleming.

'How old are you, Siddons?' Fleming had been studying him with the accusing, shrewish regard that had once brought him respect in the classroom.

'Nineteen.'

He whistled. Siddons knew what he meant. To be young at the front was both a blessing and a liability. For the older men, the ties of home were strong. But for the young, without wives or children, connections and relationships were considered less important. That they should be wiped away at this time was deemed less painful.

Valentine felt a sour rage that his life should be snatched from him in this way. He was not yet dead but he soon would be. His other existence, his writing, Putney and his parents, already seemed unreal. In his imagination they and the shadowy island that was Britain had all drifted away in the Channel's salt tumultuous waves, like a ship broken loose from its moorings. In his pocket lay the letter from Emily which had arrived that morning, accepting his proposal of marriage. Already it seemed like a document from another age.

CHAPTER EIGHT

FUNNILY ENOUGH, THE call came the very next day. It was not that Elsa had not been expecting it, but she thought a cool two days or even three, perhaps a week might elapse before that gravelly, wry voice purred down her line. Instead it came the next afternoon, just as she was flipping through *Screen International*, cheering herself up with a report on the success of British film makers in Hollywood and contemplating fetching coffee for the still silent Simon.

'Hello, is Elsa Meyers there?'

Her pulse accelerated at the sound of his voice.

'Dr Eastway. How nice to hear from you.' She hoped she sounded distant, ironic.

'Oh Elsa good, it's you. Listen I know this is very short notice, but I've got some interviews to do in London, to do with this scholarship we're awarding at the Normandy Foundation. I'm the token literary type on the panel and I just wondered if you might be free? For dinner, I mean.' He sounded, if it was possible for such a honeyed tone to sound anything but self-assured, a little nervous.

She laughed.

'Well, it depends when. Tonight, tomorrow, next week?'

'Oh, do I get to choose? Then I'll take all of them, please.'

This was not what Elsa had meant. She felt she was losing the upper hand. Brusquely, she said:

'I'm very busy at the moment. But it would be useful to discuss some of the script. When are you coming down?'

'Tomorrow afternoon.'

'I'll just check.'

Elsa reached for her diary automatically, though she knew it was blank with possibilities.

'Um, I think I'm free.'

'That's wonderful. Where shall we meet?'

'Oh I don't know. Near Paddington, so you can catch the train back?'

'I may drive. I haven't decided. So anywhere's fine. Covent Garden, perhaps? I know a very nice Italian restaurant called Dino's.'

Elsa knew it too. It was not what she would call nice. The tables were too rickety and close together, the décor cod trattoria, all red checks and plastic plants, the food indifferent. It was a provincial's idea of an evening out, a hymn to seventies culture, mediocre and middle-aged. She was amazed it was still in business. All the same, at least it was a public place so there could be no repetition of the incident in the cottage. And she preferred eating in Dino's to thinking up somewhere herself, which he might then dislike, and could tell against her.

'Fine. I know it too. Is seven-thirty OK?'

'Marvellous. I'll look forward to it.'

* * *

Simon was on the phone when she entered his cubicle with a comforting cup of coffee. He sounded as friendly as an attack dog.

'No I can't make tonight, or tomorrow . . . Or any time this week. Listen, let's leave it that I'll call you. OK?' He replaced the receiver aggressively. Though his tone suggested he was dealing with an obstructive tax inspector, Elsa guessed the call was from the statuesque French girl who had been into their office twice that week to see him. Despite her chic, expensive clothing, Elsa had detected a schoolgirlish devotion in her, a quality she had noted in other of Simon's female visitors.

What was it about him that inspired it? He was quite pleasant to look at, she supposed, with a finely boned, sensitive face and dark, sardonic eyes. He had an intriguing stillness about him, a separateness, as though he could never belong to any group. He was observant – she had often felt his cool appraising gaze on her – though he rarely shared his observations. But a date with him would surely be as warm as an evening up the Eiger.

Emboldened by the prospect of her own night out, Elsa ventured playfully on to the forbidden subject of Simon's private life.

'Fighting them off again?'

'What?'

'Is that your new girlfriend who keeps dropping in?'

'Who?'

'The French one.'

'God no,' he muttered in a staccato snarl. 'Friend of my brother's. Eurotrash.'

'Oh? Like me?'

He up looked at her for a moment, uncomprehending, then said: 'Don't be ridiculous, Elsa.' In a milder tone he added: 'What are you up to anyway?'

'I've just arranged dinner tomorrow night with Dr Eastway. He's proving very amenable.'

'That's great.' Simon was surprisingly enthusiastic. 'I've wanted to meet him. I've read one of his books, believe it or not. Have you booked for three?'

'Well, I . . .'

'Oh no. He's not bringing someone, I hope. These people seem to imagine all film makers have multimillion-pound budgets.'

'I think he was expecting just me,' Elsa continued lamely.

'He's in for a pleasant surprise, then. What's the problem?'

Unwilling to articulate exactly what the problem was, a variety of devious options flashed before her. She would ring and say she could not make it after all, then tell Simon that Dr Eastway had cancelled. She would bow out and send Simon in her place. These computations may have been momentary, but evidently they told on her face because Simon looked closely at her, then returned his attention to the papers in front of him and said: 'OK, I know where I'm not wanted.'

'It's not that, Simon.'

'Oh isn't it?' The line of his mouth twisted into a mirthless smile. 'Well I'm sure you'll get more out of him alone. It's probably best. Anyway, I have a pressing engagement with our VAT returns.'

Though she hated disagreeing with Simon and he always made her feel that she was somehow in the wrong, even this little encounter could not entirely dampen Elsa's anticipation of her night out. The following evening she left the office early, anxious to transform her persona from Grimy Commuter to something more like Sexy Intellectual. She was barely through the door of her flat when she saw the little red light winking. There was another call on the answerphone, a short stab of silence designed to unnerve her. She played it back and tried to tell from the breathy absence whether it was a man or a woman who loitered there twenty, even thirty seconds before hanging up. She tried to convince herself it was a wrong number, or a fax machine, but there was something in the ether that conveyed human intent. It was a message of sorts, she knew that.

Slipping off her clothes she stood under the shower. The hot jet of the water brought the blood tingling to the surface of her skin, making her normally pallid complexion glow. She chose a spicy scent which advertised floral notes of jasmine, undercut with a heady hint of musk and stood naked before the mirror, letting it trickle down the line between her breasts. She hated her body, which always seemed as though each part had been assembled without any reference to the rest. It was gawky and thin, the curve of her lower rib jutting out, her breasts small and high, the middle almost waistless, like a boy's. Envious people liked to assume the slenderness signified anorexia, which infuriated her and meant she had to exaggerate her femininity, rather than sticking to the androgynous jeans and T-shirts she would have preferred. That night she chose a simple, black silk dress, brightened at the throat with a floating yellow chiffon scarf which she hoped set off her sleek, shadowy hair – her best asset, Alison assured her.

After she had dressed she left the flat, late as ever and in a hurry. She had to walk some way before she could hail a taxi and so did not arrive at Dino's until a quarter to eight. The cold wind swept into the restaurant each time the door opened, making the people sitting nearby shiver and look round. Fortunately Oliver had secured a table at the back. He was straining to read a catalogue by the muted light of a candle shrouded in pink glass. The poor light made him look even older and Elsa glanced involuntarily around her hoping their meeting was not being observed.

'I just had time to catch the Longest Century exhibition

at the Barbican.' He rose to his full height and came round the table to take her hand, with an unexpected formality. 'But I think it's given me a bad case of millennial angst.'

'You don't look particularly anxious.'

'Millennial angst is the type that doesn't show. Or not until it's too late. In the first millennium everyone was expecting the world to end so they rushed out and joined strange sects and searched the skies for comets. This time round we're probably manifesting our pre-millennial tension in more complex ways.' He waved his hand stagily. 'You know the kind of thing. Moral ambiguity, heightened secularism, challenging the established authorities, the Church, the monarchy, breakdown of the family.'

'What was the exhibition like? I've been meaning to go.'

'Fascinating. When you get to the end of a century it makes you more curious about the beginning, I think. Or at least I hope so, for the sake of your forthcoming film.'

'Not to mention your biography.'

'Ah yes. I popped into my publisher's on the way, in fact. They wanted to see me and unfortunately for them they showed me the designs for the dust jacket. I'm afraid to say I rejected it. I just can't stand all those poppies. Such a first world war cliché.'

'What did they want with you?'

'Oh, I just needed to make a few tiny corrections to the text.'

'Corrections?'

'Just a couple of small factual amendments.'

Elsa's nerves tensed. She knew that now was the right time to tell Oliver of the poems on Siddons' own writing paper, but he carried on:

'God, aren't publishers the limit? Frankly we should have been celebrating because there's a very nice newspaper serialisation deal in the offing and, barring a few last-minute dotting of i's and crossing of t's, the whole book is about to be condensed on the review pages of a Sunday paper for two weeks running to coincide with publication. But with Scotts things are never simple. Always these hitches.' He gave a strained smile.

Just then the menu arrived and Oliver busied himself with

selecting pasta and wine. He seemed keen to advise Elsa on her choice, as though she had never been in an Italian restaurant before. Indeed she did prefer Japanese and Thai nowadays. But while Elsa would normally have greeted such old-fashioned condescension with withering scorn, that night she passively acquiesced. In truth she could hardly bear to think of eating at all.

Her head was ringing with the words he had whispered to her on their last meeting. What had he meant? And why had her senses quickened so in response? She recalled the way he had stroked her hair, with a swift, single gesture. Here they were, conversing again on a strictly formal footing, yet anticipation coursed through her like a drug. Though she had drunk hardly any of the Chianti, she was intoxicated already. When he looked up at her she faltered for something to say.

'And how were your interviews, Dr Eastway?'

He put down the menu, from which he had chosen melon, parma ham and linguini with baby clams.

'Well Miss Meyers, let's just say that if any of the candidates had been as beautiful as you, my critical faculties might have been severely impaired. Fortunately, they were dull postgraduates to a man, so I think we made some sensible choices. One chap studying twentieth-century attitudes to warfare and another one doing some archiving work on the cemeteries in France.'

Elsa fell silent. She wished he had not called her beautiful. What a hackneyed line. He had probably tried it on hundreds of his students, and only the silliest, most desperate and least attractive would fall for it. Yet here was she lapping it up. How ridiculous she must seem to him. And wasn't he the ridiculous one? She forced herself to look at the creases around his eyes, his receding hairline, and to think of his racing green sports car, the classic accessory of the paunchy, ageing seducer. He was just a middle-aged playboy with an academic edge.

But however much she tried to focus on his age she could not dismiss from her mind the picture of him she had seen in Lower Binding, a bold little boy, big for his age and well built, with ears sticking out either side of a crown of curly blond hair. A six-year-old smiling the great, beaming smile of the well loved. What distance had the confident boy travelled to become this world-weary charmer? Oliver filled her glass and said:

'Tell me about Durban Films. What's this Simon Pardoe like? Do you see much of him?'

'Well, yes, we work practically on top of each other. And he's fine, only a bit worried about our cash flow at the moment.' Guiltily she added: 'He wants to meet you, he's a great admirer. He almost came tonight, in fact.'

He raised one eyebrow quizzically. 'He did, did he?'

'Yes. Only something cropped up.'

'I see.'

The restaurant lived down to expectations. Not even the wine was enough to dull their senses to the wobbly table and the raucous crowd who were holding a farewell party for a colleague. A boy came to the table selling red roses and Oliver bought one, despite Elsa's insistence that the practice was cynical blackmail. The tight, folded little buds never flourished after they were brought out of their hothouses into the freezing air. They withered from inside and died before their petals opened into bloom. No Londoner ever fell for it. He listened to her tirade patiently, then proffered her the doomed flower with a smile.

He was a very good listener. With a few simple prods he had her talking about the film, her work and her ambitions, and Elsa found it hard to remember she could not be completely frank with him. The fact that Oliver was a consultant on *Passchendaele* meant that she could not be entirely open about the money problems, or the fear that the film would linger for ever in the state known as 'development hell', eating away at their budget and time, until their funds dwindled and they were forced to take on more and more part-time outside work to fill the gap.

It was far from the picture she tended to paint for Alison, when they collapsed on a sofa together with a bottle of Chardonnay to swap their woes. But Oliver was interested and informed, and he refilled her glass at pleasingly regular intervals. Delicately, diplomatically, he also suggested that he might have a valuable contact in film finance.

'It's a long shot, but he could be useful. His name's Justin Emberley. I went over to see him quite recently, when I was researching his great-aunt for my biography. He's situated in Bel Air, head of something or other for one of the studios, I forget which one, but it largely seems to entail sitting round a swimming pool all day swigging champagne cocktails. Want me to give him a ring?'

Elsa did not doubt that Oliver's friend Justin would be entirely useless to them. But this snippet of information might at least persuade Simon that she and Dr Eastway had spent the evening talking strictly business. After that, she did not hesitate to accept his offer of a lift home. His car might be a seducer's accessory, but it had its attractions, particularly when the alternative was a long taxi ride or an unappealing tube trip home, complete with the prospect of being panhandled or barracked by some drunk, or worse. She lay back in the long low seat watching the blur of the street lights flare up in front of them and pass.

'Shepherd's Bush, wasn't it?'

'Yes, I'll direct you.' She was tipsy, and could not remember if she had already confided in him where she lived. 'How did you know it was Shepherd's Bush?'

'You told me. I don't think I'm psychic.'

Watching his profile as he monitored the road in front, the Roman nose, the downward turn of the mouth's corners, she said: 'You are very like your grandfather, you know.'

'Want me to play him in the film?'

'Oh, I don't know if you'd approve of the Siddons part.'

Almost imperceptibly, his voice gained an edge.

'Oh, why?'

'Well, your grandfather's not exactly the star of the film, you see.'

He had been mellow and charming, but suddenly he sounded almost hostile. 'Valentine Siddons was not only a significant war poet, he was a hero for God's sake. He won a posthumous VC. Why should anyone want to question his achievements?'

Elsa was flustered. 'No. You've got me all wrong. I mean, he's obviously the focal point, but we're concentrating on a whole group of people. In terms of script, Siddons is only a bit part. A sort of cameo. But he is my favourite character. So inspiring.'

It was all right. He was calm again. 'I bet that's what you tell all your consultants,' he said levelly.

So that's what it's like to be proud of your family, Elsa thought.

When they reached her flat he got out of the car and opened the door for her. It was dark, or as dark as night ever gets in town, after the light slips from the sky and leaves behind it a mass of sodium-streaked shade. Oliver looked down at her almost accusingly as she stood by the opened door.

'You didn't like me saying in that restaurant that you were beautiful.'

'Oh it just seemed . . .'

'Seemed what . . .'

'Hackneyed.'

Suddenly he pulled her against his chest and lifting her face in his hands he kissed her.

'Is that hackneyed, then?'

Elsa caught her breath and summoned what she hoped was a neutral tone. 'Probably.'

'Can I come in with you?'

'I don't know whether . . .'

'Don't worry. Just for a while.'

They went down the basement steps together but no sooner had she closed the door behind him than he placed one arm across the narrow hallway, barring her way. Pushing back her jacket his hands ran down her body, along the folds of her dress, as though he was counting her bones through their thin coat of flesh. She quivered at his touch. He placed his arms around her and pulled her to him, smoothing her hair against his shoulder.

'Do you want me to go?'

She did not answer.

'You don't know, do you? How can I persuade you?'

A slow burn started up inside her. She felt herself trembling. As a distraction, almost a compensation, she said: 'I've got something to show you.'

She crossed the room to the chest of drawers and pulled

out the blue folder where she had put the poems away for safekeeping. She separated the poem written on the V.S. notepaper.

'Look at the initials, then tell me what you think.'

She could not have hoped for a swifter reaction. His face was instantly rapt, attentive. He took the sheet and looked down at it. His hands almost seemed to shake. After what seemed an inordinately long while he sat down and said: 'Interesting. "Memory's dim files". When you get to my age you know the feeling.'

'But look. Look at the initials. The same as your grandfather's. Do you think . . . I mean, I was wondering if it could possibly be Siddons juvenilia?'

'Can I ask where you got this?'

'I don't want to say, just yet. I mean I know that sounds silly, but I've got a confidence to protect.'

'I see.' He gave the poem another, thoughtful glance. Elsa was becoming impatient.

'But Oliver, what is it? I thought you'd be excited! I've got good reason to think it's connected with your grandfather and surely the fact that the notepaper has his initials on it means something?'

He laughed indulgently. 'Hold on a minute. For a start we don't know if it's his notepaper at all. And really, Elsa you can see it's not his style. Not a bit. I mean wine clouding, roses blazing. Please, do him some justice.'

'Who did write it, then?'

'Well I think it's highly unlikely it's anything to do with him. But even if, by chance, it was his notepaper, frankly it could be any one of a huge number of people. My grandmother was always having people to stay. Friends of her husband's and people who had become interested in his work and begun corresponding with her. Whether they found a piece of the notepaper at the house or inadvertently used a piece she had sent them, I can't say. But if you're not going to tell me where you found it, I can't help you, can I?'

Stretching over, he caught her round her waist and pulled her down on to his lap.

'Where did you get it, you clever little thing? Come on, I can keep a secret.'

For some reason, Elsa fought the impulse to tell him. The image of her rootling about someone else's flat, then making off with the contents lacked, she thought, either dignity or sophistication.

'I can't tell you. I promised,' she lied.

'What else do you have stashed away in that folder of yours? Are there more poems?'

'A few. But none with the initials.'

'Can I see them?'

'OK.' Dumb with disappointment, Elsa surrendered the remaining sheets. Oliver sat and read the other poems. When he finished he handed them back to her with a little shake of his head and she replaced them in the folder.

'Sorry. They're intriguing, and you were right to show them to me, but they're not Siddons. Don't be too disappointed.'

'No I'm not. Not at all. I was just curious.'

Elsa turned to put the folder back in the drawer, but as she crossed the room he sprang up and trapped her in his arms.

'Seriously, for a moment. There's something I need to know before I leave.'

'What?' If he wanted to know where she got the poems that badly, she would have to tell him.

'When am I going to see you again?'

Enclosed in his arms, suddenly Elsa's caution, which all evening had formed a brave little barrier between them, dissolved in a spasm of desire. Why should she have to resist him? Why should she not allow someone to care for her, or at the very least to make love to her? It had been long enough, after all. She let the hard edges of her body melt towards him. Sensing her surrender, he gently pulled her dress down over her shoulders, burying his face in her chest and cupping the breasts in his hands in a way which made them seem more substantial.

'To think I could have been Alan Evans,' she teased him, nervously.

'If I'd known, I would have paid him to do a bunk.'

With a deft movement he scooped her up and carried her into the bedroom, laying her down on the rumpled white sheets. He stroked a hand down her naked body, making her gasp.

'I wanted to do this the day we met. Out in my house. You wanted it too.'

For one so large and strong, his lovemaking seemed caught up in some strange private anguish. When he cried out, it was as though he was seeking comfort. When he entered her, it was as though he had taken possession of her soul. There was violence in his kisses and dominance in his grip, but beneath them he seemed to burn with some urgent need. When he had finished, he lay beside her, his arm around her and fell asleep. Elsa however stayed awake for some time, until her exhilaration slowly subsided and her heartbeat returned to its customary dull thud.

The night made her forget the anticlimax of the poems. It was not until the next day when she was strap-hanging on the tube, gazing vacantly at the damp tunnel walls flashing past, trying to rise above her role in the rush-hour's human concertina, that she remembered the folder in her bag. Though it seemed her little dream of a literary find had been dashed, she could not entirely shake off her lingering hopes that the poems might prove to be Siddons' work. So Oliver Eastway was a professional biographer and he was plainly not interested. But he didn't know where the poems came from. She need not bother him with the matter again.

CHAPTER NINE

EXTRACT FROM *VALENTINE SIDDONS: A LIFE*

In June 1915 Siddons returned after a short leave to the front. The burden of rejoining the fighting was redoubled because, for the first time, he was leaving a wife behind him.

* * *

IN THE MORNING the maid brought Connie her tea, pale gold and fragrant, with a lemon slice floating on its surface like a blank citrus moon. Setting the cup and its tray on the table by the bed, the girl hurried out with downcast eyes, giving a swift, embarrassed backward glance at the door. Connie ignored her. Listlessly she looked around the room. Since the death of Ralph's father, when his mother had departed to her London house, the manor had passed into their possession. It was a strangely ugly place.

Jacobean in origin, even the ruddy stone of that era failed to impart a warming bloom to its stark frontage. She had tried her best to cheer up the lofty panelled rooms with fabrics and furniture made by her Bloomsbury friends, screens with huge, primitive nudes in brilliant golds, reds and emeralds, vibrant cushions and drapes in dazzling patterns, bold silk lampshades painted with dancing figures. Chinese boxes and cabinets filled the drawing rooms, Samarkand rugs and lacquered screens lent an exotic aura to the manor's bare, English air. Ralph detested them of course but that hadn't stopped her. It was simple inertia which had caused her efforts to end before she reached this room, done out in aged violet chintz, its few pieces of eighteenth-century walnut furniture illuminated by a measly fire flickering in the grate.

Propped up against a heap of pillows, she realised that her depression had made her quite impassive. Her features seemed to have acquired their own pallid immobility, like the lifeless Emberley ancestors who stared phlegmatically down from the walls. It had been a shock, at first, to recognise her husband in the portraits of his relations, hung round the infinite corridors and halls of the house, all disdainful variations on a thousand-year theme. Ralph's brown, handsome visage, with its bristle of black moustache, seemed to quiver with a kind of rigorous discipline beneath which insubordinate flashes of humour or emotion were swiftly quelled, excitement suppressed and anger controlled. It was a face designed to hide its feelings, but more than a decade after meeting him she knew what he felt without needing to look. Staccato silences and pained *longueurs* stood out like Braille in the dense atmosphere which existed between them. Words were superfluous when a casual crossing of the legs, an icy glance or an irritated drumming of the knuckles could communicate so much.

Ralph was a tall, muscular man, with a passion for field sports matched only by an obsession with his own ancestry. What could have possessed him, she often wondered, to deviate so far from the path he felt destiny had mapped out for him as to marry an actress and have his union subject to everlasting social footnotes, even from those people who would never dare display the *froideur* they so longed to show? Come to that, how had Ralph even broken with tradition so far as to go to the theatre in the first place? It was frankly astonishing that he had found a space in his crowded calendar of shooting, fishing and hunting house parties, interspersed with parliamentary business in town, to see a play and fall in love with Constance Fanshaw. Unpredictability was not a familial trait she had come to associate with the Emberleys. So she supposed he deserved some credit for that. Indeed she felt a lingering tinge of warmth towards him when she remembered how he had faced off the Siberian disapproval of his mother when she was first invited into the gloomy grandeur of their home. His father had been little better, biting off the ends of his words as if he could scarcely bear them to leave his mouth, his handshake limp and cool like something recently shot.

Fuelled by their shared sexual excitement, Connie and Ralph had in their early days taken on his social circle like a

vast and hostile army, each dinner fraught with conversa-
tional heavy weaponry, each tea party in enemy territory an
encounter to be endured and ultimately won. Even the
Emberley staff, deadly infantry in the general resistance
to Connie and Ralph's union, had been worn down and
conquered, mutters and snide looks being swiftly stamped
on by Ralph, and the more obstinate dissidents dispensed
with. So comprehensive had their victory been that sometimes she forgot that her status as Lady Emberley was a
role, to be maintained with scrupulous attention to detail.

There was one detail, however, that she could simply not
master. It seemed as though Connie was never going to be
the mother of the next Viscount. The brutal good looks of
the Emberleys would come to a natural stop with Ralph.
This latest miscarriage had followed a long, miserable
pattern. The tingling breasts from the moment she con-
ceived, the tide of nausea rising up her gullet each morning,
the deadening lassitude, and then, just as she felt this one
would surely stick, the predictable cramps and the slow
spreading stain, turning to a flood of scarlet, lumpy blood,
bitter and viscous with failure. She would lie for a day
weeping, feeling the life ebb out of her and then, after the
doctor had called and performed his brief examination with
tight-lipped, unmistakable disapproval, she would feel the
energy return to her body in a surge as it expelled the last
traces of Emberley blood from her womb.

Until Tuesday, however, she had hoped for more. There
was good reason to believe it would be different this time.
Yet again she called to mind Valentine's blunt, eager face,
the downward twist of his smile, the smooth, slender torso
which tasted sharp with sweat, the tangle of clothes and belt
on the floor. How she had sat afterwards, satiated and
fatigued, barely aware of the ghost of a frown returning to
his face as he pulled his clothes to order like unwilling
recruits.

'I think you're very clever, Connie,' Ottoline had told her.
'There's something so unspoiled about him. He was still a
virgin I suppose. What a crime.'

That had been at Garsington, where she was ostensibly
helping the Morrells settle in. While Connie leaned back in

her armchair, fingering a book, Lady Ottoline absently rearranged a paisley spread left carelessly on the floor and then threw open the window so the room's aqueous, churchy light was invaded by the garden outside, drenched with rising sap, throbbing with the scent of bright, blown roses and overpowering fecundity. More than ever Connie marvelled at Ottoline. She stood there, arms outstretched on the window frames, gazing into the chill sunbeams like some bizarre pagan goddess, her face thin and bony, her huge frame draped in a confection of tassles and watered silk. Ottoline would say that she had discovered Valentine, but Connie had no fear. He seemed impervious to even the most amorous appraising glances cast on him by the women – and several of the men – among his new acquaintance. His gaze trailed Connie round the room like the eyes of a Labrador Ralph had once owned. Before he left he had begged her picture (she'd selected the image of a younger, glamorous Constance taken for the stage some years ago) and he sealed it solemnly in his breast pocket.

It seemed like an age since the September night when they'd first dined together. She'd hesitated initially. When a few weeks later he called unexpectedly at the house in Eaton Square, she decided she had made an embarrassing mistake and sent Spencer out to say she was indisposed. But a little later she wrote him a note, suggesting they meet. It had reached him just before he was sent off on training. It was hard finding time, even harder now that he had gone to France. After Christmas they had managed to meet a couple of times at the house in Flood Street, and then again, eight weeks ago at Garsington.

That last time, they didn't talk much. Once they were alone, they turned swiftly to a fierce embrace, in which they grappled and rolled like stricken swimmers gasping for air. Perhaps he thought the guilt of adultery made her silent. Maybe he felt only a physical force could bridge the chasm of age between them. Connie didn't mind at all. If she was quieter than her normal self that was not because she was so much older than him. It was because she was speechless with pleasure, all the more for it being so unexpected.

Although Ottoline favoured Valentine, to her he was no

different from all the other young men who came down from Oxford to admire at her stately feet like worshippers at the marble face of some high baroque chapel. But to Connie it was flattering, exhilarating, to be with him. True, he was absurdly gauche and unsophisticated. He carried his youth about with him like an unwelcome guest, tripping up on etiquette, airing its ignorance unawares. Connie almost preferred to see him in uniform, because it dulled the blush that still rose to his cheeks whenever they became intimate. But his tenderness and vigour replenished a withering void within her. Sometimes she pictured herself as a huge mother oak, and him the young sapling rising and twining around her.

It was ironic, really, that for safety's sake she was obliged to revive the unwelcome experience of sleeping with her husband. After a decade in which passion between Ralph and herself had chilled to a truce, she found herself coupled with a man who neither liked women, nor understood them. Ralph seemed to carry in the fibres of his large, square body some quintessence of maleness. Women were essential to him, but as foot soldiers in an army, for the orderly function of routine operations, not as beings with whom one formed anything like a spiritual or intellectual connection. Not as friends. His intimacy he reserved for the natural world. He adored rare plants and would spend whole evenings immersed in books of flora. On the few occasions when she accompanied him to the manor house stables, she had found herself watching with astonishment as he toured the horses, stroking the twitching, velvety muzzles as they leaned their long necks towards him. As he caressed their flat pelts, muttering tender nothings into their pricked brown ears, she was amazed to see again the gentleness which she had once known herself. She could think of nothing else that would recall that softness in him. Except the children he would never have.

Connie shook herself like an impatient cat. Just thinking about Valentine made her want to ignore the doctor's stipulation of a week's bed rest, and race back to her London life immediately. She took a long draught of tea, and stretched her firm, white arms. Now that the cramps had gone, it was true, her energy came pouring back, as it always did. The weather was getting hotter. Outside the gardeners were mowing the lawns and the smell of fresh grass, with its tangy promise of a long, lazy summer ahead seemed to urge her from bed. On impulse, she rang the bell for the maid. After all, with Ralph away, who was there to stop her?

★   ★   ★

Babies, they looked like, Ronald Foxley thought, from his pew in St George's, Hanover Square. He almost felt like intervening during the 'just impediment' passage, on the grounds that the couple seemed neither remotely old enough to take on holy matrimony, nor particularly cheerful at the prospect.

Emily, so thin she was almost translucent, was trembling in her ivory lace like a spring leaf, prematurely fallen, beside Valentine's tall khaki form. The pair stood in a pool of speckled sunlight before the altar, as grim as if they were facing a firing squad. The way the vicar rattled through the service there might have been a queue of couples waiting. Instead there was only a pitiful smattering of relations. The weeping, blowsy woman in the purple feathered hat he took to be the groom's mother. The father must have been good looking once, but was smug and grizzled now, like a middling civil servant. On Valentine's side there was also a toothy gaggle of what looked like cousins. The bride's side was altogether a smarter affair, though no more numerous. Apparently the happy couple had wanted something quiet in an Oxford chapel, but the father had connections here, and insisted. Presumably he had laid on something decent at his club afterwards.

Ronald loved weddings. He felt like humming.

'So romantic, a summer wedding,' he commented to Valentine's mother after the newlyweds had proceeded white faced and funereal down the aisle and climbed into a waiting taxi. The woman looked up at Foxley's smart tweedy figure with what seemed like respect. Her face was damp with tears.

'Yes, they both looked so happy. If only it wasn't for this dreadful war. You're Mr Foxley, Valentine's friend, aren't you?'

'That's right.'

'And have you been out there, Mr Foxley?'

'Not yet,' he replied in a measured tone. It was his stock response. 'Or ever,' he would add to himself, under his breath.

He had hoped the subject would end there, but was not so lucky once they reached the reception, a private room at the Oxford and Cambridge Club where good champagne was circulating in acceptable quantities and dainty asparagus rolls and salmon pieces, jewelled with winking caviare, were passing on silver platters. The air was heavy with the sickly smell of lilies thrust in huge, mournful urns.

Emily's father, an unpleasant-looking fellow with badgerish black and white sprouting hair and a fiery alcoholic flush approached as Ronald's glass was being refilled.

'My daughter tells me you're a pacifist.' This peremptory statement of fact was burdened with as much menace as a simple sentence could carry.

'That's right.'

'Yet Valentine's still a friend of yours?' He seemed incredulous.

'I sincerely hope so.'

Both looked round for Valentine to settle the issue, but he was trapped between his mother and aunt, a lean brown filling sandwiched by feathers, furs and pearls. Ronald watched the man's cheek purpling and wondered if he would stoop to violence at his own daughter's wedding. It was something he was becoming used to in the past few months. He had learned that if you offered no resistance but bent like a reed with the blow, the aggressor would desist fairly soon and wipe his fist automatically, as though defiled. Often they spat, but that seemed unlikely on this occasion. As it was, Torrence contented himself with a low growl as Ronald drained his glass.

'My son George is out there on the front line for the likes of you. I hope you're sincerely ashamed of yourself.' His jowls shuddered with suppressed emotion. Ronald fiddled with his moustache and eyed a plate of pearly quails' eggs near his elbow.

'Well it's a difficult issue . . .'

At that point, the conversation was brought to a merciful stop by the best man, one of the cousins, calling for silence for a speech. The bride's father stood to attention and Ronald lounged back, out of his orbit. Margaret, the only other of Valentine's London acquaintance to have been invited, materialised at his side, brushing her lime green velvet coat with indignation.

'I've been imprisoned by some dreadful man,' she whispered. 'Couldn't stop talking about the war effort in Devon. I feel quite faint.'

* * *

Connie was beginning to wonder whether the miscarriage had passed off as easily as she had thought. After a long, jolting train journey during which they had stopped at every tiny station, so that she had stopped bothering to look out when the steam cleared on the platform to see where on earth they'd reached, she'd felt pale and shaky when the train finally pulled into London. She was ravenously hungry. Then there was the problem of where she was to go. She didn't want to risk Eaton Square, in case Ralph was there, and Flood Street was shut up although she had the keys. But because she'd left so quickly, and packed her own small valise, she had virtually nothing decent to wear out to dinner or the theatre. There were a few things in Chelsea, true, but nothing really . . . lovely. In a moment of resolution, she decided to solve the problem with a visit to her favourite couturier, tucked away in a Bond Street mews, where she would be offered a comforting cup of tea as she luxuriated in choosing from the new season's most delectable laces and linens.

It seemed an excellent plan. A discreet gossip with Madame Jacqueline, who had run the shop for ever and who knew everyone, combined with plentiful tea and cakes, banished her feelings of rural isolation. As she toyed with an irresistible suit in fine gold linen, edged with chocolate braiding, Madame furnished her with a full bulletin of snippets concerning her London acquaintance, their parties, babies, war losses and hinted affairs. Madame had seen Lady Ottoline quite recently, and had been able to provide her

with a quite unusual peacock blue cloak, French, lined
with buttercup silk, but she was down in the country now,
entertaining some of her 'literary' friends – Madame
managed to invest this adjective with a little *frisson* of disapproval – probably none of whom was fortunate enough to
enjoy her ladyship's acquaintance. Was her ladyship up in
town for long? Perhaps she was attending Lily Southport's
bridge evening that night? Just a quiet affair, she understood
from Mrs Southport, who had been in earlier that day for a
fitting for the dress she was wearing for her daughter's
wedding. A gorgeous rose pink crêpe, though Mrs Southport
had specifically stressed that it must be understated, because
of the international situation. Not that understated meant
sparing, if she knew what Madame meant. Still, Mrs
Southport must be relieved that the new son-in-law, Lord
Timothy Boden, who stood to inherit Boden Castle in Kent,
was too mature to enlist for service.

Connie left the shop quite cheered, in possession of some
exquisite brown and white lizard-skin shoes which made
her small feet look, if possible, even daintier. But by the
time she had secured a cab, exhaustion was overcoming
her again. Impatiently she wiped away the beads of sweat
standing out on her brow and blamed the close weather.
She wanted to lie down, but she didn't think she could bear
Flood Street, all blank and shut up, with no one to make
the bed or heat the water or cook a supper for her. Perhaps,
if she went to Eaton Square instead Ralph would be out,
and she would be spared the brand of bullying recrimina-
tion, presented as concern, in which he specialised. The
idea of sinking into the fresh white sheets in her pale,
high-ceilinged bedroom there suddenly seemed desperately
attractive. Then, after a quiet evening's rest, she could
immerse herself again in the social life she had so badly
missed.

The horses trotted through Admiralty Arch and along the
Mall. The trees in London were scaly with dust, wizened
cousins of the majestic unfolding greenery in the
Gloucestershire countryside. Absently Connie watched the
figures walking under their shade. A few men in uniform
sauntering, pleased to be home, civilians hurrying,

preoccupied, about their business. And then, a face she recognised.

⋆   ⋆   ⋆

Ronald Foxley was feeling the sour jumpiness that springs from frustrated desire. Also, he feared he could be losing his famous intuition, upon which men like himself relied absolutely to orientate themselves along the shadowy sub-strata of their sexual lives. And he had been so sure. The waiter, young, thin as a whippet, gingerish hair cropped to a fuzz above a narrow, intelligent face, had given him all the signs. He had been absurdly attentive at the reception as he touted his gleaming plate of morsels. 'Would Sir care for more salmon? Was there anything else he could fetch for Sir?' The discreet brush of the bony hip as he edged past, 'Excuse me, Sir.' The sharp blue eyes that caught his for a fraction too long. They were signals Ronald knew all too well.

He had left the party, revelling in *schadenfreude* at the fate of Valentine, who had let drink reduce him to a mood of philosophical doom clutching his new bride's hand too hard, her face scared and uncertain. Truly wedlocked, Ronald had thought to himself merrily. And then, just as he stepped into the heat and noise of Pall Mall, the boy was there, at the corner, glancing back at him, clearly having finished his shift.

Ronald had followed, the champagne making his pursuit more obvious, an unconscious grin unfurling on his face. It had been quite a walk as the waiter headed down to Victoria, glancing back at Ronald now and then, but never stopping, nor, he realised in retrospect, returning his smile. In a dingy back street off Horseferry Road he almost lost him in a street market, only a bobbing orange head beyond a fruit stall keeping him on the trail. Eventually, just as Ronald's breath was beginning to labour and his armpits were soaked with sweat, the boy had mercifully stopped in front of a dank doorway.

Ronald drew purposefully level, but the boy's face remained impassive. He slouched against the wall, hips thrust forward.

'You following me, mister?'

'Is this where you live, then?'

'Might be.'

'Is it . . . somewhere we could go?'

At that moment the door behind them opened to reveal a hideous woman, with a frizz of violent red hair and a filthy apron, bulging over an enormous bosom. She ignored Ronald.

'Eric, you coming in or what?'

'Yeah. Just a minute.' He shut the door in her face.

'What are you after, mister? If it's what I think you've got a bloody nerve.'

Ronald was uncertain. At closer quarters the boy had a feral smell to him and a crop of spots clustered round his mouth. But the habitual excitement still throbbed, uncontrollably.

'You knew I was following you, didn't you? You wanted me to.'

The boy brought his face close to Ronald's and his voice sank to a vicious whisper. 'Get away from me you dirty queer or I'll call a copper.'

Ronald had turned on his heel, with as much dignity as he could muster, and retreated hurriedly up the street. The war was to blame, he reflected furiously. It had disturbed the true nature of things. People no longer said what they meant, or meant what they said.

He retraced his steps until he reached the Mall, where he turned to head back to Holborn. His best suit, worn for Valentine's wedding, felt hot and scratchy and the shade cast by the plane trees afforded no relief. He was unaware of Connie Emberley's cab pulling up alongside him until he heard his name and looked up to see her face peering out at him.

'Ronald, what a coincidence! I was going to call on you later to say what about luncheon, or tea!'

He gave a stiff little bow for effect. 'And what about it?'

He thought she seemed unusually friendly. She had always treated him with a sort of snobbish amusement, as though he were a jester or some kind of trained monkey, entertaining, but not really fit for serious conversation, let alone tea. Now her face was wreathed in welcoming smiles. He might have been the King just taking a short stroll down from Buckingham Palace.

'I've just come down from the country. I'm going to Eaton Square. Perhaps you'd like some tea now?' Anything to delay the possibility of a full-blown scene with Ralph, Connie calculated.

Ronald didn't mind. The long walk had brought on a perishing thirst. He could do with some refreshment before he went back to a quiet evening in Doughty Street.

'That would be most kind.'

*   *   *

If Spencer was surprised by the sudden appearance of Connie with Ronald Foxley in tow, he would never have allowed his face to show it. All the same, she should have given them some warning. Cook was off so the kitchen maid would have to produce tea and sandwiches and someone would have to be found to make up her bed. His Lordship was away for the night, and he had no instructions to expect Lady Emberley. He doubted whether Lord Emberley had told her where he was going, meaning that he, Spencer, would be forced to decide between the truth – racing, probably with a lady friend – or a pretence of ignorance. But after ascertaining that he was away, she did not enquire further.

On closer observation, she did not look at all well. Her skin was the colour of pale parchment and sweating visibly. She almost dropped into a chair, leaning back with her eyes closed, before with evident effort collecting herself and fixing a feverish gaze on Foxley.

'You have no idea how boring it's been in the country, Ronald. I'm absolutely starved of social life. Tell me everything that's been going on. How's Margaret?'

'Keeping very well, thank you. We've just been to a wedding, actually.'

She gave a high little laugh. 'Not your own I take it, Ronald?'

After his nasty encounter, Ronald felt the malice rising within him.

'Oh no. One of these war weddings. There's such a rash

of them. You might remember him, actually. A rather promising poet I introduced you to. Valentine Siddons. Young chap, very blond, has been over in France.'

'His wedding?' she repeated.

'Yes, to a little thing called Emily Torrence. Rather pretty conventionally, I suppose, but she seemed a bit of a milksop to me. Far too young. It does seem they're all getting married so young now.'

She was quiet, then muttered: 'He is very young.'

'Well I'm not surprised you hadn't heard about it. It was a distinctly low-key affair. And between you and me, a quite dreadful family. I almost felt sorry for Valentine. Anyway, he had a few days' leave and now they're going up to Oxfordshire, from what I could gather. The appalling father-in-law has bought them a little house up there. I think he wants to get down to some serious writing for a few days. I say, I couldn't have some more tea, could I?'

She poured for him and he noticed her hand was trembling, but she seemed to keep her composure.

'Well, do send him my best wishes. And have another sandwich. Have you seen anything of Ottoline?'

* * *

It had taken a faked headache to get rid of him, nearly an hour later. But now she did feel curiously light-headed and stumbled on her way upstairs. Her brow was boiling. Spencer stepped forward to catch her arm and wondered if she would like him to call a doctor. She felt too weak to say either yes or no, just waved him away and fell on to her bed, fully clothed. Her breasts hurt. She wondered vaguely if the miscarriage had gone off all right. She knew that sometimes things could go wrong afterwards, with the blood and such. Perhaps she was just too old. As she lay there on the chill counterpane, a single tear rolled from her burning eye.

Then, the mental screen she always built for herself around the subject of the baby seemed to crumble, so that the thought of it crept into her mind and would not be chased away. The child had slipped so swiftly away from her. She pictured it folded like a bird inside her, little sparrow bones tucked, delicate feet kicking the emptiness, tiny lost fingers with nothing to clutch at. Desolate, she craved it and even though it was gone, felt the blind maternal urge to protect it. She thought of those mothers she had seen in the posters, urging their sons off to war. She too had rejected her child. Sent it off to certain death.

For hours she lay there until sleep finally descended, digging her nails into her own, ageing hateful flesh. Though whether her rage was against herself, or with Valentine who had as good as betrayed her, she could not decide. She looked out at the bleak barren blue of the sky, thinking furiously about him and his new young wife and all the blond babies they would undoubtedly have.

CHAPTER TEN

LETTICE DE BEER'S flat was seven floors up a greying, 1930s block in Knightsbridge. Her voice on the intercom had sounded firm and agreeable, so when Simon arrived, slotting back the portcullis of the tiny creaking lift, he was unprepared for the face which greeted him at the door.

Though Lettice was only about ninety, he was instantly reminded of the blank, mummified faces of the ancient Egyptians he had often spent his lunchtimes visiting in the British Museum. It was something about the way the papery thin skin was stretched over the cheekbones, the wisps of hair brushed neatly over the balding skull, and the bones protruding from the shrunken frame in front of him. Like a leaf in its final, skeletal withering, she was becoming almost transparent with age. The knotty blue veins in her hands bulged like worms beneath the skin, and the hair, which he knew had once been a triumphant auburn crop, seemed bleached of all colour.

Looking down into her faded green eyes, however, he saw that the spirit in her was undiminished. She smiled a wide beam of welcome, a defiant grin which showed off her stubby, discoloured teeth unabashed, and motioned him inside. Her voice was bell-like and clear.

'So nice to have a visitor. Do come in and make yourself comfortable in my small domain, Mr Pardoe.'

Simon did not usually warm to the elderly. Having been bereft of grandparents himself when very young, his image of life after, say, seventy-five, was hazy. He had only unpleasant memories of being hauled around to see an elderly great-uncle in Bookham, a fat, irascible man whose house stank of cats and who always called him Norman, confusing him with his father. Uncle Edward ate tinned meals without bothering to remove them from the tin first, and shouted at visitors because of the television, which was switched on at all times, its volume turned several decibels too loud for normal conversation. Simon associated age with intellectual degeneration and generally nasty habitats. He himself hoped to die before squalor set in.

Lettice de Beer, however, seemed to differ from this stereotype. She wore a neat little peach twinset, decorated with a pearl brooch and tiny buttoned shoes made of something like crocodile skin. Her minuscule flat, clearly just a sitting room and bedroom, was immaculate, though every surface was crammed with pictures and photographs which he itched to examine. An old-fashioned gas fire burned fiercely away in one corner and tea things were laid out on a small table, covered with a lace cloth. As soon as she had sat him down, she hurried away to put on the kettle.

'So nice to have a punctual visitor for a change. My great-grandchildren always seem to think tea means six o'clock. I call that cocktails, don't you?'

Simon jumped up and looked around him. The room seemed more like a gallery than a place for living in. Every wall was hung with photographs. There were rows of beaming children, some pictures of a young redhead he took to be Lettice holding a baby and pensive adults with dated haircuts, among them some faces he instantly recognised, like Aldous Huxley, G.E. Moore, Bertrand Russell, Evelyn Waugh and John Betjeman. He stopped before a photograph of a enchantingly beautiful woman, with a cloud of dark hair, laughing up at the photographer through her eyelashes, sitting on what looked like a bale of hay.

'Ah yes, Amarine. She had that effect on all the young men.'

Lettice de Beer set down a flowery teapot on the table and came over.

'She wasn't just beautiful, she was a lovely girl too. She was a French refugee who was taken in to help out at Garsington Manor, which is where that picture was taken, and ended up running a second-hand bookshop in Hay-on-Wye. She only died a few years ago. I can honestly say there was no one who would have said a word against her, which is quite an achievement in eighty years of life. Do you have milk, or lemon?'

'Er, milk please.' Simon was entranced. 'Did she marry?'

'Briefly, but it didn't last. Right after the war she married rather a dull old duffer, Arthur Harvey, a solicitor I think he was, and much older than herself. Of course in those days, with a whole generation of young men wiped out, women did have to make do sometimes. But no one could think why Amarine did it. It could have been money worries, I suppose, but Amarine didn't seem the kind of girl who would be troubled by that and anyway, she had a small private income after her mother died. I can't believe it was love. None of us went to the wedding. He lived in Hereford, I think. Anyway, they had a child and she ran off with the baby soon after he was born, which caused quite a scandal in the 1920s. She was lucky the husband didn't sue for custody, because he'd have won it, there's no doubt. Then she opened up the shop and lived very quietly after that. I liked her tremendously.'

Simon stood sipping tea from a delicate, rose-painted china cup and gazing at the girl. The crumbly biscuit tasted faintly stale. Then realising he might seem a little rude, he turned his full attention on Lettice de Beer.

'It is very kind of you to spare the time to see me.'

'Nonsense, my dear. How many other pressing engagements do you think I have at my time of life? I don't usually talk about the past, because old people can be so boring about it, but if anyone asks me, I'm delighted to oblige. My memory is still in fairly good order. Names and dates, I'm afraid, give me a little trouble, which would be a problem if I was an historian, but of course that's not what history is really about. I can remember the events, you see, but sometimes I forget which little mental pigeonholes they came from. Each episode is there. I can still remember exactly what they meant and what they felt like, but sometimes I forget whether they came before or after something else, you know. Little things like whether I had two children or three at the time. My life largely seems divided into three stages, what I call Before Peter, With Peter and After Peter.'

'Your husband.'

'That's right. And unfortunately the After Peter stage is now longer than either of the other two. But it wasn't Peter you came to talk about, was it?'

'No, it was Garsington. And Valentine Siddons.'

'Ah, two famous names. But how many know them now? Let me see if I can find any pictures.'

She lifted up the seat of what he had taken to be a chair, and started burrowing through a stack of albums, before pulling one out. It was brown, and its pages were furled at the corners with age. Inside black-and-white photos showed a fine grey stone manor house, flanked by solid walls of yew, surrounded by a series of ornate gardens. The lawns were bisected with cypress walks and banks of wild flowers and between them women in absurd lampshade hats were playing croquet. Other pictures showed peacocks perching in the boughs of a great, spreading ilex tree and a swimming pool, around which naked men gathered, holding their cigarettes away from them in a faintly camp manner. Elsewhere marble statuettes were hidden in shady corners, and languid people were taking tea on deckchairs under shady parasols. Dense box hedges separated the silvery green lawns from the flower gardens, whose long-dead blaze of oranges and reds and mauves seemed to burst through the monochrome of the pictures, their warmth and perfume breathing back into life.

In one shot a young girl aged about thirteen lounged against a gate in full sunlight, squinting at the camera with a little scowl. Lettice smiled faintly.

'Oh dear. I don't look very fetching, do I? I was no more than a child really. I used to go down with my parents, who were great friends of the Morrells, Philip and Ottoline. There were a few children who came to stay, she had a daughter of her own of course, and my parents didn't like to be parted from me. That was very strange at the time, you know. But that's what made them bohemian, I suppose. Anyway, I was a very shy little girl and, not wanting to get in the way, I used to spend the time roaming round the fields and the farm.'

She paused and sighed.

'Garsington was a magical place, really, its own little kingdom. During the war Lady Ottoline, who was a pacifist, made it into a kind of sanctuary for people who didn't agree with the fighting. It was quite unacceptable in general society of course, where people were losing their husbands and sons, to hold forth about the war's futility and so on, so lots of people, writers and philosophers, found Garsington the only place where they really could express what they were feeling. In time absolutely everyone visited, you know. Yeats, T. S. Eliot, Virginia Woolf, D. H. Lawrence, they all stayed there. Not that I knew them well at that time. But in the latter part of the war there were conscientious objectors working on the land and men with military exemptions, so there were a lot of people around to chat to.'

She stopped at another picture of a tall, weedy, ineffectual man with thick glasses, scything a field with as much trepidation as if he had been asked to massacre a crowd of defenceless children. 'That's Aldous Huxley helping with the haymaking.'

The sunlit past evoked by the photographs immersed them both. As they sat and talked Lettice went through the pages, giving out names of the better known, smiling at others which evidently provoked some silent reflection. She came to a picture of a young blond man, with curly hair. He was at the edge of a group, and had only half turned when the camera caught him, giving him a sidelong, shifty appearance.

'There's your man.'

Simon had already recognised him.

'Valentine Siddons. Now, he's really what I wanted to talk to you about.' He didn't like to say that Lettice de Beer was the only person still living who they knew had met the poet. He was not even sure how well she had known him, having been left an inadequate briefing note by Alan Evans. But whatever grains of recollection she managed to dredge up would probably be useful.

'He went to Garsington Manor on leave in 1916, which must be when that picture was taken. Do you remember him there?'

'Only very slightly, I'm afraid. That's my only photo of him. I seem to remember he was very handsome, though he stooped a little, but that was from being in the trenches. He was rather quiet and withdrawn. I was younger than him, so I don't know if he was just unsure, or perhaps disgusted with all of them, being pacifists when he was at the front. I do recall that he played croquet with me, and let me win.'

'Did he talk about the war?'

'Oh no. They never did, the officers on leave, and partic-ularly not to a woman. They said afterwards how astonishing it was coming back from the trenches to Britain, where everyone was having civilised conversations with hardly any idea of what they were going through. One man said to me it was as though his family and friends were speaking a foreign language which simply didn't connect with his own life. They always seemed . . . slightly stunned on leave. Either that or very hearty, determined to have fun. Siddons, as I said, was the stunned variety.'

'He was married by then. Did he bring his wife?'

'I don't remember anyone with him. In fact I can remember him taking tea one day with Amarine, so there can't have been any wife there. He seemed too young to have a wife, really. Just like one's big brother. He was in Ronald Foxley's set.'

'Foxley? The one who edited a magazine, the *Journal*?'

'That's right. He was a bit louche, clearly after one thing with Valentine, if you'll forgive me speaking plainly.'

'He was gay?'

'That's not what we called it then, or indeed how we saw it. We said he was a little "so". He had a penchant for men. But no one saw sexual matters in such black and white terms as young people today.'

'And what happened to him?'

'Oh I don't remember. He's long gone.'

Her reply was sharp, almost unfriendly. Simon suddenly wondered if she wanted him to go. Old people got tired easily, he recalled, but were sometimes too polite to say so. Unfortunately, she had no pictures of Raymond Hughes or Ian MacPherson, two of the other friends who were to be featured in the film, and who had also been guests of Ottoline Morrell. Both Hughes and MacPherson had survived the war, and gone on to make small, but significant reputations for themselves in the 1920s and 1930s, Hughes as a painter, MacPherson joining his family firm of architects and becoming known for his decorative work in the school of the sculptor Eric Gill.

Lettice was turning the pages almost mechanically now. 'That's Siddons again there, digging the vegetables.'

Simon craned to see the face of the shabby man bent over a row of cabbages. It plainly was not the poet. He looked nothing like Siddons. A large floppy hat obscured most of his face and he also had a bushy red beard.

'I don't think that's him, actually.'

The old lady was looking glazed. Her wafery eyelids seemed to droop over the pale green eyes.

'Oh you're right. Well I did warn you about names and dates, didn't I?'

'I think I ought to be getting along.'

'Well really, if you have to go, Mr Pardoe.' He could tell she was relieved. The effort of revisiting her past, even for an hour, seemed to have left her enervated. As he put his coat on, he noticed her shovelling the cake and biscuits he hadn't eaten back into a tin. His usual appalled disgust at the old seemed to have deserted him.

Walking back to the office, Simon wondered if he would get to ninety. Life-prolonging drugs seemed to make it more than a remote possibility. The prospect horrified him. There was no chance he would end up like Lettice de Beer. He would be fouler, crabbier, more alone. Which friends would he look at in his photograph album – let alone family? It seemed impossible that he would ever find anyone he could stand for long enough to marry them. Or who could stand him, as he had been unkindly informed by a few previous girlfriends. He just didn't seem to be able to communicate with people. Or didn't want to. And then when he did meet someone half tolerable . . . For a moment he thought of Elsa's pale face, plastered with freckles, her smile at once teasing yet affectionate. Well, anyway.

He was turning out like his father. Lots of women had been initially attracted to Norman, the beleaguered daddy squiring his motherless sons. Some had even seemed determined to win him, braving the practical jokes and sniping from the older boys, a fierce resentment born of the fact that these women did not and never could replace their true mother. Only Angus, Simon's younger brother, who could scarcely remember his mother, snuggled up to the women, seeking affection indiscriminately like a dog. Disdaining this approach, Simon and Andrew emulated their father's manner towards women. Sarcastic, dictatorial, impatient. Just three tiny markers on the old genetic material, but enough to ruin your love life, Simon reflected grimly.

Chapter Eleven

Dinner with Alison Joliffe had not seemed such a bad idea when she first suggested it. But now that they were all sitting there in Alison's post-modern Islington flat, admiring the air plant display and the Masai tribal rugs hanging on the milk-white walls, the atmosphere was as warm as the ice in their glasses of Australian Chardonnay. The angular metal chairs round the aquamarine glass dining table seemed designed to add physical awkwardness to the atmospheric unease. Alison's minimalist décor and disinfected surfaces created a tense, hospital effect and under the glare of expensive halogen lamps, her bleached calico armchairs threw shadows like escaped prisoners frozen in the floodlight.

It was also getting late and Elsa was feeling increasingly hungry. Alison, with her habitual insouciance, had left the cooking of the dinner to the last moment, and was now completing it in front of them, like a Japanese chef. The mixture of salad and cold, marinated chicken looked distinctly insubstantial, but then the only raging appetite Alison possessed was for gossip. And a liaison with Dr Oliver Eastway, the TV don, was an irresistible morsel which deserved to be savoured with nothing less than a dinner party, she had announced, when Elsa imparted the news to her on the phone two days before.

'An older man, Elsa! You are a dark horse. This I have to see. How long has it been going on?'

Elsa knew that if she said 'months' Alison would be affronted at being the last to know, but if she truthfully replied 'weeks', somehow her relationship would seem less important, even to herself. Yet in a strange way, time seemed a meaningless measure when she was with Oliver. So she settled for: 'Some time now.'

'Ooh. It must be love.'

Yet again, as her friend talked on, Elsa marvelled at her discovery of Alison Joliffe. Loud, over the top, exuberant and insincere, her brash confidence and confrontational aggression bubbled together dangerously like some risky chemical experiment. She and Elsa had been friends from the day they met, as producers on the same chat show, united in mutual contempt for the host, whose sexual harassment, like his toupee, was all too laughably visible. Both had slogged their way up the grades, and both had agreed that friendly rivalry, unlike destructive competitiveness, enhanced rather than spoiled their friendship. That philosophy of course took a dive last year, when their plans to resign and form their own independent production company went so wrong. Openly, Elsa agreed with Alison, that nobody could be expected to throw up the chance to host their own show. *Good Relations*, the afternoon relationship counselling programme, may have had a small audience, but it thrust Alison into a spotlight she had never enjoyed as a producer. She had even appeared in *Hello!* magazine, and had borrowed a smart relative's flat, replete with marble floors, *trompe-l'oeil* pillars and overstuffed sofas for the purpose.

Privately, Elsa believed that no friend should entice you to resign a securely paid job and sit through endless talks with bank managers, only to leave you in the lurch at the eleventh hour. Elsa had not enjoyed having to beg a job from the lecherous Alex Durban and then endure Simon Pardoe's obvious dissatisfaction with the arrangement when Alex left the country. What made the betrayal worse was the dismaying sight of Alison, whose grooming and personal wardrobe had always been reassuringly drab, crawling out of her cocoon and spreading her creased linen wings as a glistening minor celebrity, complete with gleaming blonde bob, short, tight little skirts, and a toned up, slender shape. She was so busy she lost a stone and a half. She took up weight training at a new gym and abandoned her old habit of consuming whole Mars Bars and two bottles of wine at a sitting. She did, it must be said, acquire an unattractive chain-smoking habit, but then live, emotional, inarticulate audiences with personality problems were notoriously tough to handle, even for seasoned presenters. And Alison was good at it, Elsa was forced to admit. She was professionally, if not morally justified in ditching their joint venture.

But the nagging ache of Alison's career had been anaesthetised for Elsa in the weeks since she met Oliver Eastway. More then that, she realised guiltily as they chatted over the office phone, for the first time she wholeheartedly wanted Alison to succeed.

'How are the ratings?'

Alison uttered a theatrical groan.

'Still going downhill, unfortunately. It's either the Catholic priest, the hospital soap on the other side or it's Prozac. They reckon half the audience is on it now. Whereas they all used to slump there Valiumed up to the eyeballs, they now feel tremendously happy and fulfilled and they've left their husbands for toyboys. I do wish the manufacturers would think through the implications responsibly when they put drugs like this on the market.' She paused reflectively.

'You're not on Prozac by any chance, are you? Or is it just love which is making you sound like a Stepford wife?'

Elsa laughed lightly and Alison thankfully changed tack: 'How's Mr Grumpy? Lost any more employees recently? That's one man who'll never need to worry about naso-labial smile lines.'

As if he divined he was being discussed, from across the room Simon cast Elsa a surly glance. Alison chattered on.

'If only he wasn't so good looking. What a waste. I mean I like the strong and silent type, but he's a walking Pinter play. He was certainly way down the queue when the social skills were being handed out.'

'Don't.'

'God, he's not listening in, is he? I suppose he objects to you making private calls on business lines. Spare us.'

Elsa viewed Simon covertly. He was smoking as usual, like the before picture in a government health warning film, the glass on his office screen filmed with the amber ectoplasm of a thousand dead cigarettes.

'We must get together soon.'

'And I must get to see this new man of yours. I'm green with envy. No sooner do I get a job talking about other people's relationships than my own go down the Swannee. You know, I hear myself sitting there saying, "Avoid like the plague immature, irresponsible men who are only interested in one thing" and all the time I'm thinking, "Where are these immature, sex-crazed monsters? Let me at them!" You remember that bald psychiatrist I was seeing? Woody Allen without the laughs? Well, it's all over. I told him I loved Jewish men with beards and he told me I needed therapy. Said my reliance on irony was an immature denial mechanism. I mean, please. He's the miserable divorcee with two dys-functional kids, not me. Still, no such problems with Oliver Eastway, you lucky girl. He's not even married, is he? Why don't you bring him to dinner? Can you make Thursday or Friday?'

'That would be lovely.' How would Oliver respond to Alison on full volume? Elsa wondered with trepidation.

'Who shall we get to be spare man? No, don't suggest anyone, I've just had a brainwave. I'm going to invite your boss. I want to see if he's as bad as ever.'

'I don't think that's much of a romantic prospect.'

'Maybe not, but I'm desperate. Siii . . . mon!'

She began to shrill down the phone, forcing Elsa to motion Simon to the phone and hand him the receiver. His conversation was curt. 'Hello . . . yes . . . well if it's this week I can only do Thursday.'

After a few moments he replaced the receiver with distaste. 'What's she after? She practically press-ganged me into dinner. Thank God you're going too.' As an afterthought, he added: 'I'll give you a lift over, then?'

Evidently, Alison had not mentioned that Elsa would be accompanied. She decided that now was not the time. 'No, I'll get there on my own,' she said.

When she telephoned Oliver, to tell him about Alison's dinner proposal, she thrilled at the thought of her call penetrating his book-lined sanctuary.

'Yes.' He sounded abrupt when he answered, but as soon as she spoke his voice softened. He explained he had a student with him and could not speak for long, but was delighted at the idea of coming down to London.

'I was going to suggest something like that anyway,' he said. 'I've got another meeting with the publishers that day. I hope you haven't made any plans for the weekend.'

'No, but I'd better warn you about Alison, she's a bit loud.'

'Alison Joliffe, eh? *Good Relations*. Perhaps I should call in to her programme then. Get some hints on dealing with loud women at dinner parties?'

Elsa laughed, slightly surprised that he was familiar with the names of afternoon TV hostesses. 'I'm sure you'll manage.'

That Thursday evening, when Oliver's long green car slid into its accustomed space in front of her flat, Elsa awaited his arrival with unmixed excitement. Already this relationship felt different from any that had gone before. She had passed the tingling, early stage of infatuation where the body pulses like an exposed nerve and the appetite vanishes. The day after he stayed the night in her flat, she had received by special delivery a first edition of Siddons' poems, with an inscription from Oliver himself and some lines from 'Still with Me', one of Siddons' best-known works. She was touched by that, knowing such first editions to be rare and rather valuable. Perhaps what he said was true. That he did feel differently about her.

He had mentioned he liked women with 'understated elegance', so Elsa had ardently attempted to achieve this effect. After a sweaty half-hour specifically allocated for her customary dress rehearsal of revisions and indecision, her best shot was a shirt of silver-grey silk, whose soft, heavy folds fell like cream on her skin, and tight black satin trousers which emphasised her narrow hips.

Oliver walked through the door wearing an old mustard checked tweed jacket and a silk cravat inside his shirt collar. But he also appeared to be in an unfamiliar bad temper. He bypassed their usual, urgent greeting, in which he would fold her into his arms with unexpected strength, and gave her instead a terse kiss before heading for her small collection of drinks and selecting a whisky.

'What's wrong?'

He uttered a growl of frustration. 'My publishers. All these people with their nit-picking, time-wasting, middlebrow problems. Give me strength.'

Ominously, he didn't want to discuss the meeting any further, just saying he hoped Alison Joliffe's other guests would not be the usual television bores. Elsa had never seen him annoyed before and it had taken a fair bit of wheedling to restore his usual sanguine charm.

It was a beautiful evening, with a light, lemony sunset fading over Hyde Park. But as the car nosed through the evening traffic towards Islington, Elsa's misgivings about the dinner party intensified. Why had Alison asked Simon? And why had Elsa not been brave enough to tell him that Oliver Eastway would be there? The awkwardness of having to explain to Simon that she had allowed a professional relationship to develop rather swiftly into a personal one was embarrassing. It wasn't as though she was a doctor, or a teacher, she told herself resentfully. There was no unspoken client etiquette to be transgressed in the lowly, jack-of-all-trades position she now occupied. Yet she knew with absolute certainty that Simon would disapprove. That Simon would take upon himself some kind of spurious moral authority he neither possessed nor deserved and that disapproval would manifest itself in more of the leaden silence that weighed in the office air heavier than the eternal roar of traffic from outside.

When they reached the tall, terraced house where Alison lived Simon was already there, his long, gangly frame lolling on one of the calico sofas, grilling Alison on her career with a plausible expression of interest. Another couple, workmates of Alison's, joined in. If Simon was surprised when Elsa and Oliver entered, Oliver with his arm lightly encircling her waist, he concealed it well. But as he stretched out his hand to Oliver, telling him how much he had looked forward to meeting the eminent Dr Eastway and how grateful he was for his assistance on the film, his grey eyes swept Elsa's face quizzically. Alison was just as bad as Elsa had feared.

She beamed at Oliver, extending a bowl of root vegetable crisps. 'I'm a relationship counsellor, so I'm allowed to ask nosy questions. Where did you two meet?'

Oliver, however, gave an easy laugh.

'Elsa came to ask me about my grandfather's life. I'm afraid she's still more interested in my grandfather than me, but I'm hoping to change that.'

'And your grandfather is who?'

'Valentine Siddons, one of the poets of the first world war.'

'My God, he's your grandfather? How thrilling! Did you know him!'

'Oh dear, I don't look that old, do I?' Oliver smiled politely.

'He died in 1917,' added Simon, quietly.

Alison hit her forehead in an actressy gesture. 'God I am so stupid. I knew, I knew of course.'

'Where is he buried, by the way?' asked Simon.

'His grave is in the Tyne Cot military cemetery near Ypres. One of about twelve thousand. He's also commemorated on various war memorials, one at his old school, one at his college and he's on the little village war memorial where he lived in Oxfordshire.'

Simon was interested. 'Have you been to see the battle-fields? I went out there when we first thought of making this film, and I was amazed at how much remains.'

Oliver looked dubious. 'Really? That's not how I recall it at all. There is that little tinpot museum I suppose, where they've preserved a few trenches and stuck some tin hats and gas masks in glass cases. And there are the memorials. But most of the battlefields have either been turned into cemeteries, or melded back into the countryside . . .'

Simon interrupted: 'But that's not to say they've dis-appeared. The grass is grown over maybe, and the villages have been rebuilt, but there are so many reminders, aren't there? Whenever the fields are ploughed they come up with iron and bones, apparently. The trees are shot so full of shrapnel, you still can't cut them without ruining your axe. It's rather sobering, really. History's physical persistence. As though nothing is ever completely erased.'

Oliver gave a quiet chuckle. 'Oh with respect I think that's a rather romantic view. I hope we don't believe there is anything so simple as objective historical truth, appealing though my students always find that notion. Or that any kind of documentary or forensic evidence means we can understand exactly what went on?'

'Well . . .' began Simon, but Oliver swept on.

'We can never know how things were. Each generation remembers only what it chooses to remember. And uses history to its own ends. To illuminate the future, justify current policies, or whatever. You'll know Simon that heritage is very much the thing at the moment. Piecing together selected historical fragments to present a pleasing image of some imagined yesteryear. I mean it's not truth, is it?'

'But historical artefacts have their own validity . . .'

'Oh yes. Your so-called historical truth may appear to linger on in wills, maps, testaments and so on, but these things are only a source, aren't they? And all sources must be filtered through our own preoccupations and apprehensions. We can never see history as it actually was, only as it is.'

No one seemed to know what to say to this. Fortunately Alison swooped brightly back into the conversation, depositing some long-awaited plates of food on the table. 'So you've written a biography! Seriously, how is it going? Tell me all about it!'

Sitting next to Oliver, the occasional brush of his thigh sending a charge through her flesh, Elsa was relieved at how self-possessed he was, how different from the other, younger men with whom she had had relationships. The brash ones who tried perpetually too hard to assert their intelligence and knowledge. The timid ones who attempted to hide their innate insecurity with a veneer of cynicism. Most of all the adoring ones, who deferred to her and let her do all the talking. Oliver seemed to treat other people's ideas with respect, holding them up to the light and examining them for their individual worth.

Simon, by contrast, had relapsed into a scowling silence over the chicken salad. He was just so . . . awkward by comparison, Elsa thought with exasperation. He seemed to be taking no interest at all in Oliver's views on the decline of the BBC. After a few minutes, Oliver made an obvious attempt to reintroduce him to the conversation, breaking off to ask: 'Did you ever hear anything more of that Alan Evans chap? Where did he disappear to?'

'Off the face of the earth by the look of it,' said Simon shortly.

'How intriguing. Do you think he may have had an accident or something?'

'Oh no. He sent a perfectly formal resignation letter.'

'What a shame. He seemed a pretty well informed fellow.

Well educated, too. A UCLA graduate, wasn't he?'

'Yes. We did try to contact him actually, or Elsa did. She went round to his house, but they had no idea whether he'd gone for good or not. Just bloody inconsiderate, really.'

'You went to his house?' Oliver turned to her. 'You didn't tell me that.'

Elsa smiled fondly. 'I hardly thought you'd be interested.'

'But presumably he wasn't there.'

'Well no, but I did gain entry. I didn't spend all those years in TV journalism for nothing. I had a good look round but there wasn't any sign of where he'd gone, or why.'

An unexpected flash of anger contorted Oliver's face. 'For God's sake, no wonder silly young girls get murdered in this city, creeping around and breaking the law. Don't you know it's risky, going to a strange man's house? You should never have done that.'

A sliver of silence hung like a knife in the air after this outburst. Then Simon said:

'I'm sorry. I suppose Evans' vanishing must have wasted a lot of your time. You never actually met him, did you?'

'Well we spoke – and corresponded, of course.' Recovering himself Oliver took Elsa's hand under the table and beamed at Simon: 'Not that I'm not delighted he disappeared if it meant me meeting his replacement.'

Later, as Alison returned with a plate of kumquats which no one attempted to eat, he turned to Elsa and said softly: 'I'm sorry. I didn't mean to be cross. I just don't like to think of you doing anything dangerous.'

Simon left the dinner party early, pleading overwork. The next day, when Elsa arrived at the office, he was already at his desk, head down and ear fixed to the telephone. He glanced at her briefly and Elsa felt a pang of regret. But almost immediately she reprimanded herself. She owed nothing to Simon. As Alison would say, she should stop seeking male approval for her decisions. Of course he wouldn't like Oliver Eastway. Simon would think he was too smooth, or showy, or something. But that was only because he didn't understand him as she did.

She settled down at her own desk to attend to the script. She was adding a scene in which Hughes, MacPherson and

Siddons met at the Continental restaurant in Calais. All had just returned from leave and were waiting to go into line, Hughes and MacPherson, both officers with the 2nd Manchesters, were headed for Beaumont-Hamel, where they would meet appalling carnage but survive. Siddons, who at that time had just nine months to live, was off with his regiment to Bapaume and one of the most harrowing experiences which the western front held. The restaurant scene was simple, a few minutes in duration, a flashback to record the last time that two of the friends saw the poet before his death. The scene was not really necessary, but Elsa had decided to insert it on balance because she knew a marvellous hotel in Brighton which would be perfect for a location, dripping with wedding-cake ceilings, palms in pots and rich brown Edwardian paint.

She reached for her copy of the Siddons notebooks for reference, opening it at the flyleaf photograph of the poet himself, dated only 1915. He seemed almost the ideal of the upright young officer, his curls tamed and centre parted, the Sam Browne pulled tight across his khaki chest, his ruddy, handsome face bearing the proper military half-smile of mingled humility and pride. In vain Elsa had searched that smile for a reflection of the more subversive, youthful defiance that emerged in Siddons' poems, that disdain for the English society that sent its young men into the war, then insulted them with Horatio Bottomley's exhortations about God and duty from the comfort of its national armchair. Nor could she see any premonition or shadow in that portrait of the end that was marked out for him when the battle of third Ypres was unleashed on those men spared the unspeakable slaughter of the Somme. The life in the face seemed to vanish as she looked at it, the elusive connection that spanned the years retreating too.

But, if she admitted it to herself, what interested Elsa most about that face was its resemblance to his grandson, whose own smooth, knowing smile and inscrutable looks now dominated her thoughts.

The work absorbed Elsa, so she scarcely looked up when Michelle called across that she was going to lunch. 'Do you want to come?'

'No I'm fine. I'll get something later.'

Waving her arms significantly, Michelle seemed to be attempting to send her a message in semaphore. As Elsa tried to decode it, Simon left his own office with his coat, gave a brief nod in Elsa's direction and said: 'Let's go then, shall we?'

'We'll be in Alfredo's,' said Michelle, speaking as though Elsa was slightly deaf.

'Great. Have a nice lunch.'

It was only fifteen minutes later that Elsa remembered the last time they had visited Alfredo's, the Italian restaurant situated directly under the office. Then it had been Michelle's birthday and today, 5 April, if she was not mistaken, was Simon's. Either that or they had gone out to celebrate the last day of a very disappointing financial year.

'Oh God.'

She jumped up from her desk, and then, on reflection, picked up her bag, with the little blue folder in which she had stored the stolen poems. She clattered down the stairs, combing her hair and preparing her apologies as she went. It was too late to buy Simon a birthday present but letting him into her little literary mystery might be adequate compensation for the time being.

Either Alfredo's good cheer or the quantity of wine they had already drunk had put Simon's mood somewhere between amiable and jovial. He looked up with amusement when Elsa entered.

'Simon, happy birthday. I completely forgot.'

'I didn't like to say.' Michelle did not look too pleased at the sudden interruption of their *tête-à-tête*. 'I thought you knew.'

Simon smiled brightly. 'So how's the great poet's greater grandson?' His voice was thick with sarcasm, which Elsa decided to ignore. 'I must say, Elsa, that was quick work. Bit old for you, isn't he?'

'I don't think age is relevant in our relationship.'

'Oh, really. It seemed pretty relevant from where I was sitting.'

'What's that supposed to mean?'

'I mean I can see what he gets out of it, but I didn't know you were into the older man.'

'There's a lot about me you don't know.'

She glared at him and Simon smiled back. Elsa tried to remind herself that this was a birthday lunch. 'So you didn't like him?'

'He was pretty much what I expected.'

With great effort Elsa bit back any retort. Instead she took a quick look at the menu.

'Listen, Simon, I didn't mention it at the time but there's something you might like to have a look at. I found it when I went to Alan Evans' house.'

She took out the blue folder and spread the poems on the table in front of him. For several minutes, he sat there reading them all, in silence. The he looked up at her:

'You stole these from Alan Evans?'

Almost effortlessly, Elsa found herself rewriting the past. 'I didn't steal them. They were in that book I retrieved. My copy of the Siddons notebooks.'

'And have you tried to contact him to let him know what you found?'

'No, but remember, Simon, he hasn't contacted us, either.'

As usual when his interest was aroused, Simon's face was suffused with excitement, his general expression of sarcastic indifference quite gone.

'What the hell do you think they are? Not Siddons', surely?'

'Well I don't know. You see the initials on the notepaper. But when I showed them to Oliver he said they were amateurish and of no interest at all. Even if the notepaper was Siddons', it could have been used by anyone.'

Simon's face darkened. 'Delighted to hear you showed them to him before your own business partner. They were definitely in the book, you say?'

'Folded all together inside the cover. I didn't discover them until I'd left his flat.'

After a moment's contemplation, he said: 'Are you sure it's not just professional jealousy on old Eastway's part? Frightened you might upstage his biography?'

'I hardly think "old" Eastway, as you call him, has got anything to be jealous about. He said they weren't Siddons' style.'

'Well, he's the expert, but I'd have thought styles change in a writer's life. And if they're nothing to do with Siddons, what the hell was Alan Evans doing hanging on to them?'

'Well unless we find him again, which seems highly unlikely, they will just have to remain one of life's little mysteries. Like the Rosetta Stone.'

'They deciphered the Rosetta Stone,' Simon reminded her, drily.

*   *   *

It was Michelle who noticed it first. They had all been back in the office for around half an hour, lethargic and giggly from the wine and from Alfredo's tuneless rendering of 'Happy Birthday' when he brought the cappuccinos. Sounding slightly mystified, Michelle said:

'Did you leave the door on the latch when you came downstairs to lunch, Elsa?'

'Now, you can't get me on that. I thought about it, but then I distinctly remember locking it.'

'In that case,' said Michelle, looking hard at the assortment of papers scattered on her desk, 'considering that it was on the latch when we came in, and that someone has obviously gone through my drawers, I'd say we've been burgled.'

CHAPTER TWELVE

EXTRACT FROM *VALENTINE SIDDONS: A LIFE*

It has been noted before that the period of Siddons' greatest creativity coincided with what was effectively a mental injury. Though he sustained just minor wounds, the effects of the shell which exploded just as he was taking a German pillbox on the western front in early 1916 were severe enough to induce what was then called neurasthenia, or more commonly shell shock. Fortunately for posterity perhaps, Siddons was recuperating in Britain during the worst episode of slaughter of the entire war, the start of the Battle of the Somme, the point which marked a sharp downturn in British popular idealism over the war. A hastily trained infantry of volunteers, led by too many junior officers and often short of shells, was mown down frequently before they even saw who they were fighting. There were 20,000 British deaths on the first day of the offensive. By August the shock of the Somme's casualties had filtered through to the British public so that the publication of Stanzas from Battle and Beyond, *with its despairing, sardonic and often shocking imagery of war, met with considerable critical success.*

At the end of his recuperation, Siddons was invited to Garsington Manor, the country home of Lady Ottoline Morrell, whose London salon he had visited at the start of the war. He accepted with alacrity, eager for the chance of exposure to some of the most stimulating minds of the age.

★   ★   ★

HESTER MORIATY REACHED the brow of the hill and stood there like a target, leaning on her parasol with her limp hair streaming out behind her and pearl necklace whipping in the wind. She wore orange morocco leather boots and had knotted a scarf in gypsy fashion round her head. Her curiously piping voice failed to carry, but it was just possible to catch the gist of what she was bleating as she surveyed the

Downs, supine and still before her. 'Do you think that one can truly love landscape, in the same way that we love a man or a woman? I think I do. I think I love the curve of that field, you see, the way it bends round and seems to embrace the house. I think landscape is such an . . . active thing, don't you?'

Behind her Valentine hovered, silently noting the plumes of smoke rising from the farm dwellings into the mouse-grey sky, the peaceful fields scarred only by the plough. Across the valley, crows shot coarse boasts from their ragged nests. It was a scene he would have liked to paint, but he had developed an instinctive dislike of standing up on hills. The bitter autumn wind made his eyes sting and water. He wondered what the best reply was in order to get them home as quickly as possible.

'It's getting cold, Hester. It's going to rain.'

He felt tired. It had been a nightmarish walk. Hester had insisted on passing through the villages, nodding to the women who stood at the gates with curious children laughing and pointing, bidding cheerful good afternoons to the old men who sat, sullenly smoking their pipes at the door of the inn, impervious to the ludicrous figure she must cut in her velvet and jewels. He felt as though he was accompanying a circus. He should never have come. But it was a relief to get away from Emily, who had nursed him with tireless and exhausting attention in the past few months. She had been jealous when the latest invitation came, but refused to admit it. Instead she insisted that he bolster the slender reputation which the publication of his first book had brought. It was good that he was being lionised by the right people, she told him. What a joke.

Droplets of rain hung in the wind. In the distance, over by Garsington Manor, mist hugged the horizon. He considered the house with a fascinated bitterness. It had been strange coming back again. Once it had seemed so enchanting. From the stately mullioned windows of the Cotswold stone manor one looked out over a series of formal gardens, ponds and orchards to the silver gleam of a huge, oblong pool, shielded by dense, clipped box hedges, the location on summer nights for naked swims. Ottoline's original approach to décor, which might have seemed out of place in a grander house, only complemented Garsington's quaint cobbled beauty. Now everything about the place seemed to boast of its separation from the dull world of conscription and leave-takings and amputees invalided back from the front. A shifting population of visitors appeared as if on a stage, all colourful, declamatory, unreal.

That evening Hester wanted him to sit again for the portrait she was doing. The idea made him shudder, but at least it meant abstaining from the intense meanderings about life and literature which were held in front of the roaring fire after dinner. The swollen stream of educated musings, which Emily believed he so relished, would flow over him as he sat there, silent as a stone. They could be difficult conversations to join in at the best of times. Only the afternoon before he had been lurking by a window, staring absently out, when a celebrated writer came to stand beside him. The man, who was much fawned over by the other guests but whose books Valentine had thus far failed to read, was small and weaselly with a cravat and an angry moustache. He regarded the vista before them with a savage snort.

'It's vanishing, isn't it?'

Valentine strained to refocus his gaze on the misty distance. 'What is?'

The writer turned accusingly, as though Valentine was being deliberately slow-witted.

'England. The whole country is being trodden under the heels of swine. There'll be nothing left soon. Nothing. Just a drab little graveyard where a civilisation lies buried, with only the rubble left to stub your toe on.'

By the time he and Hester had crossed the valley, bridged the stream at the end of the grounds and walked up the sloping lawns to the house, they were drenched. Kicking a wet peacock out of their way he noted with malicious satisfaction a tidemark of mud creeping up Hester's scarlet cloak. From the courtyard at the front of the house came the scrunch of gravel and the shrill of

voices, alerting them to the arrival of yet another consign-
ment of visitors. Valentine grimaced at the thought. The
place was continually filled, it seemed to him, with guests.
Some, like him, were invited for an indefinite stay, others
appeared just for random meals. They streamed through
the house like a marauding army, dispelling the quiet with
their continual cries, eating up the food and cluttering the
bathrooms. A contingent of conscientious objectors were
lodged in a separate house where they were often to be
glimpsed through the windows drinking coffee and talking,
loftily ignoring the taunt of 'Slackers' emanating from
passing village boys.

Envisaging yet more pacifists or Slade girls, he was
astonished when he rounded the corner, to see Ronald
Foxley emerging from a sea of coats and bags. His lank,
greying hair was cropped short, his monocle replaced by
glasses.

'Ronald, I don't believe it!'

'Nor do I, I assure you, old man. I've been conscripted.
I'm in the Artists' Rifles but I can't tell you how hard I tried
for an exemption. I've been in some godawful camp in Gidea
Park for the past three weeks being turned into a man. This
is my first weekend leave, and I intend to enjoy it.'

Even after the conscription rules had been tightened that
spring, embracing married men and raising to forty-one the
upper age limit for those liable to be called up, there was still
no shortage of fit men who managed to avoid service.
Normally Valentine had nothing but contempt for them, the
men who sought safety in civilian jobs or scurried after
medical exemptions on the grounds of bad feet or a nervous
twitch. But the sight of the flamboyant Foxley finally
subdued and ready to be dispatched to the human mincing
machine of the western front, brought a momentary surge
of regret in Valentine.

'You're looking well,' added Foxley, clasping him round
the shoulder. 'I was sorry to hear about your trouble, but it
looks to me as though you're over it.'

Valentine paused. What did 'over it' mean? There was no
answer to that. Nor was there likely to be. Although the
Garsington set relished debates on the merits of spiritual

versus carnal love and the true meaning of Expressionist art, they were unlikely to welcome an exposition on the psychology of battle-weariness. So he said simply: 'Well the hand's still there and it was good for a blighty I suppose. When you're ready we'll sit by the fire and have a talk.'

Foxley beamed. 'And I'll tell you what a very eminent friend of Mr Churchill has been saying about your book.' He looked outside at the darkening sky, where the rain was now lashing down, and gave a shrug. 'Pity you couldn't have been here this summer. Ottoline had the most gorgeous young things posing as nude living statues round the pond.'

* * *

Droves of people meandered through the house, passing through the long gallery with its ancestral portraits in dusty oils, its antique vases and primitive sculptures, and congregating in the drawing room, where a huge log fire sent shadows leaping over the Venetian red walls and heavy glass bowls of pot-pourri scented the warm air. Foxley ejected a pug from a large leather chair in the corner and plumped himself down. Valentine pulled up another chair and lit a cigarette which he held in his numb hand. Whatever he told Foxley about the war, it would never be the truth. Some men, he knew, came back from the front and were full of it, but far more, like himself, returned from their leave with something like relief. The war turned family into mere acquaintances and those acquainted with the true nature of battle became one's only real family.

Besides, how could he describe what he had seen? The trench mortars bursting in the sky overhead, the skeletons of buildings and the mutilated ruins of men? The French countryside raped by battle, its woods filled with German batteries, its peaceful nights shattered by the spangled green flashes of Very lights. Or the howling of the shell just before it hit, followed after a deathly pause by the dreadful shrieks and moans of its victims. How he still woke every night, sweating and trembling. Of the worst day, he had never been able to speak.

It came after nearly a week of lull, in which the men had

existed, uneasy, believing a major offensive was on the way. The company's orders, when they finally arrived, were to move up to the front from where they would capture a small section of woodland, perhaps two hundred yards from the line. The advance had been successful, but estimates of German strength at that section of the line were wildly off course. The enemy returned fire with far greater ferocity than expected and half the men in Valentine's company were wiped out before they even reached the wood. Enemy mustard gas and high-explosive shells turned the horizon into a crawling mass of flame. Before long, it seemed as though they were advancing towards a flickering cliff of fire. He, Davidson and Grey had succeeded in taking a pillbox, which they shared with the remains of two Germans, one blown in half from the grenade Davidson had thrown in before entering. The other German, still whole, was infinitely more disturbing. He had been sitting when the explosion hit him, and in death he reposed slightly thrown back with startled eyes and just a smear of blood running from his mouth, so that he resembled a man poisoned at his restaurant table.

But almost as soon as they took it, the pillbox had come under intense fire. The first shell cratered the ground beside them and the second hit the box itself, taking off the wall. The three of them, faces coated white as wraiths with mortar dust, began to leave. Valentine went first, adopting a crouching run through the howling darkness, and Grey following. As a third shell blasted down they threw themselves face down in the earth. After a minute, Grey called out softly, saying they should go on and Valentine reached out and felt Davidson's arm. He tugged, to signal that he was moving, but the arm dropped from his grasp, inert. In the dark he had to reach some distance to find the rest of the shattered remains of Davidson, a sticky diaspora of flesh and mud.

They got back to their own front line somehow. But when Valentine arrived, they found that he had sustained a small shrapnel wound to his left arm. He was also half blind and gibbering. He remained unaware of anything until he was lying in the casualty dressing station behind the line. From there it was a nightmarish trip by hospital train across the French countryside, jammed in with hundreds of men, talking, moaning and reliving the horrors of the front. Even when he got back to England, he had lain for weeks in the hospital, drifting and hallucinating, listening to the other men in the ward playing gramophone records or card games over and over again.

Then, weeks later, when the arm was healed and just as he felt able to return to Oxfordshire and sit at his little desk in the cottage, or perch outside at an easel, drawing and redrawing the countryside below, the book he had submitted was finally published. The reviews were good. In the chastened climate of 1916 even his cynicism, they said, would not offend the public mood. For Valentine, the sight of the poems on the page was a strange relief because after his first, indecently hasty arrival at the front, he had feared he would never write again. The shock, the cold, the continual trench foot and exhaustion had made poetry seem obsolete. But then, unfettered by boredom perhaps, or long dull hours behind the lines, the words began to flow again, a perverse, grudging little rill maybe, muddied with despair and bitter with hatred, but poetry for all that. And it was poetry of an entirely different nature. It was as though his eyes had been dashed with acid and he saw with a searing clarity. The dustcloths of his early life had been stripped away.

The admiration that greeted *Stanzas from Battle and Beyond* took him by surprise but he could not really enjoy it. He felt as if he had scrambled his way to glory on a pile of corpses. Then after July, reading the reports of the battle of the Somme which had wiped out three-quarters of his battalion, he no longer even felt fraudulent. He felt empty.

Yet Emily would try to talk about it. To understand it. And even when her questions ceased there remained her wan, uncomprehending gaze, raking over him like salt on a wound, her silent reproach and her attempts at cheer probing him alternately like needles. In bed it was even worse. He was impotent with her. Night after night in the shadows of their narrow bedroom, looking down at the pale gold hair spread across the pillow, the eyes half closed and the eager mouth parted like a succubus for his kiss, it was as though she was trying to suck the life out of him. He was incapable of laying himself open, because she would try to dig in, to extract some piece of him like a wriggling crustacean on the end of a pin. The inner part of himself was of necessity sealed and because she could not know what he had known, so she could not know him.

Garsington at least had promised respite. Here the inhabitants were bright, exotic creatures, like exquisite tropical fish, floating in their own enclosed, dreamy, aquarium world, impervious to the hell and darkness beyond. They didn't seem to have a clue what went on, or even want to know. Indeed he liked thinking that this was what he was fighting for – the teas on the lawn, the games of croquet, the Hesters, Laetitias and Erics. It made the futility of the front more savage, the sublime sacrifice more ironic.

Garsington's guests were not, of course, uniformly awful. There was one bright-eyed, rosy-faced French girl called Amarine whose willingness to join in games of chess, or merely sit companionably talking, had been one of the few consolations. Their hesitant discussions of Shakespeare, Keats and Shelley reminded him of distant days in Herbert Kelly's study at Oxford. Now from across the room Amarine glanced at him as Hester's voice rose above the drone of conversation, calling for volunteers for a performance of somebody's new masque set in fourteenth-century Florence.

'Who's feeling Florentine?' demanded Hester. Amarine rolled her eyes.

Foxley, following his gaze, said:

'Pretty young thing over there. Anyone I should know about?'

'Amarine. She's French. Her parents sent her here hoping she would be able to mingle with the cream of English society. Funny, that.'

'On the subject of the cream of society, that reminds me,' said Foxley feeling in his jacket, 'I've got a message for you.'

The envelope, marked only with Valentine's name, enclosed a thick sheet of writing paper, headed 53, Flood Street, Chelsea.

Dear Valentine,

I would very much like to see you again. Ronald tells me you are staying with Lady Ottoline. Would you have time to call in before you leave? I will be here until Sunday.

Yours ever,

Constance Emberley.

'Thanks Ronald.' Valentine's face was like a mask. He placed the letter in his pocket as carefully as a loaded gun.

★ ★ ★

The next morning was cold but sunny. A gilt frost crusted the grass and the air was sharp with promise. Valentine had his valise packed and, leaving a note for Lady Ottoline, took the first bus from the village to Oxford, boarded the train, and was in London by the afternoon. Basking in the autumn sunlight, the city was crowded and unexpectedly gay. Streams of men in uniform made their way down the Strand and groups of chattering office girls headed for the underground. Valentine caught a bus to Chelsea. The Flood Street house looked more deserted than he had remembered it, the curtains drawn. As he rang the bell, he wondered what he would find as he entered. He imagined his own un-answered letters stacked surreally high on the hall table. The copy of his book he'd sent her unopened and unread. A cat came and curled itself around his legs, sniffing his boots.

She opened the door herself. He did not know whether, like other families, she had heeded the call to release all staff for war work, or whether she just wanted to be alone. She looked momentarily startled but swiftly recovered her composure.

'Valentine. It's you. I'm so glad you came.' She took his hat. 'Can I get you some tea?'

He assented, mutely. He felt again like the gauche undergraduate in her presence. She showed him into the drawing room. Hunched forward on a sofa, he nervously lit a cigarette, holding it between his knuckles and taking savage little drags at it. He could think of nothing to say. Neither did she give any hint of why, after more than a year of silence, she had contacted him. For half an hour they sat there drinking tea and discussing the war in the way that people who knew nothing about it would talk. She mentioned how the new British wonder weapon called the tank, which Valentine had already seen on the battlefields, was now being hailed as the key to ending the fighting. She said her husband was gloomy about the prospects of Prime Minister Asquith, who had become the subject of endless sniping and criticism in *The Times*. It was a smear campaign, inspired, her husband claimed, by Lloyd George, who wanted to take control. She confirmed that most of the servants had been discharged for war work, but that Cook remained at Eaton Square, for which they were thankful.

It was all irrelevant to him. He watched her small red mouth moving, her eyes not meeting his own. But it was not until the afternoon light drained from the sky and she rose to light the lamps, that Valentine felt able to scrutinise her properly.

She had aged in eighteen months. But then he was an old man compared to the youth he was when he had last seen her. She looked smaller, somehow. Her hair remained a rich, chestnut colour, but pulled into a loose chignon rather than piled up on her head. Her skin was still as clear as petals but a tracery of fine lines was visible round her eyes. Her dress was of some shiny, dark orange stuff, shot with gold thread at the neckline, and she wore a necklace of heavy amber beads. Valentine found himself looking at the tiny cracks in the stones, thinking of how flies became embedded in amber and how like a stuck fly he himself had felt for months. Immobilised.

'I suppose I understand why you didn't answer my letters. But why did you want to see me now?' His voice was dry and hoarse.

She went on round the room, adjusting the lamps so they burned low. After a moment she said brightly: 'Perhaps I wanted to congratulate you on your success.'

'But what about before? It was so sudden. You didn't contact me and I didn't know what to think.'

'Really? Oh I'm sorry.'

'Please . . .'

Still avoiding his gaze she said quietly: 'I was ill for a while, and then yes, I did think that it was best we didn't meet again, in the circumstances . . . I mean, I heard about your marriage from Ronald.'

'So that was it . . .'

'Oh please don't misunderstand me. I was delighted for you.'

'Listen, what could I have said?'

'You could have told me.'

'There was nothing to say. Nothing worth saying. Nothing that affected us.'

She just looked at him and he thought he saw pain there and was seared by it. Then her face closed again. In an effort to reach her he said:

'Connie, it's hard to explain, but she believed in me. Believed the best of me. I wrote to her – asked her to marry me – the day I first went to see you. You were out. Or perhaps your husband was there. Anyway, I didn't know what to think. Then, when I met you again, when we were together, I knew I could never love her. But I couldn't let her down.'

She cut off his outpouring with a wave of her hand.

'Valentine, let's not waste time on these . . . recriminations. It's in the past now. I read your poems and I thought how silly it was not to tell you how much I admired them. You're quite famous now, you know. Quite the thing. Everybody's talking about you.'

Her eyelids fluttered flirtatiously. She was like a stranger. He wondered if his poems had really communicated anything to her. He searched her face. 'Connie, do you have any idea how much . . . how much I've wanted you?'

She gave him an absurd, polite little look and suddenly he felt something that had been dammed for more than a year beginning to creak open and unleash itself. He had not allowed himself to feel anything but anger, but now some ferocious desire, mingled with rage and pain, was forcing itself out of him. He pulled her down beside him and she did not resist. He felt how small she was as he crumpled her into his arms, seeking her mouth with his and he was momentarily afraid of hurting her. He feared the aggression rising within him, which seemed indistinguishable from the aggression he had made himself feel over there. Then he felt himself harden, felt the selfishness of lust overtake him. As she reached for his belt he lost all restraint: his body, toughened by more than a year of hard, manual life took over, his fingers, desperate and clumsy, grappling with the buttons of her blouse, laying her down beneath him, prising her legs apart with his knee. He felt a sudden, strange pride in the functioning of his body, and its wholeness, having seen how easily substantial flesh just like this could be shattered and destroyed. How perfectly it served him, how strong and invincible it seemed. Even his hand. In an act of final self-control he steadied his fingers to undo her amber necklace, delicately placing it on a table beside them.

★   ★   ★

After they had made love he raised himself on an elbow and watched her, relaxed beneath him, her silky hair loose over her face, her breasts rising and falling, her small white belly slack. He reached over and lit another cigarette. They talked about the petty banalities of wartime, the Londoners' fear of Zeppelin raids, the scarcity of sugar which was so severe now that jam-making was officially forbidden.

'How's your husband?'

'Always busy. Supervising the conscription laws. I don't see much of him.'

Busy sending other men to their deaths, Valentine thought, feeling the old revulsion rising at the back of his throat.

'I have to report at Victoria tomorrow afternoon.'

Her grip tightened on his arm sleepily. 'But we'll have a day together, won't we?'

'Of course we will. Just like before.' He caressed the curve of her cheek. 'What was this illness of yours? Nothing serious?'

'Nothing serious.'

'I wish I'd known. Did he look after you? Your husband?'

She gave a slow smile and closed her eyes. 'Husbands. Wives. Let's not even think about them, Valentine.'

'But that's right. That's what I wanted you to understand. They could never touch what we have together. And I could never betray that. Nor could you.'

He extinguished his cigarette and coiled himself to her, as tight as a seagull in the air that carries it, as close as a shadow on the earth. That night, for the first time in six months, he did not wake up trembling.

CHAPTER THIRTEEN

EXTRACT FROM *VALENTINE SIDDONS: A LIFE*

During his final leave of 1916, Siddons paid a brief visit to London, where he became acquainted with the debate that had begun to circulate about the post-war order. Had he survived the war, there seems little doubt Siddons would have become a leading figure among these artists and intellectuals, with whom he felt an instinctive sympathy.

* * *

'UNCLEANNESS IN A MAN is a curse and burden to his wife and future children. It is a moral blot, an invisible evil which can breed subnormal, even idiot offspring. I urge you now, ladies, if you suspect your loved one is tainted, insist that he consult a doctor for the sake of you and your babies.'

The preacher of this oblique message was a frowsy female aged around forty-five. She was enfolded entirely in a shiny, black material, tight as a butterfly's pupa, which seemed close to bursting from the effort of constraining her formidable flesh. Grey jowls juddered with the importance of her subject. The speech was on the dangers of venereal disease but so impenetrable was her address, to the Chelsea Towns-women's Guild, that the bulk of the audience appeared more puzzled than shocked. The twenty scattered women perched like roosting chickens on their hard chairs blinked back at her, not seeming to appreciate the urgency of her message. With a steely glare, designed to impart what mere words could not, she rounded off her lecture with a warning of the sometimes terminal nature of the moral stain, so easily contracted when men were away at war.

Valentine, smoking dully at the back of the hall, thought of the barmaid he had seen in one of the French estaminets – just-a-minutes the men called them – the tiny bare bars where soldiers would congregate to drink coarse beer, or wine so rough it sandpapered the throat. That barmaid was almost certainly in possession of the invisible evil. He had come upon her when passing through a back room on his way to urinate in the yard, and had not realised until it was too late what stood between the soldier, rocking rhythmically with his legs apart and the dank wall. She was so small, she was almost swallowed up by the huge, shuddering khaki form. He remembered the tiny rolls of grime like little grey snakes on her arms where she had pulled up her sleeves. The bored look in her eyes, neither embarrassed nor surprised, which followed him over the soldier's thrusting shoulder.

Not for the first time he wondered what he was doing there. This was not the way he would have chosen to spend his time with Connie. They had most of the day free together but Connie's idea of a free day did not coincide with his own. Had it been up to him they would have spent the morning in bed, then taken a walk through Hyde Park and along the Serpentine, lunched in Knightsbridge and perhaps visited a gallery. Instead, as they lay together that morning, the day before them a map of infinite possibilities, she had firmly removed his arms from around her in order to come here. And while every minute he spent with her still seemed a forbidden excitement, her world, of which he knew precious little, seemed as busy and as alien in its own way as that of the front.

The townswomen's meeting, for example. She had been obliged to attend because she was chairlady of the Guild. There really could not be any question of missing it, she had pointed out as she poured his tea over a hasty breakfast. She had suggested Valentine meander in a nearby bookshop while it lasted and, if he returned early, wait for her at the back of the hall.

After the speech, she hurried from her place in the front row and caught him by the arm with a conspiratorial smile. 'It's all right. No one here will recognise you. Now I've got a treat in store.'

'Being alone with you is the best treat I can think of.'

'But this is important, Valentine. I want you to meet some people who think the same way as you do. They're a new generation, planning the future after the war.'

Valentine did his best to sound neutral. 'And when's that?'

'Very soon, so many of them believe.'

At that moment, the fat woman came bustling up. Connie turned to her, wreathed in smiles. 'Geraldine, what a marvellous speech.'

The woman's small black eyes fixed beadily on Valentine. 'And this must be your son, Lady Emberley.' She realised her mistake almost instantly and became flustered, attempting to cover her tracks. 'How silly of me. I mean, a nephew, perhaps? Won't you introduce me?'

She showed no sign of recognition when Connie murmured his name, and swiftly disappeared, but the incident was embarrassing. As they walked down the King's Road together, side by side, Valentine wondered for the first time what people thought of them. Tiny and exquisite though Connie was, he realised how much older she must look. She was different, too, from their times before. There was something brittle in the lightness of her step and the fixity of her smile. The well of unhappiness he had first divined in her seemed to have been sealed over. Yet it was hard to believe this was a result of their reunion.

Connie's treat was a short cab ride away in a Soho basement. Down an unobtrusive flight of steps, she led him into a crepuscular gaslit room, the front half of it filled with tables, the far recesses done out with armchairs and bookshelves and carpeted with rugs. Rough portraits and still lives dotted the walls. Loud-voiced young men were lolling in the chairs, their legs slung over the arms, while others sank behind newspapers. A tiny fire flared fitfully in the grate.

Connie led the way to a table and eventually attracted the attention of a nonchalant-looking girl, who sauntered casually over.

'Lunch is soup, fish and jam pudding. All right?'

'Lovely,' said Connie brightly, with an enthusiasm disproportionate to the unexceptional ingredients. She reached over and took Valentine's hand. Awkward at such a public show of affection he withdrew it to fumble in his jacket for a cigarette.

'I just had to have you see this place,' she breathed. 'It's a new club. A meeting place for poets and writers and artists. A whole group of people who have instinctively come together because of the war and the desire for a better society.'

Valentine concentrated on lighting his cigarette. The match spluttered out like a little dead dream.

'You don't know how much it has meant to me, coming here.' Connie's voice was hushed, as though enfolded in some private rapture. 'The war has been so dreary and things have been so stifling. Ralph keeps insisting I stay in the country because of the bombing raids in London. Besides . . .' She raised her unblinking eyes to his. 'For a long time after I last saw you I felt so miserable I could have died. Then I was invited here and met some interesting people and really felt I'd come alive again.'

Valentine looked around him at the would-be architects of England's post-war utopia. To him they seemed little different from the Garsington types, or the assorted oddities he had met at Bedford Square two years ago. There was a sprinkling of the cropheads he had met and despised at Lady Ottoline Morrell's salon, with their blackened eyes and paint-pot lipstick that would look better on a clown. A pair of tall, plain-looking girls with severe bobs were huddled with their heads together at an adjoining table. From what Valentine could overhear they were discussing the novels of Joseph Conrad. The plainer girl ventured comparison with another eminent novelist and her friend laughed dismissively. 'Oh no, my dear. He's very much yesterday's man. I hear his sales are right down.'

It was difficult to know what to say to Connie. But the memory of last night made him try. 'How did you find this place?'

'Through friends of Ronald's, actually. There were some people, contributors of his I think, who have stayed out of the war for one reason or another, and they wondered if I'd like honorary membership. Ralph of course doesn't know about it, but I've met some tremendously inspiring people here.'

Two bowls of watery soup were plonked on the table in front of them. Lumps of cabbage cruised the surface. As he took his first mouthful, a shabby figure approached.

He was a tall man of no more than thirty, with a starved face and a complexion which bore all the signs of a hormonal riot in his youth. He had regular features and straggly blond hair and if Valentine thought of such things, he might have admitted he was handsome in an effete sort of way. For a bewildering moment, he imagined the man was giving him a sly, lascivious wink, until he realised he had a nervous twitch. He looked as much like a tramp as was possible while possessing a well-cut suit and an aristocratic manner. He bent and kissed Connie on the cheek.

'Constance, my heroine. I demand your congratulations. I'm safe. Unfit. Preserved from barbarism by a nervous tremor and highly strung disposition which would mean a full-scale breakdown if I were to venture within a mile of a gun. May I?'

Without waiting for an answer he pulled up a chair and sat down, reaching over to read the label on the wine bottle.

'I should escape altogether now. I was certainly due some luck. I'm making barely a bean from reviewing nowadays. I dressed as badly as possible, ate virtually nothing for a week so I was practically a skeleton, and the medical committee handed over my exemption like lambs.'

Connie laughed, but uneasily. 'Colin. I think you should meet Valentine Siddons. I'm sure you've read his work. He's home on leave. Valentine, this is Colin Seabrook. The journalist and reviewer, you know? His father's cut him off because of his opposition to the war.'

Valentine warmed to Seabrook senior as Colin's voice took on a shrill, declamatory tone. He did not appear remotely embarrassed at meeting a serving officer.

'I say. All hail to the great poet! I've read absolutely everything you've written. We're honoured to have you in our midst. What brings you here? I hope you're joining our club.'

'I don't know. What's the club for?'

'We tend to think of it as a meeting place for like minds, I suppose. We read papers and essays to each other, you know, discuss the issues of the day in congenial company. It's a sort of army of the avant-garde. For all those who feel betrayed by the Victorian generation.'

'And what are they going to do about it?'

'Why – fashion a new tomorrow, of course. We shall storm the ramparts of class consciousness like the revolutionaries in Russia – with just a little less bloodshed, I hope.'

He leaned forward confidentially and Valentine caught a strong whiff of alcohol. 'I trust that doesn't sound too ambitious. Didn't Shelley say something about poets being the unacknowledged legislators of the world? Well it's time we were acknowledged. It's time for us to be the ruling class. After all, whatever you soldiers out there believe, the war has changed everything profoundly. When you all come back you'll find England will never be the same again.'

Valentine wondered if Colin Seabrook was one of those who Connie would describe as 'tremendously inspiring'. Certainly she seemed to glow in his presence. Her arch, feline features turned to him like a flower following the sun. He watched her as she laughed with him, placing an empathetic hand on his arm. He badly wanted to like Connie's friends, but how could she stand these people?

As Colin talked on, he felt all his nervousness at being with Connie and his irritation at the way the day was turning out, collect into a ball of anger within him. He had a vision of himself running Colin Seabrook through with his bayonet. Indeed, as his imagination quickened, he pictured himself turning on all those fey young men and women and lancing them down, lining them up in front of a machine gun until their blood coursed the walls. He had thought that if he could write about the war in plain, straightforward, layman's language, while it might not end it, at least it might make people back here understand. Instead, not only did they remain plain ignorant, but some seemed to hold those who were fighting personally responsible for the mess.

After another half-hour of Colin's plans for the nation's future they left the club and wandered up to Piccadilly, gazing half-heartedly in the shops. Connie seemed skittish and distracted.

'You don't believe all that stuff about ending class consciousness?' he asked her.

'Oh yes,' she said distractedly, turning over a pair of buttoned kid gloves in Swan and Edgar's. 'Within limits, of course.'

Of the real future they discussed almost nothing.

It was an unexpected relief to return to the impersonal bustle of Victoria, where he was due to rejoin the leave train. By four o'clock hundreds of men were swarming round the carriages as they grunted and wheezed in preparation for the journey to France. Wives, sweethearts and mothers kissed and hugged. Children cried, or stared open mouthed at the tumult.

Valentine's train was on a far platform, next to that reserved for staff officers, who would direct the fighting from the safety of battalion headquarters behind the lines. Inside its glowing dining cars, he could see the officers being guided to their tables, waiters already taking orders for drinks. The other trains, bearing troops and regimental officers bound for the front, were very different. Dimly lit, they were crammed with men wearing bulky packs on their backs, huddling together either cracking jokes or merely gazing glumly into the distance.

He found a spot by the window and set down his luggage. As the train pulled out through London and into the suburbs, he saw above one field a dark cloud of migrating starlings, eager, unlike the flock of men beneath them, to be heading south. In the parks and gardens autumn leaves were circling down from the trees to lie mouldering in the grass.

Valentine stared as the trees slid past. It occurred to him that his own body might well die and rot away in France before the leaves in England's fields had finished falling.

Chapter Fourteen

SIMON HAD DECIDED not to call the police about the burglary. Michelle had said that was unwise, and could affect the insurance policy on the office, but Simon pointed out that the insurance policy was still paid, or probably not paid, by Alex Durban. Besides, it was hard to establish whether anything had actually been taken. Their most valuable possession, the fax machine, was intact, the broken photocopier hunkered uselessly in its corner, but otherwise there was very little to steal. The sole decorations in the office consisted of framed posters and artwork for films made by Alex Durban, an etiolated cheese plant and a dusty plastic rhomboid presented to Simon at the British media awards for an exposé of illicit uranium sales published when he had been a young investigative journalist. But after Michelle raised the alarm, all three went through their desks and looked for further signs of intrusion. Simon's inspection took only a couple of minutes.

'Nothing gone. In fact I'd say nothing even touched,' he concluded, closing a drawer as tidy as a shop window before replacing with a satisfying click two freshly sharpened pencils on their lonely expanse of clean desk.

'Looking for money, probably.' He gave a hollow laugh. 'Well they chose the wrong place here.'

For Elsa, the search was going to take longer. Certainly, her desk looked as if it might have been burgled, but then it always did. The dusty heap of papers, wrappings, writing instruments and newspapers decomposed quietly, like the organic mulch of a forest floor, with only its top layers occasionally disturbed. Unlike many people with untidy desks, she did not pretend to know exactly where everything was, but usually burrowed impotently, trying not to upset the whole edifice, before giving up her searches. Now she scanned the desk momentarily, before realising the hopelessness of her task. Besides, she reasoned, if she could find nothing on her desk, it was unlikely a total stranger would do any better. Unless he or she knew what they were looking for.

'Nothing here either, I'd say,' she muttered.

Simon raised his eyebrows, but did not comment. Michelle, however, whose drawers had been closed, and now stood ajar, was still unsettled. She was examining the door lock which, as Simon knew from personal experience, was so weak it could be opened with the old credit card trick. He did not mention it, though. No need to suggest that he had prior knowledge of the vulnerability of the office to bad elements.

'It's so awful to think that we were just sitting downstairs, enjoying ourselves, when it happened,' Michelle wailed. 'You feel violated, don't you, to think someone's been through your things?'

Simon's voice betrayed an edge of exasperation at the way Michelle's generally professional air seemed to have deserted her. 'What exactly has been taken, then?'

'Well that's just it. I don't know. I mean I know what's in every drawer, and it's filed alphabetically and everything . . .'

'So it should be clear what's gone.'

'Well, nothing really. I mean, I can't imagine that anyone would take Inland Revenue forms or the location queries. There's all the correspondence from Mr Durban of course, under D. And from Mr Eckstein under E. Then I keep a separate record of useful names, telephone numbers and things in my Rolodex in case any of you lose them.' At this she cast a reproachful look at Elsa.

'What's this?' Simon had taken over the search and was pulling out each of the drawers in the filing cabinet in turn. He held up a sheaf of yellowing newspaper cuttings.

'That's background research details. You know, whenever any of you chuck over things and say file this please Michelle, that's where I put it.'

'There's rather a lot of it.'

'Well there was all Mr Evans' stuff there too, of course, which he didn't take with him. I didn't know if it was still wanted so I kept it.'

'Huh.' Simon grunted. 'Can you tell if any of it's gone?'

'Doesn't look like it.'

'Well if they were looking for anything valuable they won't have had any luck,' said Elsa, in what she hoped was a comforting, yet authoritative tone. 'Perhaps we disturbed them.'

'It's like rape, isn't it?' sighed Michelle. 'You don't understand until it's happened to you but burglary's such an intimate intrusion.'

'Don't be ridiculous, woman,' snapped Simon; then, seeing the look on her face said, 'I'm sorry. Why don't you make us all a cup of coffee?'

Michelle decided not to take offence and only muttered darkly, 'What a terrible thing to happen on your birthday.'

Elsa and Simon returned to their work. But Elsa felt detached from the routine details, reading contemporary documents, completing her research, polishing the script. It was not that she was disturbed about the burglary, rather she was in a state of euphoric exhaustion. She had not slept more than a couple of hours the night before. In the time that had passed after the dinner party, lying on her bed, encircled in Oliver's arms, she seemed to have unloaded the events and feelings of a lifetime.

It was strange how the profound understanding which had grown up between them had leapfrogged the conventions of romantic relationships. They had known each other only a few weeks. Yet through his relentless interest in her, his urge to know everything about her down to her childhood diseases, the books she had read, her travels, her feelings for her family, it was as though he wanted to become part of her. And she felt herself responding. It seemed to her that the boundaries between where her life ended and his began were slowly eroding, as though she were a river running into the great, salt enormity of the sea.

But when it was her turn to probe, and she asked about his past, why he was not married or had ever been deeply in love, he brushed her off, laughing.

'I'll tell you if you really want but it's meaningless now,' he replied, his head nuzzling her neck. 'I don't want to look back. What's past is past. All that matters is that I've found you.'

And she had not protested at this inequity. She had wondered instead how he, unlike any other man, had managed to trigger the surrender of her inhibitions, as though she herself was unlocking a fortress within her. Did this come with experience? Alison had called him 'an older man' and the label sang in her head like a reproach. Yet there was no denying it. His arms were weathered, his face a chickenwire of lines. He had the confidence and security of one who was sufficiently established in his work to admire the discoveries of newcomers. He seemed entirely generous, ever willing to believe the best in people.

Even the most mundane activities were transformed when she was with Oliver. He had arranged several times to be in London, so he could see her at lunchtime or after work, when they would meander along stopping at bookshops or cafés. Once she had visited Oxford and he had taken her to the Botanical Gardens.

'You were worth waiting for,' he had told her as they walked along the gravelled paths. 'If that old Eastern belief is true, that the soul splits in two at birth and spends the rest of its life scouring the earth for the lost partner, then it may be that we've found our other halves.'

'You're forgetting there's about two decades between our births,' she teased.

He gave a slow smile. 'Oh you know what I mean. We complement each other.'

'How?'

'Well you know all about this film business, which I admit is a closed world to me.'

'And what part of your world is closed to me?'

'I'd say the world of botany, to start with.'

It was true. She loved the way he knew about plants and flowers, not only their Latin surnames but intimate details of their hidden, earthy histories. He strolled the garden as though it was a library of his own donnish devising, pointing out relations and derivations, inspecting the perfection of a camellia or stroking a furry leaf's hide. Like a consultant on his rounds, he would stop and cup a tulip's sulphurous crucible or split open a pod and show her the pearly multitude of seeds ranked within. The sight of such fecundity frightened her, though he evidently imagined she would be inspired.

'Wouldn't you rather live in the country?' he asked.

'Oh no. I'm incurably urban, I'm afraid,' Elsa replied instantly, feeling the comforting thrum of the traffic as it pounded along and taking an appreciative draught of sooty afternoon air. She had thought no more of it at the time.

* * *

She flicked on her answerphone, which she saw had registered a couple of messages. It was the pause again. She was certain of it, though he had never called the office before. The silence of the unknown caller seemed to have acquired a breathy, exasperated rasp. The click with which he replaced the receiver, a tiny explosion of sound, seemed to Elsa to express a tightly coiled aggression. It was a relief after that to hear a voice, the shaky, genteel sound of an elderly man, with the stuttering uncertainty of one unused to dealing with technology post-1970.

'Hello, er, I take it there's nobody there just at the moment? Well, in that case I'll leave a message. My number is Hay-on-Wye 2553 and I wonder if you could call. Oh, my name is Harvey, Mr John Harvey, by the way.'

Then, after a second click, came Oliver's soft voice curling reassuringly out at her.

'Hello, Elsa. I've just finished my lecture and I thought you'd like to know I was just sitting in my office thinking about you and last night. How are you, my love? Do you mind me making regular checks on your well-being? Call me.'

Elsa picked up the receiver to dial the Oxford number which she already had by heart.

He was not in his office. Perhaps he was already on his way back to London, she realised, with a comforting glow. She noticed that Simon had come over to her desk and was looking down at her.

'Busy?'

Damn Simon. How did he manage to sound so accusatory?

'Quite, why?'

'You were playing back the answerphone.'

'Oh sorry, yes. Some man from Hay-on-Wye. Didn't say what he wanted. Sorry, Simon. The other message was for me.'

Simon wound back the tape and listened to the message, scrupulously switching the machine off when Oliver's voice came up.

'John Harvey? Hay-on-Wye? The only thing I can think of is . . .' His voice trailed off as he scribbled down the number. He returned to Elsa's desk a few moments later. 'Elsa, this might prove interesting. Remember I went to see Lettice de Beer the other day? About the Garsington set? Well she mentioned a woman who had been there and met Siddons. A French woman called Amarine, who later retired to run a bookshop in Hay-on-Wye. Lettice was a nice old dear, very efficient, and it seems she got straight on to the bookshop and asked them to give us a call. It's run by the son now, after Amarine died. He wasn't much use really, though he obviously thinks of himself as a bit of an oral historian by the sound of it. Either that, or business is slow. Anyway, he didn't know any of our key people personally but he was desperately keen to witter on about it.'

'So?'

'So you might just give him a call. Find out if he's coming up to London any time. See if you can squeeze any colour out of him. You could even go up there if you have the time. The bookshop's called Harvey's. It's near the clock tower, apparently.'

Traipsing down to Wales was not high on Elsa's agenda. Still, she thought to herself, it might be nice to go with Oliver. Make a weekend of it. Simon was still hovering.

'You know, Elsa, those poems have got me interested. I think I might go and have a look down at the Normandy Foundation and see what I can find. It would be amazing if we'd found something significant. Sorry, I mean if you'd found something significant.'

He smiled and Elsa thought how different he could be when he was intrigued.

'You won't find anything,' she warned him laughing.

'It's my birthday. Indulge me.' He paused.

'Are you busy tonight?' he asked.

Elsa was. She and Alison were to join Oliver at the London film festival, where Oliver's friend, the film producer from Los Angeles who might be able to help them with their funding, was attending the première of a movie he had worked on. For some reason she did not feel like telling Simon this.

'I am a bit. Something boring. But aren't you going out for a birthday celebration?'

'Oh no. Nothing planned. Probably drop in on Norman.'

Elsa had divined that the relationship between Simon and his father was a classically English one, full of repressed and confused emotions, of which the warmest manifested itself in a fleeting, dry handshake. She felt sorry for him.

'Maybe later in the week?'

'God, no. I just wanted to see the new Tarantino. No problem.'

Simon watched Elsa bow over her work again, her dark hair curtaining her face, her shoulders hunched in concentration, and cursed himself for the question. She probably thought he was asking her out. And perhaps he was. What an idiot. She was bound to be spending another night in the arms of that appalling academic. Eastway was old enough to be her father. Elsa would be picked up, used and dropped like a hot potato, just as he had probably done to a long line of simpering women. A waste, really. Still, it was her life. On the way out of the office he made a mental note to replace the locks. There might be nothing for a burglar to steal, but it was unpleasant to think that just anyone could wander in off the street and riffle through their things.

* * *

Alison was in her element at the première. The film itself, called *In the Blood*, was quite terrible, a Gothic horror about a vampire joining a dance studio in modern-day Los Angeles. It was supposed to be funny and scary in turns. But even among the invited audience, which included some of the cast, crew, teams of producers, backers and their friends and families, the occasional suppressed snigger could be heard during the scary bits and a leaden silence

143

accompanied the jokes. The smattering of applause which greeted the ending lasted barely long enough to cover the final credits. The audience drained away through the exits like a lava flow. Elsa felt embarrassed for Justin Emberley, who was with them, and shrank back into her seat so she should not have to turn a congratulatory, hypocritical face to him as they left. What could she say? She could not think of one element which she could wholeheartedly praise. She need not have worried. Alison on overdrive said more than enough for two.

Alison had arrived in an extraordinary brief, fuchsia-coloured dress with little spaghetti straps which left voluptuous indentations in her firm flesh. The neckline swooped halfway down her chest, which looked unusually plump and enticing. It was the kind of dress she would have been far too uncertain to wear in her earlier incarnation. Elsa was amazed.

'Isn't it a bit, you know, small? There's not much of it, is there?'

'Quite enough for my purposes,' Alison had smiled, smoothing the sheath down a couple of inches over her well-honed thighs.

Elsa did not know whether it was the dress, or the fact that some of the audience had recognised her from the show, which caused a ripple of pointing and smiling as they passed. Detecting a scintilla of celebrity, Justin had instantly placed Alison next to him.

At the end of the film she turned and beamed at him. 'I bet you're proud,' she said, in a soft, gushing voice.

'Oh, let's just see what the box office says first,' Justin replied, amazingly untroubled to Elsa's mind. 'But we certainly had a ball making it.'

Elsa had recognised his type the second she set eyes on him. The public school education, recreational drug habit and trust fund were as obvious as his elaborately casual movie mogul clothes. He had a strange, unconvincing transatlantic accent, such as people pick up over a decade in America. He sounded like Tony Curtis impersonating Cary Grant, only less amusing. Elsa could not work out how someone like Oliver could be friends with Justin.

'I told you. We got together when I was writing the biography,' Oliver had insisted earlier, during the brief half-hour before they had left for the cinema. He had a key to her flat now and had been waiting when Elsa came home; he enfolded her in kisses as she walked through the door, pulling her towards the bed.

'He told me all about Constance Emberley.'

'Who?'

'You haven't heard of her, then? I thought you might have come across her in your research for the film.'

'No. Who is she?'

'Oh no one really significant. She knew Siddons. She was an actress, before she married into the Emberleys. You've heard of them, surely? As in Emberley's merchant bank? They're a hugely grand family. They own hundreds of acres of Scotland and absolutely hate publicity. Justin's the black sheep but even so, he's very loyal to them. I was just pleased I managed to get something out of him.'

Elsa was lying on her front, her face turned towards him on the pillow. 'I hate the way you say "no one significant". That's not a very professional approach for a biographer, I would have thought. Everyone's significant in some way, aren't they? Am I not really significant?'

He ran his palm down her back, following the dips and ridges of her spine down to its furthest hollow, causing her to arch appreciatively under his hand like a cat. 'Just at the moment my darling you're the most significant person there is to me.'

'You mean I'm your significant other.'

The way he surveyed her evoked in Elsa a peculiar, confusing thrill. 'Do you mind that I'm so much older?' he asked.

'No, I like it.'

'Tell me why you like it.'

'I don't know . . .'

'Yes you do. I think you do. What was your father like?'

'Paternal.' What a small word to hide a multitude of sins.

'I'd like to have been your father. I feel fatherly towards you. Then when I see you like this . . .' he slid her naked body down towards him; 'I feel both things at once. Like a father and a lover. All very Nabokovian.'

He said this directly, with no sign of embarrassment, and Elsa, who did not permit herself to reply, answered his kiss with an ardour she had never known.

He continued running his hand over her body. 'Do you know what I want to do with you?'

She laughed. 'I've got a pretty good idea.'

'No, not that. I want you to live with me.'

She wanted to tell him not to be hasty, that they barely knew each other. But she knew that would not be true. He knew something about her which no other man had divined.

'It's too early.'

'Not for me.'

'Well, I'll think about it.'

'I mean it.'

The excitement his words roused in her had lasted all the way through the film, so that when Justin suggested they all go and 'chill out' somewhere, she felt momentarily frustrated that she would have to wait another few hours before going home with Oliver. However, Oliver had implied that Justin might be able to help them with the 'right' kind of film, and Justin had agreed that Hollywood was 'hot for heritage', so she tried to assume a more professional state of mind and concentrate on extracting if not an actual pledge of financial assistance, at least some interest from him.

Outside the cinema in Leicester Square, a small straggling crowd had collected obligingly behind a barrier erected to give the audience a sense of its own celebrity. The crowd scanned the passing faces with a kind of critical interest, as though attending an identity parade. A few eyes locked on Oliver, then looked away, as though unconvinced of his familiarity. Alison, who for some reason had left her coat off, shimmered in the neon glare of the camera flashes, her skin silvery and sleek as a seal's, her hair slicked and gleaming. Justin pressed up close to her as though they were old friends.

'Where shall we eat? Where's good nowadays?' he asked.

Oliver smiled at Elsa complicitly and shrugged. 'Don't ask me. I'm not the metropolitan sophisticate around here. I live in an ivory tower in a provincial town, remember?'

Across the square, Simon was leaving the Tarantino film with his old university friend Alistair. Alistair was the kind of person who was always on for last-minute invitations. Deciding on a Chinese meal, they paused on their way up to Chinatown to survey the exodus of guests from the première.

'I hear it's a real turkey,' said Alistair happily. 'Fifty million dollars down the pan. Deep gloom at Universal.'

Simon's eyes were fixed on the group of four emerging from the flashlights. He saw Elsa and Oliver holding hands, exchanging a quick look. He watched as the quartet headed away, towards the south corner of the square.

Alistair was revelling in the bad press the film had already attracted.

'Apparently, in the final scene the heroine almost dies but then the vampire sacrifices his own life, and it's all meant to be tremendously tragic, but the reviewers were actually weeping with laughter.'

'Good,' said Simon, thoughtfully.

CHAPTER FIFTEEN

ELSA LOVED ALISON. It was nothing she would expect a man to understand. She loved her light gold, burnished skin, her wide toothy laugh, her fingernails like neat ovals of mother of pearl, her bold, unfrightened stare. She felt approving of Alison. Proud. She didn't understand why men didn't flock to her. Now that they'd got over the frosty interlude in their friendship, that ugly hiatus of jealousy and hurt feelings, things seemed better than ever. Although Alison was undoubtedly busier than Elsa, they had just spent a lunch hour as they used to, patrolling an enclave of clothes shops they liked, cruising the rails in silent, military inspection of a jacket here, an impossibly short dress there. Elsa's selection was curtailed somewhat by Alison's diagnosis of her as a Winter Person – meaning that only a palette of greys, blues and dismal pinks suited her complexion – whereas Alison's skin tones made her a Summer Person, free to flourish parrot-like in bright, show-off shades of orange and red.

It was two days after the film première and they were sitting in one of their favourite bars, drinking coffee beaded with globules of glistening cream and examining their purchases with indulgence. Alison had bought shoes, a few wisps of strappy leather balanced over precarious heels.

'Whore's shoes,' she said happily. 'Just the thing for the man I have my eye on.'

'The psychiatrist's definitely over, then?'

'He's archive,' said Alison briskly.

'So what's the new one like?'

She sighed. 'Oh about the same age as me but you'd never guess it because he smokes like a chimney and drinks like a fish and has a pot belly.'

'So tell me the bad bits.'

'He's a journalist. A European Union specialist based in Brussels. But I know he's serious about me because he's dropped his grand plan to sleep round the EU.'

'What?'

'Oh a girl from each state, plus one from each would-be member, like Turkey and Morocco. Fortunately, when I met him, he'd only got as far as Belgium. And she seems to have exercised her veto.'

'Sounds very romantic.'

'He is. Anyway, there's no time to lose for single thirtysomethings. We don't all have professors panting down our necks. I saw you in the cinema.'

'He's not a professor. And thank you for the dinner party the other night. It was fun.'

'Well at least two of us enjoyed it.'

'Oh, I'm sure Oliver and Simon . . .'

Alison rolled her eyes. 'Elsa, they hated each other. Didn't you notice? They were like Stalin and Churchill at Yalta. Barely civil. Seriously bad chemistry.'

'But you like him, don't you? Oliver?'

Alison paused to stab a strawberry on the top of her cake. The iron discipline of her body reshaping diet appeared to be wearing thin. She licked the flakes of pastry adhering to her lips and paused to savour the forbidden delight.

'Mmmm.'

'Go on. Answer the question. You're the relationship counsellor.'

'Well I haven't exactly got much to go on. I think he's fascinating.'

'But what? You don't look very keen.'

'I am. I am.' She reached a hand towards the cake on Elsa's plate. 'Are you eating that?'

'No. No. What about Oliver?'

'Well he seems a bit, oh I don't know, a bit of a control freak. Not that that's a criticism. I wish someone would try to control me more often. No, he seems great.'

'You don't like him.' Defensiveness rankled in Elsa. What should have been a joyous post-mortem of the evening they had spent together had soured. Refusing to admit any iota of her friend's criticism, Elsa fell silent. But Alison was unwilling to let arguments over men cloud their own friendship.

'Elsa, don't be boring. He's fantastic. I'm deeply jealous.'

'Really?'

'Yes. He's got everything, hasn't he? I just want to know why he's not married already. What is it, mother from hell? Latent homosexuality? Refusal to grow up?'

'Now you're being ridiculous.' Elsa was laughing. 'He just never met the right girl.'

'Well he obviously thinks he has now, judging by the looks he's giving you.'

Within herself Elsa clenched, like an oyster that refuses to give up its pearl. Something about Oliver frightened and thrilled her at the same time. But she couldn't say what it was.

'Well he's shattered my illusions in one respect.'

Elsa told Alison about the poems she had found and of Oliver's disappointing response. Alison was predictably, gratifyingly enthralled. Her eyes gleamed like the buttons on her red satin jacket.

'Let's get this right. In the course of burgling a house you just happen to stumble on some pieces of paper which turn out to be valuable literary heritage? My God, Elsa, this sounds fantastic. You're in the right job after all. And here was I thinking the film business was all about talking to faceless men in power suits and shades who bore you with how many co-production deals they managed to do at Oliver Stone's last pool party.'

Alison's burlesque assumptions about the film industry, in which she had after all intended to forge a joint future with Elsa, caused a flicker of the old irritation to rise which Elsa repressed in the interests of harmony.

'Well it just goes to show, doesn't it. Except you're forgetting what I've just told you, which is that Oliver, who should know better than anyone, insists they're not Siddons'. Not nearly good enough.'

'But you have your doubts.'

'Not really . . .' said Elsa slowly. 'Well, take a look. Some of them just seem to fit his situation so well.' She extracted the bundle of poems from her bag and handed Alison one called 'After.'

Like the barrel of a gun in the hand of a spy,
The sun regards us with a dispassionate eye

We're in the unambiguous world of After
Where the cloudless landscape doesn't lie.

Here at the rainbow's end the ground is frozen
The inauspicious November rose is blown.
The ice on our path will never now be broken
What might have been will never now be known.

After the last leaf falls like an ultimatum
After my letters all unposted lie
After our future words have died unspoken
I will no longer wonder or ask why.

I will no longer wonder or ask why
We could not follow those lanes that lead to the sky
We could not once more walk under Oxfordshire
  poplars
On land where You are not You and I am not I.

'OK so it's hardly his war poems, but I mean he lived in
Oxfordshire. And then there's the mention of the Poplars,
which is the name of his Oxfordshire home. And the clincher,
to me anyway, is that one of the other poems – there, there,
that one – has his initials on it: V.S.'

Alison seized the bundle and put on her reading glasses
to peruse them. The round, hornrimmed spectacles gave her
an air of attractive gravitas and made her look more than
ever like an American psychotherapist. As appearing like a
qualified practitioner is more important on television than
actually possessing any qualifications, the producers of her
programme had been keen to have her wear the specs on
air, but Alison's vanity shone resiliently through this ruse.
'I'm not looking like Miss Moneypenny for anyone,' she had
told them firmly. 'Not on what you pay me.' And she was
probably right.

Now she whipped the glasses off and turned to Elsa.
'They're rather cryptic, aren't they? Almost like a puzzle.
You are not You. I am not I . . . he sounds a bit inhibited. I
detect a hidden love affair.'

'You've got him on the couch already, haven't you?' Elsa

laughed. 'Whereas I was more excited by the publicity value it would give my film. But anyway, Oliver assures me we're barking up the wrong tree, so what does that say about your psychological assessments?'

Alison tossed her glossy hair dismissively and glanced at her reflection in the window. 'I've been spending too much time with depressive balding shrinks, that's what it says. I think I'm quite right to go for a journalist this time. They're so self-obsessed to start with they won't have the time to analyse me.'

'Let yourself go,' said Elsa. 'You deserve it. You've worked for it.' Both women smiled at the mantra which had become a well-worn joke between them.

'Oh God,' Alison looked at her watch and downed the last of her coffee. 'It's late. I'd better get back and start reading.'

'What's tomorrow?'

Elsa was not faking interest. She loved watching *Good Relations*. Alison's guests were mostly plain, synthetic-fibred men and women who sat quietly on the sofa before her, their dull skin pansticked, their blank eyes dazzled, their hair stiffened cruelly by the make-up girl's wand. In quiet, suburban voices they would relate the astounding emotional contortions of their lives, the suppressed hatreds and alliances which seethe beneath the life of every ordinary family, but were now extracted, bottled and labelled with chemical titles like Lesbian Sex Triangle or Step-Siblings: Incest or In Love? Secretly Elsa wondered in what category her relationship with Oliver would be pigeonholed. Perhaps, Father Figures: Desirable Deviants or Dangerous Dads?

Alison picked up a tan leather briefcase the size of a small television. 'Tomorrow we've got False Memory Syndrome.'

'What's that?'

'Well it's quite a big ethical question in America. It's all about like, can you really trust what people say they remember? In the States people are finding that they recover memories – things like being raped by their father or sexually abused by their grandmother – under therapy, and then they go and present this in court as evidence. But now it turns out that you can plant memories in people's heads. False memories. And yet to the people who remember them, they're no different from their real memories.'

'It might not be such a bad idea,' said Elsa, 'if it could work the other way. You could plant happy memories. I'm sure everyone does that to an extent anyway. I mean we all airbrush out the nastier parts of our lives. Or the embarrassing bits.'

'Mmm,' Alison seemed unconvinced. 'Strains of *Brave New World.*'

'But why is it so important to remember the actual truth? When it comes to families, recognising what really happened doesn't necessarily make people happier or better adjusted. Look at *Hamlet.*'

Alison paid the bill and shrugged. 'Frankly darling, I'm not sure *Hamlet*'s on my question sheet.'

Elsa perserved. 'But aren't all memories false in that they're subjective?'

Alison stood up and gave her an exasperated smile. 'Elsa, this is daytime television not rocket science. We're only doing this false memory thing because we've got a hysterical eighteen-year-old who believes she was sexually abused by her father, and he's a well known plastic surgeon who has mysteriously agreed to come on and argue it out with her. If she's lying or being brainwashed by her analyst no one really cares just as long as she cries nicely and we don't get sued.'

* * *

After Alison had hurried off, Elsa sauntered back to work through the London streets. She felt no urgency to get to the office. Even in the shabby heart of Soho, there was a vibrancy in the air. The raddled newspaper seller seemed to smile at her and the handsome Italian in the delicatessen where she stopped to buy pasta joshed with her, asking if she would make him a candlelit dinner for two. No chance, she explained, laughing, it's for my boyfriend. Lucky man, he replied, but Elsa thought, no, I'm the lucky one.

She dawdled at a bookshop window, but the titles glazed over and she stood gazing curiously at her reflection in the glass. What a find. Could it really be true that in the space of a few weeks she had stumbled across the ideal man? He seemed to have found a hole in her and filled it with happiness. And just being happy made her a better, more considerate person. Unlike Simon, for instance, who dragged his discontent around with him like a calliper. Generously she hoped that he would also find someone, but she feared he was just too critical with women, spiky and uncomfortable, as though they could never possibly meet his high standards. No sooner had they fallen for him than they would be stung by a sharp reply or a stab of sarcasm.

Oliver was Simon's living opposite. He drew people to him. Everything about him as he enfolded her in his tall, solid frame, the soft brush of his moleskin trousers, the weathered cotton of his shirt against her skin, his hands feeling out the territories of her body, made her feel wanted.

'He makes me feel colonised,' she had told Alison.

'You mean he's possessive,' her friend simplified brutally.

Alison's chill summary was like a cloud passing over the sun. Elsa was unwilling to admit to any flaws in her discovery. But 'possessive'? Her father had been called that too. It was not something she associated with love.

By the time Elsa became aware of it, it seemed that everything about her mother – her forgetfulness, her gaiety, her very untidiness, the colourful, ill-matched clothes and streams of dangling, dark hair – was a defiance of him. Any time she spent with the children, reading or playing everyday games, felt like a conspiracy against their father. Back in the tall, narrow house of Elsa's childhood, crammed with too many people and too much noise, the children would often cluster with their mother in the upper drawing room to avoid disturbing their father's work. Yet frequently the talk grew too loud or an argument arose and he would burst furiously through the door, shouting at them to be quiet in his German-accented English, yelling at their mother to control them. Away from him their mother bloomed, like a plant brought into the sunlight. With him she was curbed and cautious. People said he was possessive of their mother. But in reality he wanted to control her, and the children's own pure selfishness meant that he ruled at best over a divided kingdom. Suddenly she understood one of her sharpest resentments against her father. He had taken her mother away, and Elsa missed her.

On the corner of Museum Street she passed an expensive florist's. Snaky foliage, vivid clusters of fat roses and tulips invaded the pavement. On impulse she picked out some pale hyacinths from a steel bucket and bought them. They were Oliver's favourite flowers. She had discovered a bowl of them in his bedroom a week ago and when she remarked on them he had leaned over and breathed their scent greedily, their great, bruised violet blooms the colour of the shadows under his eyes. Elsa was not used to men who bought flowers for their own bedrooms and she struggled against the thought that there was something unmanly about it. But he had always had flowers for his room, he explained simply, his large hand caressing a knuckly hyacinth bud. His mother brought them for him when he was a child and the habit stuck. Something about this image of the boy and his flowers had struck her as so solitary, so vulnerable, that she was propelled all the more swiftly into his huge, meticulously clean, white bed, and did not torment herself, as she usually did, with thoughts of all the women who had lain there before her.

Chapter Sixteen

EXTRACT FROM *VALENTINE SIDDONS: A LIFE*

In February 1917 Stanzas from Battle and Beyond won the prestigious Publishing Society award for a first volume of poetry. Unexpectedly Siddons was granted two days' leave to attend the presentation, which was held at the headquarters of the Royal Society of Arts. Emily Siddons, though painfully shy in the company of her husband's more famous friends, was persuaded to make the trip down to London to see the literary establishment pay him handsome tribute.

★   ★   ★

VALENTINE COULD HARDLY take his eyes off her. Even now, the mere sight of her was enough to send his senses singing with anticipation. The way she leaned forward, chin cupped in her hands, eyes ardent with interest, when he took the small gilt medal and made his brief acceptance speech. Her smile at once demure and knowing. She really was an enchantress. Her simple chocolate linen dress concealed curves and crevices all the more enticing for being remembered before revealed. He'd not have much longer to wait now. Tonight, surely, there would be time.

'Valentine, I'd be awfully glad for you to meet Mr Archie Brown from *The Times*.' The secretary of the Publishing Society motioned towards a small, shabby man before him, a few wisps of hair straining over a gleaming skull. 'He's writing a special report on the soldier poets at the front. Then there's tea, as you know, in the library. I'd be delighted to take your parents in while you two talk.'

Taking his cue, the little man produced a pen and notepad and looked up at him expectantly.

'Are Art and War mutually exclusive Mr Siddons?'

Connie gave Valentine a secret smile before disappearing

with Ottoline into the adjoining room. He was beginning to distrust Ottoline's influence. Her wispy feather collar lent her the appearance of a vulture swivelling its long, balding neck.

'I'm sorry. What?'

'Could you summarise the function of Art in wartime?' The man looked at him expectantly. Valentine could see he had written 'Art and War' on the top of his pad.

'I don't know if I've really thought about it in those terms. I mean I hope passionately that my poems say something, however limited, to people back home.'

The man did not write this answer down. His pen remained poised inquisitorially above the paper. Valentine laboured on.

'You see it's impossible to communicate what it's like . . . out there, but any small glimpse – through poetry or painting or whatever – has to be better than nothing. Because we're all involved in it.'

The man cocked his head quizzically. 'Do you see your writing as part of the war effort?'

If it wasn't for the prospect of seeing Connie, he'd never have bothered with trying to get forty-eight hours' leave. Tripping off for some trifling literary ceremony was hardly the thing to go down well with the men. But there was every reason to think she meant to see him tonight, because she had inveigled one of her husband's friends from the War Office to make the presentation. It was that which had swayed his commanding officer to let him go. 'Can't disappoint the top pen-pushers,' he'd told Valentine, signing his pass with a curled lip. 'Put a good word in for us.'

Seeing Connie meant sending Emily back to Oxfordshire early, and Valentine felt bad about that. But Connie must be looking forward to tonight as much as he was. If only he could get a moment to talk to her. He wrenched his thoughts back to the aggressive Archie Brown.

'Can er, artistic works like yours ever communicate anything meaningful about War? Because in my humble opinion Mr Siddons, I'm not sure most people would understand what your poems are trying to say. Even on quite simple issues – should we prosecute the war or back the movement for peace, for instance – I don't feel your position is entirely clear.'

Out of the corner of his eye Valentine saw a solitary Emily standing against a marble pilaster. She looked small and sulky, clutching on to a teacup and surveying the vast, classical proportions of the hall. He felt a pang of baleful guilt.

'Well Mr Brown, one thing I'm trying to say is that if only people like you understood the reality of war, you wouldn't ask questions like this.'

'Don't mistake me, Mr Siddons.' The little man huffed up his shoulders. A fraction too late, Valentine realised what he was about to say. 'I think I understand the reality of war all too well. Both my sons fell at the front.'

* * *

Really, Emily thought, fingering her new shawl defiantly and accepting another cup of tea and a macaroon. If she hadn't absolutely insisted, Valentine would have stopped her coming down at all. He said it would be boring, claimed she'd hate it. He even dared imply that she might find some of the people there intimidating, because they were older or better educated. As if! Wasn't she absolutely desperate to escape from Lower Binding and have some fun once in a while. What did he think it was like having your social circle confined to the vicar's wife and the local farmers' families? With the occasional, pitying call from one of her friends from Oxford. It had, after all, been Valentine's idea to take up the offer of a cottage in the middle of nowhere and because she had been so keen to please him, she'd put her own preferences aside. As soon as the beastly war was finished she would tell him straight they were to take a flat in London.

It was so nice to be here. She breathed deeply as though the air itself was pregnant with sophistication. Granted, she'd thought it might be more of a party than a restrained little tea, but there was quite an impressive crowd. A pair of very polite old fellows from the Publishing Society and some extraordinary literary types. They all seemed terribly keen on Valentine. She thought she recognised a couple of famous authors, whose books they had back at the cottage, though Emily had not got round to them. And the women! Very modishly dressed some of them, especially the large lady with the feather collar and a sort of little hat like a fez. Her friend – another very smart woman, Lady something – must feel terribly dull beside her. Emily felt sorry for her. She must be the wrong side of forty and she was wearing a very plain mud-brown outfit which did her absolutely no justice. Emily's own pink paisley suit looked far prettier, she knew, though she bet it cost a tenth as much to make. It didn't actually look as if either of the grand women were going to deign to chat to Emily but all the same, wait till she told her mother about this. She would be green.

Truthfully, when she married Valentine, Emily had imagined there might be more of this sort of thing. Obviously it was hard with being away at war and everything, but Valentine had spent much of their brief courtship entertaining her with enticing, slightly mocking stories of the eccentric, artistic people he had met and the parties he'd been asked to and, frankly, Emily thought she'd soon be coming too.

Fat chance of that now. Even though she hadn't seen him for months, he'd been utterly withdrawn when she met him off the train last night. The weather was freezing, with flurries of snow folded into the wind, and it had been hard to talk as they soldiered back to the boxy little hotel in Mayfair where Valentine had insisted on staying. He had refused to stay with his parents, which in principle Emily didn't mind, but the hotel was cheap and poky and the food was horrid. Supper, served in a dismally empty dining room, was limp boiled cod in parsley sauce followed by suet pudding. When they'd finished the meal they had climbed the narrow stairs to a bed as hard and narrow as an ironing board and Valentine made love to her, his gaze focused blankly beyond her face, making her feel as if she didn't exist. Afterwards, the time when she'd been led to understand most married couples enjoyed an intimate talk, he rolled over as usual, taking most of the sheet with him and pretended to sleep.

Emily sighed. He was not actually unkind to her, she thought carefully, it was more that he seemed perpetually cross with her, or more specifically cross with himself. It hadn't always been like that. In the early days before the wedding, when he wrote poems about what he called her ethereal beauty, he had seemed to place her on a pedestal and she (perhaps unconsciously) had responded with an air more grave and dignified than was her natural mien. All his talk of modern values and philosophy brought out an earnestness in her that she hadn't known she possessed.

Married life had started all right too. When they first saw the cottage her father had bought them, Valentine had been enchanted with it. He adored its honeyed stone walls that seemed to glow from within under the evening sun. He loved the rambling garden with its winding grass walks. On that first day he leant at the window of his study and gazed at the landscape for ages, as if he was trying to fix it in his memory and then toured the small rooms, with their sparse furniture, repeating again and again that this was just what he needed. And on their first night, as Emily lay still but expectantly beneath him in their marriage bed, he had deflowered her with halting but undeniable enthusiasm.

Thinking back, if she had to put a date on it, things had really changed for the worse during his convalescence last year, when he was forced to spend months in England recovering from the incident with the shell. He had lost the feeling in half of his hand as a result, but when she tried to look on the bright side, saying how lucky he was that it was only his left hand and so would not affect his writing, he had shot her such an unpleasant, sardonic look that she had made him apologise. He refused to talk about what had happened in any detail, and even when she invited over some of her best friends, who obligingly came out to the cottage with copies of *Stanzas from Battle and Beyond* for him to sign, he had seemed unwilling to engage in anything but the briefest conversation.

Eventually Emily's misery forced her to confide all this to her mother, as they stopped for tea and cakes at the Randolph hotel during an all too rare shopping trip in Oxford. She had expected her mother to take it as justification for her original disapproval of their marriage, but instead she seemed to side entirely with Valentine. She cautioned Emily that there were plenty of men coming back from war in the same condition and it was the job of their women to be patient, understanding and compassionate. This condition was called nerve damage and it was certainly being taken seriously because there were several hospitals opening up to treat it. When Emily pointed out that her brother George managed to be perfectly cheerful and he had lost a whole foot, her mother said quite sharply that she should remember all men were different and she was lucky enough to have a husband who wrote her the most beautiful love poems.

That was true at least. The love poems which had appeared in his collection were beautiful. Emily had taken the book to bed with them one night, and read aloud her favourite, 'The Enchantress', almost as a ruse to reawaken the romantic feelings Valentine plainly cherished for her. It was useless of course. She could have been a haddock on a fishmonger's slab, for the perfunctory way he ran his hand over her body, the prelude to a hasty, hopeless coupling and yet again, 'I'm sorry, I'm sorry,' muttered into her ear like a curse.

In a way she was secretly relieved they wouldn't be spend-ing tonight together, though she wouldn't let Valentine know that. He had insisted on bundling her on the last train this evening, which would mean rushing, with no opportunity for shopping. Not that there was any money to spend anyway. Emily had thought an award would surely mean some sort of cheque, but it turned out to be nothing more than a minuscule medallion on a ribbon. Still, going back early meant she needn't spend any more time with Valentine's parents. Lunch with them at Simpsons had been a real trial. She did like Mr Siddons, who tried to engage Valentine in hearty conversation about military tactics, but his mother was a bundle of nerves. She barely touched her dressed crab and kept on about what they would do after the war, the holidays they could all take, though it was plain from her face she believed her son was doomed to die at the front. Emily felt precisely the reverse. Some people went by the laws of statistics in these things but she preferred a medical analogy. If Valentine had survived this long, there had to be some sort of natural immunity protecting him.

A tall blond man leaned over her, interrupting her thoughts.

'I'm so glad your husband is not a patriotic poet. Patriotism in art is so vulgar, don't you think?' He had an elaborate, drawly voice, swilling every word round his mouth like wine. Emily thought he sounded suave and aristocratic. Although his suit wasn't much to look at, you could tell he was distinguished. But she didn't know whether to agree with his assessment. It was good to be patriotic, surely?

'Valentine loves his country,' she said staunchly.

'Oh of course, absolutely. I wouldn't doubt it. We all want what's best for our country after all. Forgive me, I've not introduced myself. Colin Seabrook. You might have read my essays. In the *Journal*?'

'Um, possibly, yes.' She held out a white gloved hand.

'I'm Emily Siddons. Oh, but of course you know that.'

'I wish I'd known sooner. And may I say how lovely you look. Fuchsia is such a brave colour. But you carry it off so convincingly. Why does Valentine keep such a bewitching wife hidden away in the country? Do you despise the town? Is that it?'

Emily laughed. 'Oh not at all. I love it. I'm having such a good time today. It's just there's so little opportunity to come to London.'

'What a shame. It is simply so frightful to be entombed against one's will in rustic solitude. I do sympathise. My parents are always begging me to come up to their place in Leicestershire but I would rather hole up in one room in Fitzroy Square than pace around a freezing estate trying to shoot anything that moves.'

Emily thought Colin Seabrook sounded fun. No reflection on Valentine, but some men were so good with women. Interested in them. You felt you could confide in this man. Seeing Valentine's mother approaching, she turned further towards him and said: 'Do you know all these people? I'm afraid I know practically no one.'

'And you want to know what you're missing. Well of course.'

Willingly, Colin launched into a biting commentary, making her giggle at the defects of the other guests, their pretensions, absurdities and social inadequacies.

'See that old fellow, Osborne Davies,' he gestured to a

flushed, portly man complaining loudly about the Zeppelin raid which had damaged his house. 'Trots along to every function the Publishing Society holds, though he hasn't written a thing for twenty years. Just shows anyone can be a man of letters if they live long enough.' Given Valentine's imminent return to the front, Colin's remark might have seemed a little insensitive. But Emily was preoccupied by a more uncomfortable image, of an ageing Valentine, cooped up in the cottage, angry and stagnant with writer's block. She tugged at Colin's elbow.

'Who's that lady over there by the door?'

'Lady Ottoline? Our feathered friend? I fear she's a little put out today. Had a little tiff with one of her admirers.'

'No, I meant the lady with her in the brown dress. I was introduced but I . . .'

'Constance Emberley? Now she really is a darling. A highly discerning woman. She's married to Viscount Emberley y'know. She's a very close friend of mine. She's my guest tonight as a matter of fact. I'm hosting a small dinner party at my debating club to discuss the Russian situation. What a shame you're not staying. It would be such an honour to have you and Valentine along.'

★　★　★

The compliments and civilities and little circulating plates of cakes were over all too soon and swiftly the guests dispersed into the bitter evening. Wistfully Emily watched them go, like bright candles snuffed out by the encroaching gloom. Snow was falling in gusts of spiralling ice, eddying round the Royal Society's high brass door as they stood saying goodbye to Valentine's parents. Emily pulled her old rabbit fur collar tightly round her ears. Mrs Siddons was taking an age, clinging to her son's neck, trying to conceal her tears. His father, stamping his feet on the periphery, turned to Emily awkwardly and said, 'Well keep your spirits up, little lady.' She smiled tightly. At last Valentine detached his weeping mother and tugged Emily to his side.

'We'd better hurry if you're going to catch the 6.15.' Emily huddled gratefully into the warmth of his greatcoat as they walked.

'Don't you wish I was staying over tonight?'

'Doesn't make sense. I have to be off so early tomorrow.'

'That Mr Seabrook invited us to his club this evening.'

'What a ghastly thought.'

'They're discussing the Russian situation.'

'Really? You probably know as much about it as they do.'

'All the more reason for us to go. I could do with a nice supper.'

Valentine didn't answer. His uncertainty over that evening's arrangements distracted him. Stupidly, he had been unable to make any definitive plan with Connie at tea, because Ottoline stuck to her side like glue. Now he was going to have to look for her. Where on earth would she be? Most likely, he decided, she would be waiting for him at the Chelsea house, preparing for a quiet night together.

Unconsciously he sped up. He wondered how long it was going to take to get Emily on her train.

'Valentine! We're not on a route march now. You're almost running.'

'Don't want you to be late.'

She looked up at him crossly, this small, irritating appendage, whose life had so disastrously tangled with his own. As he hurried her along, Valentine was struck by a feeling quite different from his usual brew of resentment and guilt. He felt remorse. She was so young to have a husband in love with somebody else. Taking her slim, gloved hand in his own he placed it in his pocket where it banged against something hard and cold. He took out the medallion.

'Here. You have it.'

'Really?'

Emily stopped and took the Publishing Society medal with its relief of a laurel-wreathed Adonis in her hand. Carefully, reverently, she placed it round her neck.

'I've misjudged her,' pondered Valentine uncomfortably. Emily tucked her stole over the medal to keep it safe.

'It might be silver after all,' she thought.

CHAPTER SEVENTEEN

THE NORMANDY FOUNDATION was ensconced in a tall eighteenth-century light-filled house set on the south side of a London square. Through its long windows, rays of morning sunshine filtered, warming the shoulders of the readers at their desks, illuminating the high stacks of books and glinting off the odd gold-embossed spine. Simon moved through the pools of liquid warmth, pacing the shelves slowly, stopping occasionally to inspect a title. He thought how many years of human life were represented in these accumulated millions of words, packed as tightly as grains of sand in a rock, stiff with the civilising smell of learning. Libraries, like gardens, evoked in him a deep unhurried content, such as most people knew in the long sunlit days of childhood but rarely found thereafter. He thought what growth and endeavour was embedded deep in these shelves, what flowering of knowledge must be folded in its leaves.

Becoming another year older had depressed him. He could not help comparing his own paltry progress with that of some of his university friends. Whether lawyers, bankers or brokers, somehow they were all strangely alike. He met them, increasingly infrequently, at dinner parties, where they arrived late with their low-five handshakes, loudly complaining about their working hours, boasting of the deal, or the case, or the treatment, and bearing the hallmark of success like a smart school tie against their sharp, high-salary suits.

Whereas Simon had abandoned a promising journalistic career for what? An obscure production company in a low-rent office above a greasy spoon. A daily, down-at-heel struggle against financial nemesis. Numbed, hardened and immured in the rat race he had once so carelessly despised. Yet, as if that was not enough, he knew there was something else troubling him. Something missing, something he wanted but was unable to pin down. Every day he awoke with a surge of panic, indefinable fears disappearing like car thieves into the taunting shadows. Indigestion burned in him like an acid assault. He didn't know what the problem was, but frankly, there was plenty of material. His private life was a desert, his family life dominated by Norman's dyspeptic eccentricity. And as for his career, well it didn't bear too much consideration.

But the library's shelves were a salve to his mind. By the time he arrived at the section devoted to first world war poets he was calm, almost relaxed.

Collecting an armful of volumes, he went over to one of the big tables and started to read. He had not thought much about the war since university, when its epic slaughter and its shuddering impact on the twentieth century first aroused his horrified imagination. The Passchendaele film had been Elsa's idea of course, and he had largely concentrated on raising the funds to make it possible. Looking now at the photographs again he thought how alien the faces of the soldiers appeared. In the harsh light of retrospect their innocence was as strange and shocking as the old advertisements for cigarettes which promoted tobacco's health-giving qualities. He found it impossible to imagine himself in the apocalyptic landscapes with their charred sticks of trees. He could not see through the frozen black-and-white layer to the living, coloured reality within.

The poetry made a difference, though. Voices like that of Siddons, which spoke with a contemporary, deceptively casual tone, cut like a knife through the formality of letters and dispatches from the front. The thought that Durban Films might be in possession of some of the poet's unpublished work, though both Eastway and Elsa seemed to have disregarded the possibility, still hovered tantalisingly in his mind. What a coup to launch a film with. He had already mentally sketched the process of ringing his friend James who worked on a Sunday newspaper, and how the ensuing, exclusive full-page layout would appear: 'War Poet's Early Work Unearthed – a forthcoming film about the first world war has delighted scholars with an important find'. Or 'Universities bid in auction of original Siddons manuscript'. Or even, he indulged himself, 'Film maker tells how he discovered valuable new manuscripts relating to war poet

Valentine Siddons', though admittedly, with that tack, he would have to gloss over a few of the facts. But the main thing was, if the poems could be genuinely verified as Siddons', the money for the film might come flooding in.

The Normandy Foundation library was the biggest collection of first world war documentation in the country and if there was just one clue to the Siddons poems, a single pointer to the existence of some undiscovered writing, then it would surely be here.

Simon hauled out the first collected edition of Siddons' poetry and prose and began to read doggedly through it. Generally he admired Siddons, but that morning the poet aroused in him a niggling irritation. It was not until he turned to the front of the volume and saw the frontispiece portrait that he realised why. He had seen that blank, slightly superior stare, the knowing smile and handsome, receding hair as Oliver Eastway had strolled arm in arm with Elsa off into the night.

As he was brooding over the picture an inscription caught his eye. It was a dedication, a single line, scrawled neatly across the top of the facing page.

For Arthur Winelees, with best wishes from Emily Siddons.

Underneath, the library had inserted its own line:

Donated by the family of Arthur Winelees. June 1966.

Winelees. Simon had seen the name before, somewhere in the research notes. Wasn't he the young corporal in Siddons' company who had been left some paintings in his will?

Strange that Siddons was a good painter, too. Good amateur, anyway. That two creative talents should co-exist. Idly Simon wondered if they expressed different truths about the artist, or what he represented. Different ways of seeing.

Well, evidently Winelees merited a first edition of the collected poems and prose, too, when it was posthumously issued some years later. The gifts were unusual. From what he could remember, men of different ranks did not often strike up the kind of friendship which led to legacies and suchlike. How well had Winelees known Siddons? Obviously, the man himself would be long gone. Indeed it looked pretty much as though he had died in or before 1966. Yet the friendship seemed to have been important. Perhaps the Winelees family might know something. He took the volume up to the desk, filled out a form to borrow it for a fortnight and had a quick look through the donation records.

After consuming a steaming cup of kipper-coloured tea and a ham sandwich in a small café nearby, Simon headed for a telephone box. The warmth of the day and his new sense of resolution had lightened his mood a few shades. Elsa answered the phone, but as soon as she realised it was him her voice sounded uptight, as though she was being cold-called by a fitted kitchen company. It was exactly the voice he used when his own father phoned requesting some unreasonable and trifling errand. Simon tried smiling into the receiver, which he had read could make the voice sound friendlier.

'Elsa. How are you? Burglars not returned I hope?'

'No. Though Alfredo says he's had some bag snatches recently, so I suppose our episode was linked to that. Are you sure we shouldn't tell the police?'

'No. Listen, Elsa, are you busy?'

Elsa thought it unwise to reveal that she wasn't.

'Well, I did as you asked and contacted that nice man John Harvey, in Hay-on-Wye. He did seem charming. You're right, he didn't know Siddons, but he met quite a few of his contemporaries. I fixed to go down and see him anyway. Why? Where are you?'

'I'm in London. Listen. How do you fancy a trip to Kent?'

'When?'

'In about half an hour?'

Elsa had been planning to take the train to Oxford for the evening, but Oliver had that instant called to tell her he was entertaining some dull guests to High Table that night and that she would do well to miss the event.

'Well, OK then. What are we doing?'

Using the library records, Simon had established that the donor of the Arthur Winelees book was a son, the Reverend Andrew Winelees, vicar of St John's, Faversham.

'It's a stab in the dark really, but I thought we'd look up the Winelees family. Siddons' friend from the front, remember? The one he left the paintings to. We could see if they recognise the poems.'

'Oh Simon. You're not chasing after those? Oliver says they're certainly not Valentine Siddons'. I mean, he'd know, wouldn't he?'

Elsa's immediate deferral to Oliver Eastway provoked the Pavlovian annoyance in Simon.

'Just bear with me, Elsa. All right?'

'Well I've never seen Faversham. It's supposed to be very pretty.'

'Fine. I'll be there.'

★   ★   ★

It was so good to see Simon happy, Elsa realised, as they sped down the M2 in his rusting VW Golf. It meant she did not have to work so hard to conceal her own quiet exhilaration. She could not keep her mind off Oliver's request. Should she move in with him? Secretly she had always fantasised about living in Oxford again. Yet she had known him just a couple of months and much as she liked the idea of leaving the damp little coffin she currently owned, relationships could be far more oppressive in their way than the narrowest west London basement. Unfortunately, this was one topic she could not discuss with Simon. No point ruining such a glorious afternoon.

Instead she gazed contentedly out of the window. For April, the weather was defiantly summery. The warm air was impregnated with the smell of the first cut grass of the season. Elsa drank it in, invigorated, like wine. The crops were shouldering up through the earth, trees unfurling their leaves like relaxing fists.

Though she thought their journey was probably a wild goose chase, she silently decided to indulge Simon about the potential of the poems. Indeed, she rather hoped they would never discover the identity of the writer, if it meant he'd be too disappointed.

'How's Norman?'

His father was the sole area of Simon's personal life about

which Elsa had managed to extract some detail, but even then it was like drawing teeth. She knew that he, more than either of his brothers, visited Norman in his small, terraced home at least once a week and ensured that he had everything he needed. It was plain the old devil had descended prematurely and with pleasure into a crusty old age he felt he much deserved, after the epic endeavour of bringing up three boys single handed. Elsa had not met Norman but she had seen him once, when he turned up unannounced at the office. He was wearing a seedy cord suit and fraying shirt sleeves, but was rather younger than she had imagined. He smoked incessantly and his face was creased and stubbly, but she could see that once he had been an attractive man. His eyes had raked down her short skirt and legs in an automatic, appreciative way. She wondered if Simon would look like that in forty years' time. It was hard to envisage.

'He's all right. Drinking a lot. I told him to lay off the phone-ins or we'd never be able to pay the bill.'

From what Elsa could gather, in his latter years Norman had taken to making regular calls to phone-in programmes. Armed with a whiskey bottle and packet of cigarettes, punctuating his sentences with a raspy cough, his major topic was the state of the Government, about which his views were articulate, nihilistic and frequently sensible. On most stations he was either banned or patronised, in the way younger people generally treat old people with strongly held views. But in some places Norman's calls were welcomed, and he was greeted like an old friend. Even then, though, he had a tendency to ramble.

'I bet he takes no notice. The turn-off's coming up here, I think.'

They drove into Faversham like tourists, remarking on its peace and prettiness. St John's turned out to be a robust Victorian building lying at the far end of the town. Across the road from the church, the vicarage was a soulless, modern box, wearing a shroud of Virginia creeper as if to disguise its uninspired design. It squatted hideously alongside a splendid redbrick house, plainly the original vicar's home sold off at some low moment in the church's finances.

Elsa and Simon parked a little way down the road and sat

in the car. Suddenly, Elsa felt that the futility of their mission was almost overwhelming.

'So what do we do now? Just stroll in and say, tell us everything you know about Valentine Siddons?'

Simon waved the borrowed edition of the collected prose and poems from the Normandy Foundation as though it conferred validity on their visit.

'They'll probably be delighted to help. It'll remind them of their small part in literary history.'

The vicarage did not look as if it had a place in history. As they approached it they saw ruched net curtains at the windows and artificial flowers in a pot in the porch. Inside Elsa could see Dresden shepherdesses picketing the mantelpiece, at their feet china dogs frozenly frolicking. The doorbell played 'Onward Christian Soldiers' in a glockenspiel trill.

'Hello?' The woman who opened the door wore a blue gingham housecoat, and restrained a yapping dachshund by its collar. She looked slight and kindly.

'We were looking for Andrew Winelees, the vicar?'

'Oh my husband's out at the moment but he won't be long. He's just nipped across to the church with the surveyors. The never-ending steeple issue, I'm afraid.'

'Could we wait, perhaps?'

'Of course, dear. Only I hope you haven't come for the class?'

'Well . . .'

'Marriage preparation? Because it's Tuesdays, you know.'

Elsa suppressed a peal of laughter. Simon glanced at her crossly.

'No, I'm sorry, let me explain. My name is Simon Pardoe, this is my partner Elsa Meyers. My business partner, that is,' he added hastily.

'Oh dear, I am sorry. Have I put my foot in it? It's just that whenever we get a young couple coming to the vicarage it's usually either marriage or a christening that they want. Come in anyway. Let me get you both a cup of tea. He'll be back soon.'

Inside the tiny front room the two sank down in capacious patterned armchairs and looked around them. Bibles, concordances and religious guides filled the bookshelves and the piano top. The carpet was busy with tangerine and purple swirls. On the coffee table beside her, Elsa saw several copies of a book with a lurid pink cover, *Visited by an Angel*. The name on the spine was Andrew Winelees. On the walls were a number of Alpine scenes in gilt frames and posed photographs of the Winelees family. But over the fireplace a quite different and more beautiful picture had pride of place. It was a watercolour of a summery English countryside, grassy meadows shimmering into the turquoise distance, lazy cows grazing the far fields and red flowers marking the foreground with an angry arterial splash. Simon stood and examined it.

'It's one of his, you know.'

After a few moments, Mrs Winelees returned with a tray and set it down.

'Now if you don't mind very much, I'll just get back to the kitchen, because we have the parish council meeting tonight, and though it's not supper, they still seem to expect an awful lot of cheese sandwiches and flapjacks to go with their cups of coffee. Andrew shouldn't be a moment, and I'll tell him you're here Mr Pardoe and Miss . . . er, mmm.'

While Simon sat crunching biscuits, staring at the watercolour thoughtfully, Elsa picked up a copy of *Visited by an Angel*. Overweight and balding, Andrew Winelees grinned out at her from a smudgy black-and-white photograph. His face above the dog collar had a florid complexion and a wide, friendly grin revealing terrible teeth. Hair swept in lanky streaks across the shining pate. Why did vicars so often look the part? She tried to imagine his face in a more fearsome guise, a Nazi perhaps, or a hangman, but it didn't work. The Church of England, in all its glorious warmth and banality, was unmistakable. And that was what she loved about it. Her own father was a Lutheran, a creed she associated with coldness and distance. She remembered the clean, clinical chapel they had frequented in her early childhood, with its whitewashed walls and relentlessly modern wooden furniture. How well it suited her father, whose acid bath mind stripped religion of all its glamour and mystery and soupy sentimentality. If he had to believe in a God, and as a reasonable man he was perfectly prepared to keep an open mind, he believed in being straight with

Him. Prayer for him was more a polite exchange of pleasantries than some undignified begging session.

Elsa winced. Even thinking about her father was something she tried to avoid. It was dark terrain, mined with emotions still unnamed and unexplored. She recalled his icy anger with her, when she refused his advice to study science or economics and read English literature at university. He had paid her way, but distastefully. Earlier, when she had declined to accompany the family back to Germany, his parting comments were as sharp as a severing blade.

'Elsa,' he had said over a stiff farewell drink in the airport bar. 'You believe I have failed you as a father.'

She blinked back at him. It was unlike him to be quite so direct. 'Don't worry,' he continued, 'it is a natural feeling, but the failure lies within yourself. You cannot expect people to conform to your notions of how they should behave. Recognising that is the first step in taking responsibility for your own life.'

She hated him at that moment. 'So I take it you won't miss me?'

He looked at her, bored, exasperated. 'Of course I regret you're not coming with us and the family is being split. But I have never had any doubt that you will manage. You are much tougher than you seem. I think there is iron in your soul.'

Now, she wondered, if she moved in to live with Oliver, would her father be impatient to meet him? Somehow, she doubted it.

The door opened, and the bustling figure of Andrew Winelees entered the room, rubbing his hands on his jacket.

'Forgive me, I wasn't expecting visitors. This isn't to do with the steeple appeal is it, by any chance? I'm afraid our little fund-raising barometer seems to have got stuck halfway. And as I've just been saying to the surveyor, there's an awful lot of bring-and-buys between here and £50,000.'

He gave Simon a damp handshake.

'Reverend Winelees? Sorry to descend on you like this, out of the blue. I'm Simon Pardoe and this is Elsa Meyers. I hope this isn't an awkward time, and you may be totally unable to help us. It's hard to know where to start.'

'Fire away Mr Pardoe, fire away.'

'Well, I understand that your father Arthur fought in the Ox and Bucks light infantry. And that he was friends with, or at least knew, the poet Valentine Siddons. That's one of his watercolours, isn't it?'

'You're right, it is. They knew each other in the first world war. He left my father his entire collection actually but if that's why you're here, you're out of luck, I'm afraid. Until a few months ago we had Siddons all over the walls but we auctioned them off. For the steeple, as a matter of fact. That's the smallest one and we only kept that for sentimental reasons. They're not valuable, I hasten to add. Rather amateurish, the experts would probably say. Are you some kind of art dealers then?'

'No, no. We're making a film about Siddons.'

'Mmm. Really? There was a documentary which featured him, oh, when was it?' He called out into the hall. 'Susan, when did we see that programme on the BBC? About Valentine Siddons? Must have been the seventieth anniversary of the Armistice, 1988 I suppose. But of course he didn't get the whole film to himself. Couldn't expect to, of course, when there are people like Wilfred Owen around. Are you from the BBC too?'

'No, we're er, independent. What we wanted to ask you was more something about his life.'

'Oh.' Was it Elsa's imagination, or did his tone cool slightly? 'Well, there I can't help you. I'm afraid my father told me very little about him. So if that's what you've come for, I'm afraid you've had a wasted journey.'

Simon exchanged a look with Elsa, but persevered. 'You see I found this book of his poems in the Normandy Foundation library which was donated by your family.'

Andrew Winelees cast a cursory glance at the book. 'That's right. My father was given it by Emily Siddons, his widow. We thought a proper library was the best place for it. It might be useful to scholars, you see. It's a first edition.'

'Well, the thing is, this book claims to be the collection of all Siddons' poems written between 1913 and 1917.'

'Yes?' It was beyond doubt now. The vicar's ruddy,

overworked complexion had hardened; his manner had become more terse.

'You see, I think despite what it says in the book, we've discovered something rather interesting about Valentine Siddons. I don't think this book does represent all the poems he wrote.'

With a sudden movement, surprising in one of his bulk, the vicar got to his feet, and went over to the window. His voice was level and controlled, but it had lost its friendly edge. He rocked on his heels, his back towards them.

'Listen, Mr Pardoe, I really don't want to be offensive or difficult, and I appreciate you've come a long way hoping to get something out of this. But frankly I feel very tired of people like you, coming down here, asking about Valentine Siddons. I understand your interest, but I really know nothing and have nothing to say. I repeat, nothing.'

He moved towards the door.

'I hope I'm not being rude, but I am rather busy and if that's all, I'm afraid I shall have to bid you good-day. I'm expecting some of my parishioners here shortly.' He smiled thinly. 'Goodbye.'

Elsa and Simon walked back down the crazy paving and silently returned to the car. Simon lit a cigarette. After a moment's thought he said: 'Well that just about confirms it.'

'What does it confirm?' asked Elsa, bewildered.

'The poems are genuine. That's the only explanation. He knows about them. Other people have been here. Sniffing around. Just a shame they obviously badgered him half to death. God, how exciting. Oh damn.'

'What is it?'

'I've left the book in there. I suppose I'll have to go back and get it.'

He had to ring twice before Mrs Winelees' cautious face appeared round the door. Her former friendliness was clouded with worry.

'I'm afraid my husband . . .'

'No, it's just that I've left my book here.'

'Oh, is that all. Just a tick.'

She left him waiting in the porch and hurried away. When she returned she held on to the brown volume for a moment, so that Simon had to step forward to take it. As he did, she brought her face close to his. Simon smelt a comforting aroma of rosewater and furniture polish as she almost whispered: 'I'm afraid I don't know what you're doing, Mr Pardoe, and I don't care, but I would just like to tell you the truth. Whatever they say about Valentine Siddons, don't listen to it. He may have done a terrible thing, and I'm sure it's not for us to judge. But Valentine Siddons was a good man.'

CHAPTER EIGHTEEN

EXTRACT FROM LETTER SENT BY CAPTAIN ANGUS MCCALL, OX AND BUCKS LIGHT INFANTRY, AUGUST 1917 TO MR FREDERICK AND MRS ROSEMARY SIDDONS.

I would like you to know that I spent some time in our front line trench talking to your son before the raid into enemy trenches which he led. He was extremely cool and calm, good humoured and a great inspiration to his men. It was partly owing to the leadership of Second Lieutenant Siddons, as well as the impressive discipline of the men, that they made such splendid progress. He returned from the raid successfully, but in an act of simple heroism went back to No Man's Land to rescue another man. That act was, for your son, the supreme sacrifice. I would like to record the deep sympathy of the whole battalion for your loss, and pray God that you will suffer it with some pride.

* * *

'HE WAS A good boy.'

Yet again, with a wince, Valentine recalled the sight of Foxley's face. The white, slightly paunchy folds of flesh, which had once made him seem so amusingly debauched, now looked merely sweaty and fat, the fashionably long hair had gone, to be replaced with a crude boyish cut, as short as a labourer's. Like everyone else he stank, but he had tried to cover it up with some appalling embalming fluid of a cologne. Foxley's company had billets in the same village and Ronald had come over to the cottage they had taken for a mess.

It was not the whole cottage, of course, just the front room, but nevertheless it had a homely feel. It was luxuriously equipped with several battered armchairs and tables, and despite the smoky stove which gave off choking dark clouds of soot, they had closed the green shutters to preserve as much peace as possible. Along the mantelpiece a child's dolls were ranged and above them, bizarrely, some sort of ploughing implement had been hung up on the wall.

There were three of them in there, smoking, and apart from carrying out a gun inspection that lunchtime, Valentine had hoped to have another six hours in the armchair before they were obliged to move up again.

The other men, Fleming and Leo Cowley, were playing cards. Foxley's arrival had interested no one.

'Just a boy, Valentine. He was seventeen. He lied about his age.'

'They all do. Or used to anyway.'

Foxley had been attached to the Ox and Bucks. His company had been billeted in an even smaller village, about two hundred yards further away from the line. Foxley said he and six other officers were sleeping in a former pigsty. The original inhabitants had long since become bacon, but the rain still caused fetid fumes to rise from the damp straw. That accounted for a lot.

Suddenly, two streaks of tears rolled down Foxley's pale face. He was crying, damn him.

'I say, old man,' Valentine extended a hand uncertainly and rested it on Foxley's shoulder. 'I know it gets a bit much but . . .'

Foxley honked, a great, moist, porcine sniff. 'Stop it, Valentine,' he said thickly. 'It's not me that needs your bloody sympathy.'

The story was a depressingly familiar one. Several days earlier a private in Foxley's company, Reggie Addison, had been found asleep on duty at advance post. Addison, a butcher's boy from High Wycombe, with blunt, straw-coloured hair and a wide, ever-smiling face, was considered a little simple by the other men in the company, Foxley said. He had appeared completely unperturbed to be found asleep, and merely promised it would not happen again. That indeed might have been all, had not a captain in Foxley's battalion related the incident in the presence of the company commander, Colonel Frank Rowe. Colonel Rowe, a bureaucratic, bank-managerish figure, had a highly nervous disposition which he concealed by generating mounds of paperwork, in an attempt no doubt to simulate the conditions of his peacetime occupation. His present obsession was that the battalion was becoming riddled with dangerous insubordination. Hearing the story, he ordered a court-martial immediately.

Foxley was at the front line when the orders reached him. He stood in his dripping dugout, reading the papers over and over again, with hatred and dumb anger rising in his gorge. How it was that Addison heard of his fate before he was arrested, Foxley did not say, but the terrified boy ran away. He made it back to the village where the company were last billeted, and hid in the cellar of a local house. He was easily located however, as he cowered in the dungeon-like space, by his very audible wails and screeches and whimpers.

The unusual aspect of the trial was the appearance of Field Marshal Douglas Haig, who happened to be visiting that area of the front after the victory at the Messines Ridge. He did not arrive in time for the hastily convened court, at which Private Addison, in his soft country drawl, put forward his defence for falling asleep. He had just, he said, 'felt tired'. His act of desertion only confirmed the cowardice. But Haig was there in time to sign the warrant.

The execution was ordered for dawn the next day. A patch of ground on a railway embankment, just a few hundred yards away from the battalion headquarters, was selected, a tree serving as a stake. Addison spent the night before in a tiny room at the HQ, being helped to compose his final letter. Foxley went to help him.

'He was just so worried because his parents couldn't read. He kept asking if I thought we would be able to find them someone to read the letter out sensitively.' Foxley's face creased in pain.

Yet in some ways, once sentence had been passed, Addison acted in a calmer way than the men detailed to kill him, Foxley said. Finding a firing party was a struggle. At midnight he left the boy with a bottle of brandy, taking a fitful sleep in the cell, and went to wake the men. As well as an officer, they needed a sergeant and ten men, but when the unit was asked they all cursed and pleaded to be exempted, as though it was they who were to be killed.

'Don't make me a murderer, sir. I like the boy,' said one, with a desperate gleam in his eye.

Another was more mutinous. 'I won't do it, so don't bother asking me,' said the huge, puce-faced man, a farm labourer who came from the same area of town where Addison's family lived, and had known the lad since childhood.

Eventually Foxley made them cast lots. The ten unlucky men swore among themselves, though the gloom induced by the execution meant that they dared not swear at Foxley. He would not have cared if they did, he told Valentine. Two of them were to have live ammunition in their rifles, and Foxley was to carry a pistol for the *coup de grâce*.

By dawn the brandy had done its trick. Reggie Addison had sunk into a stupor. The priest, sent to see him an hour before, had shaken him awake, and kept shaking him to discuss repentance and the kingdom of heaven. Foxley saw, with something approaching relief, that the boy was staggering and reeling on his feet, his head lolling on to his shoulder. Then, said Foxley, he made his request. 'He asked me to kiss him.'

Valentine was slightly appalled. 'Good God. Did you?'

'Of course I bloody did. I put my arms round him and held him and told him to imagine I was his mother.'

At that point he had placed his head between his hands and taken a few audible breaths. Valentine waited queasily for the story to continue.

'The thing was, as long as he was drunk, I thought I could bear it. We got all the way to the stake and I pinned the white cloth on his heart and he said nothing. But when I tried to put the blindfold on he went mad, crying, calling out. I just couldn't—'

Foxley stopped talking and swiped the mucus dripping from his nose with a savage blow of his sleeve.

'Couldn't what? What did you do?'

'I left the blindfold off.' He looked at Valentine, his eyes blank with misery. After a few moments he said: 'So what about that then, Val? What about this goddamned stinking, fucking pit of barbarism we've fallen into? And that strutting, heartless bastard of a Haig, may he rot in hell.'

At this, Fleming and Cowley had raised their eyes from their cards.

'Keep your voice down, there,' said Fleming, neutrally.

'What are we doing killing our own people? Our own children? Because we're like their parents, you know. That's how I feel about my men. We're the ones who watch them dying and cradle their heads in our arms. We're the ones who call them by their Christian names when they need it. Oh, the real fathers remember them as upstanding heroes, going off to war in their uniforms. But when we see them at the end they're like babies again.'

Alarmed by the rising cadences of Foxley's hysteria, Valentine leaned towards him and put his hands on the other man's shoulders. He didn't know what to say. He felt clichés bubbling unbidden to his lips.

'Look, Ronald. It's the war, isn't it. It's hateful and disgusting, and we've just got to concentrate on lasting till it finishes or getting out. Roll on duration, eh? It sounds bloody awful what happened to that boy and it's understandable that you're feeling . . . rotten about it. But you've got to take that anger out on the Boche.'

Foxley gave him a look of disgust. 'I can't believe I'm hearing this from you,' he said.

Valentine could not believe it either. But he was angry at the role Foxley had cast him in. The educated apologist for the war. The officer with the moral answers. Nothing could be more ridiculous.

'What did you expect to hear?'

'Oh I don't know, a bit of common humanity, a bit of that exquisitely intelligent poetic sensitivity that dear Connie Emberley is always babbling about. But I don't know why I expect you to show any judgement when you carry on with her. She drops you and then when you get the tiniest bit of celebrity with your book she picks you up again. Her little soldier boy on the side. It's the likes of her and her husband we're fighting for and dying for. You're stuck out here, and what about her? Well if you want to know, Valentine she's being squired round London in your absence by some new young lad now. An essayist, I heard.'

A gas attack could not have had a swifter impact on

Valentine. He felt it like a physical shock. The thought of Connie melded with the image of Ronald Foxley kissing the condemned boy in the cell. Misery and revulsion seemed to choke him. He shouted furiously at the snivelling man before him.

'Ronald, what the hell do you want? How many deaths do you think I've seen? We've all seen it, every day. But you come in here snivelling over some . . . private . . . and you expect all of us to throw away our arms.'

Perhaps it sounded more hostile than he had intended. Either way, Foxley stood up so suddenly the chair toppled over behind him and stumped out into the rain.

* * *

The next morning, the company was returning to the Ypres salient where a big offensive was planned. They had a few hours' march north to the station, where the troops were to load the stores on to the trains before boarding themselves *en route* for Poperinghe. The rain had cleared, at least for the moment, leaving behind it what Valentine thought of as school holiday weather. The air was washed and pungent with evaporations of rosemary, thyme and lavender, the sky a high, still, infinite blue. Hot sun burned the flesh on the back of his neck and warmed the fur of the odd stray cat arching across a broken wall.

Valentine and Fleming went along together. An easy, companionable feeling had grown between them. Fleming was the only man who knew the truth about Valentine's experience with the shell and how it had shattered things far less substantial than flesh. He knew about Connie too, and had appeared to pass no judgement.

There had been no chance to see Constance since the disappointing day of the award. She was away now, holiday-ing at their lodge in Scotland, entertaining her husband's fishing party. On his last leave, Valentine had been confined to base with Emily, lurking inside to avoid stray spinsters from the village who were liable to ask brightly whether he was longing to get back to the front.

Some amputees, he had heard, returned agonised by sensations in their vanished limbs. He, however, was still whole, but numb. Emily chatted on about the local people, in an obvious, but ill-judged attempt to keep his spirits up. Sometimes she varied the routine by lowering her voice and in hushed tones running through those women she knew who had lost 'loved ones'. He watched her scurrying and fluttering around him like some dreadful small animal. Her pinched porcelain skin seemed almost transparent and her face had lost all its puppy fat, making her powder-blue eyes even larger, glistening sometimes with easy tears.

She was more beautiful then ever but what did he care? He was dead flesh anyway. A carcass in khaki, going through the absurd motions of life. When she stopped trying to chat to him they would sit in their little drawing room in silence, Valentine reading while Emily sewed or gave the odd pathetic sniff. Marriage, whose acid accretions and dismal insights had so swiftly eroded affection, seemed calculated to destroy the feelings that inspired it. Sometimes at night in bed he tried to connect with her, but there were continents between them. It had seemed all the more bitterly ironic to him then that brute life had asserted itself and Emily found herself expecting a child. When she told him, Valentine felt it had almost nothing to do with him. It was as if she mentioned she was expecting friends to tea, or expecting to go down with the cold everyone else had caught. He tried to picture a child, a small solitary boy like he had been, but he failed. All he knew was that he was trapped now, like a rat in a cage.

It was a relief to hear Fleming, with no relations to speak of, talk about his life. Fleming went on a lot about his 'enthusiasms', of which there were many. Valentine supposed that was a result of being single, with time to spare. That morning, Fleming was discussing one of his greatest enthusiasms, archaeology. He had spent his holidays before the war on field trips at Knossos with Sir Arthur Evans.

'And what did you find then?' Valentine asked, with a flicker of interest.

'Oh, well you know there's an ancient Minoan palace there. Really quite magnificent. In the fifth year I had a great piece of luck. I found a fragment, on my first morning, as it happened.'

'A fragment?'

'Yes, definitely late Minoan. About four thousand years old. An oil lamp probably because of the handle, though we weren't able to be entirely sure.'

'You went for five years, and all you found was a bit of broken lamp,' Valentine scoffed. 'That was well worth it, then.'

'I thought so,' said Fleming with quiet satisfaction. He pulled something out of his breast pocket. It was a scrap of cloth, from which he drew a russety piece of pottery, bruised dark with earth. He handed it carefully to Valentine.

'This is it? It's thousands of years old and you brought it to war?' Valentine was incredulous. Fleming shrugged, apologetically.

'I know. It is frightfully unorthodox of me, but I couldn't bear to leave it there.'

Valentine turned the piece over in his hand. 'Shame it's broken.'

'Well yes, you're right. It is only a fragment, as you say, and of course, much less valuable than the whole. But you know, I think I prefer it that way. I mean, it's like all history, isn't it? We only have fragments to go on, but somehow the imagined whole they conjure up is more beautiful than it would be if you'd pieced it together. A sort of Platonic ideal.' Fleming halted. 'Well, that's how I think anyway.'

Though outwardly sceptical, Valentine was privately intrigued by Fleming's pursuit. When he talked about early Aegean life, his brown eyes brightened. His worn, teacherly face, dull as a school textbook, looked almost attractive. Dimly, Valentine understood how appealing it might be to uncover an ancient civilisation. To think that people who had once formed communities, made marriages, borne children and fought wars, people who thought that their society was the peak of human achievement, now lay buried beneath the flower-studded Cretan hillsides. Fleming told him how all of them, from the kings who had sat on the fabled throne of Knossos, to the scholars who developed the new script, Linear A, to the slaves who filled the oil lamps, had been destroyed by earthquake and fire, overtaken by other, stronger, claimants to the dubious title of civilisation.

It was a comforting thought. Somehow it helped to blunt

the sharp actuality of their own experience. The idea that perhaps, in a few centuries' time, someone might come along and dig them all up again, and reflect, under peaceful skies, on the self-destruction of the antique European powers. He wished he could go on like this, walking and talking to Fleming, for ever.

They were a subdued company that day. The men tried to start up songs, but there was no enthusiasm for it and after a few verses they died away. Valentine could not stop thinking about Foxley. He seemed ridiculous now. That fat frame, the easy sentimentality. What had he said? 'I told the boy to imagine I was his mother.' A hot anger ran through him but he did not understand why he was angry. Perhaps it was because it was going to be hard to eradicate the story of Reggie Addison from his mind.

Some way down the road he found himself looking into a sallow unfamiliar face. A company of Chinese labourers, part of the Chinese labour corps who had been shipped from their homelands and recruited to maintain the roads, stared up from their tools as the troops went by. They had an impassive, inscrutable expression on their faces. Dumb insolence, Colonel Rowe might have called it. The clang of their pickaxes on the roads sent little eddies of noise into the great stillness around them, where fields of hops and potatoes lay open and peaceful to the sky.

By the time the train arrived at Poperinghe it was early evening and the weather had changed dramatically. Pewtery rain clouds shrouded the horizon. Above them a grey observation balloon drifted. Valentine had orders to take his men straight up the Ypres road to the line. Nine British and six French divisions were to move forward on a fifteen-mile front. As they walked, the roads alongside were pocked with shell craters and to one side a mass grave was being dug, the pile of bodies humped in a messy line behind as if convened for some routine, pre-burial inspection. Most of Valentine's company had already seen some action, but the sight of bodies not yet black, returned from the place for which they were headed, still had the power to shock them. Straggling lines of men and ambulances came past them down the road, some of them giving a gesture or wave. As the road forked and dipped down to the support trench, the first fat drops of rain fell from the sky and bounced, spattered, skidded on the churned earth.

All that night the rain lanced down, teeming on to the field, filling the trenches to knee level with liquid mud. Beyond them ground that had been pounded for the past three years turned to a treacherous soup. In the darkness, where they were trying to sleep standing up, Valentine's company drew their oil sheets round them. Some attempted to bail out the narrow little corridors with their tin mugs. Valentine and Fleming had found a small hollow of mud to serve as their dugout and Fleming, who seemed to sleep through anything, had nodded off in a semi-reclining position. But for Valentine sleep was impossible. He sat staring at the portion of sky visible above the trench, watching the edges of it turn from the colour of rifles to mother-of-pearl. After a while he took out his small leather notebook and pencil. He always kept a notebook with him. He looked at this one for a moment, running his fingers protectively over its black hide, the gold glint of a V and S in its bottom right-hand corner. He thought of the slender, jewelled hands that had thrust it into his, as though it were a bible and she a salvationist. 'I want to see what you write in it,' Connie had said. Her voice was tender, mocking. He could not say if she would see it now. He wrote the word *Betrayal*, and under it scrawled:

> He vowed to serve his country
> For King and common good.
> But no pledge prepared him for the foe he met
> Stumbling out there in the mud.
> Betrayal advanced without warning
> The struggle was hellish and hard
> Like prising the wind from the rain it carries
> Splitting the bone from its blood . . .

At zero hour, half past four exactly, the sky seemed to burst into flame. The first barrage had begun, hundreds of British guns setting off their volleys into the unresponding darkness. For a while there was no retaliation. In the distance, a line of falling lights was all that indicated the location of the Boche trenches. Shells roared and flashed and spat fire from the British side, revealing the jagged ruins of Ypres in sudden, sharp silhouette against the blazing curtain of rain.

'Christ,' said Valentine softly.

'Not long now,' replied Fleming, his eyes still shut beneath the lid of his tin hat.

It was, however, another day of nervous acid apprehension before a runner splashed his way up the communication trench, bringing orders from divisional HQ to move forward. They were to mount a midnight raid on enemy trenches, a few hundred yards away in a small section of what had once been a wood. The aim of the raid was to capture a few Germans. HQ liked prisoners, although Valentine had previously found they often refused to give out any information, or worse still, imparted false news. But a raid the previous night had captured a Hun who informed HQ, correctly, that the Germans were unready for attack. Now they wanted to know Jerry's next tactic.

Valentine, Fleming and Cowley, who had been deputed to lead the raid, had changed into the uniforms of privates. Since the previous night's bombardment, the Germans had been jumpy, sending over frequent Very lights to check for activity. The men, most of them with blackened faces, gathered silently in the trench until Leo Cowley gave the signal to go.

'Let's bloody hope they keep Jerry's head down with some cover if he catches sight of us,' said Fleming, in a low voice which he intended only Valentine to hear.

'Shut it, will you,' barked Cowley, in an angry whisper.

It was a moonless night. They moved forward stealthily, stumbling over the clumps of earth, eyes straining for the wire. Valentine's wire cutters hung from his belt, banging against his leg. In places the mud was sucking at his boots, almost pulling them off his feet, and when he reached a patch of firmer ground he tripped over something soft and was unable to see whether it was flesh, or earth. His pulse seemed to be jumping in his throat, making his breathing almost painful. The men fanned out cautiously towards the wire which lay between them and the enemy trenches, situated in a solid line behind the first ragged stumps of trees. Ahead of him, someone fell and there was a metallic clang, provoking the sound of German voices. A moment later, the silvery green light of a flare burst over their heads, bathing the party in stark, crystalline illumination. At the same time as they threw themselves down, a machine gun raked the air. As Valentine raised his head, he heard the scream of a shell in his ears and a burst of stinging shrapnel burned his face.

'Sir?'

He recognised the voice. It was one of the men, Winelees. His soft Kent burr. He liked him.

'I'm all right. Go on.'

The German guns were still puncturing the air above their heads. Winelees shuffled closer. He squinted at Valentine then reached over and touched his head.

'Sorry, sir. Lot of blood.'

Valentine felt the liquid creeping over his face. It dribbled from the spattered shrapnel wounds down into his eyes.

'Best get back, sir,' whispered Winelees.

Valentine said nothing, but the pressure of Winelees' hand on his arm intensified very slightly, an infinitesimally tiny push. Valentine turned round towards the trench as the howl of shells filled the air.

His wounds were superficial, just a gash on the temple, where a piece of shrapnel had insinuated itself under his hat, and a peppering of cuts on the face. He stanched the wounds himself with a field dressing from his pocket, leaving the blood caked ghoulishly over his face. A few minutes later Leo Cowley was brought down, one hand and one foot blown off. Valentine could see the white of the tendons protruding out of the red meat. His face was grey and he was muttering quietly, between clenched teeth. Aghast, Valentine bent down to hear him.

'Thank God. Thank God. Thank God. Thank God.'

'Pleased with your blighty, Cowley?'

'Thought it would never come. I've been waiting for this for two years. Thank God, thank God, thank God.'

Two stretcher bearers carried him off to the dressing station.

188

Over the next hour, the party straggled back. Of fourteen men, eight returned. Fleming did not appear. From what they could see by the light of the flares, no one had penetrated the wire, let alone the trenches. Valentine loitered, waiting for more faces to appear over the top. Then one of the men, peering through a periscope fixed to his bayonet said:

'Looks like the buggers got one of our lads caught on the wire.'

'Can you tell who it is?'

'Not an officer, sir.'

'We were all dressed as privates,' Valentine snapped. 'Can't you see the face?'

'Got his back to me, sir. He's moving, I'm afraid. Unless it's the wind.'

Valentine felt the nausea rise in his throat. He turned and made his way back down the trench. Then, as if on impulse, he stopped. In a small hollowed-out niche, a ladder had been let into the mud wall. He scaled it, froze for a moment, a man-shaped target, inviting the gunner's eye, and then plunged forward.

It was the first time Valentine had ventured into No Man's Land in anything like daylight. In the darkness, death had seemed to come from nowhere, with no sight of the enemy, but in the silvery half-light of approaching dawn its leavings were plain to see. There were bodies everywhere, the Germans, their uniforms grey against the mud, sprawled like seals slaughtered on a beach. Alongside them a few Gordon Highlanders lay, their kilts skewed unmanfully above their thighs. In the middle distance a burnt-out tank keeled, like a shipwreck in the mud, with the charred figures that had once been its crew scattered around. On everything the cold rain fell, burying the bodies in the enveloping mud. Though the battle had receded, it was not silent. The noise of the guns and shells was replaced with a worse sound, cries and moans of the dying, some soft, others ugly with pain. Placing his foot close to what he thought was a corpse, Valentine felt a hand pluck at his boot, and looked down aghast to see the eyes of a man widen with appeal. He shook the hand off and went on, retracing his steps cautiously, half crouching, half running, making for the figure on the wire who must be Fleming.

But even before he got there, he realised it was not. As he neared the wire, the wind did his job for him, turning the body gently, so that he saw the side of the face with its blood-filled eyes. It was a dead face with the soft cheeks of a boy. Valentine knew him but could not remember his name. He stared at the crucified figure as it hung there, head jerked back, mouth agape. It was Reggie Addison, wasn't it? No, Addison had been shot.

He was on his way back when he found Fleming. Through the gloom he saw him lying in a shell crater, half out of the water, like a man relaxing in a warm bath. A stray, uniformed leg lay torn beside him. He must have been caught directly by a shell. In Fleming's blackened face, behind his shattered spectacles, the eyes were swollen shut, the lashes and eyebrows singed off. A soft gurgling issuing from below him suggested he was slowly sinking into the mud as he bled to death. Valentine braced Fleming's back with his rifle and crouched down beside him, taking off his glasses gently.

'Fleming? It's me, Siddons. Robert, d'you hear me?'

Fleming's black face did not move, but his raw, scalded lips flickered as the cold rain dripped down on them. Valentine knelt close. A suspiration seemed to issue from his mouth, the burnt, swollen tongue fluttering as if in speech.

'MMMmm.'

It could have been anything. Mother. Maybe. Mud. But then there was nothing. When he thought of listening for a heartbeat, he found that the clothes were melted on to Fleming's flesh. His stump stuck out awkwardly, a bloody tangle of cloth and bone. But in the haversack which lay beside him were his iron rations and water bottle.

For a long time, Valentine crouched there beside Fleming's corpse, the rain gradually filling the shell hole around them, rising to meet the glistening clods of earth around its rim. His map, which might have shown him the way back, had turned to a watery pulp.

He felt dazed. The loss of blood from his head provoked a faint, floating sensation. How odd it was to have risked his life for Fleming, who had no wife, no children, no one at all to miss him. To run a heavy risk of getting lost and then being spotted in the quickening daylight and cut down by the waiting guns. Why had he done it? For Fleming, of all people. Fleming had called him 'poet' laughingly, but admired his work. Fleming understood him, and now he had died.

Valentine did not know if he himself would live. He knew the stretcher bearers would be sent out, and that Jerry normally held his fire for them. Fleming's obliterated face had fallen back, so that the water was lapping at his sparse hair. Above them, the sky hung bruised and empty, but in the far corner, pink gleams tinted the watery dawn. They seemed fragile as eggshell as he fixed his eye on them, willing the pink to deepen to scarlet. He tried to think of the rhyme. Red sky at night, shepherd's delight, but red sky in the morning, shepherd's warning. Lucky there were no shepherds left round here, only soldiers. And soldiers died in any weather. He felt very calm. Images coasted through his mind. He remembered how his mother had given him a boat to sail on the pond in Kensington Gardens. He loved that boat. He had not thought of it for, what? fifteen years, but the image of it remained there, tucked in the whorls of his brain, its jaunty red sails, and his mother shouting 'Be careful', as he leaned over the water to push it out. Then the deep rose perfume of her skirts as he buried his face there after some slight accident. Good boy. The strong enveloping arms. He wanted to feel them and he wanted to fight them. Connie's arms had encircled his waist, her hands smoothing down over the flesh of his stomach, cool on the hard, springing organ below. Foxley had told Reggie Addison to pretend he was his mother. Had put his arms round him and kissed him.

He felt a deep desire to sink down into the earth, to die and disappear, at one with the horizon. He wondered if it was true that a soul was waiting to wrench itself, light as a Renaissance angel, from his cooling flesh. Or whether his being depended solely on the continuing quiet conspiracy of his beating heart and lungs. He lay there for a long time, until his hands, falling on Fleming's water bottle, raised it to his lips and he found rum. The taste of it ran like a shot through him. A rancorous acid burned in his gullet. Later another thought occurred to him. Reaching into Fleming's breast pocket he tucked there his small leather notebook. In exchange he withdrew a piece of pottery wrapped in cloth and Fleming's round, metal identity disc, the only recognisable remains of what had once been his friend.

CHAPTER NINETEEN

October 1917

Some weeks later, Emily Siddons woke at six o'clock in the morning, unusually early for her. She lay for a while, watching the chill light that washed round her tiny room brighten and mellow as the sun rose. It was going to be another fine day. The birds had been up for hours, swooping and calling in the fruit trees. She could hear the cows in the distance, lowing for their morning milking, banging their warm flanks against each other as they queued by the gate. She felt a dismal empathy with their bovine forms as she shifted her large bulk on to her other side with a grunt and felt the baby start up its tiny hammering inside her. I am twenty-one, she told herself again, a thought that could be relied upon to bring a prickling to her eyes. It was a time she had always associated with glamour, what her father called coming of age, pictured in her mind as some glittering round of parties, cigarette smoking, dancing and romance. Trips to London, engagement dinners perhaps, and above all fun. Being a pregnant widow had not been part of her plans.

The unfairness of her situation encouraged the first of the day's hot tears to roll down her cheeks. Valentine had not been easy, had not even seemed particularly happy in the short time that he had lived in this house with her. But the thought that he would not be coming back at all made her entire daily routine seem all the more futile.

The cottage had only three bedrooms and it had been deemed too small for a maid to live in, so a girl came up from the village every day. Emily, who had grown more desperate for company since moving to the country, attempted desultory conversation with her but it was extremely limited and confined largely to subjects that Heather, the good-natured daughter of a local farmer, was expert in. These included pregnancy, babies and childbirth, but Heather's lurid tales of other women's experiences, and in particular the length and awfulness of their 'pains', had only increased Emily's apprehension. The girl was also full of superstitions, most of them to do with the way the clouds were massing or birds behaving, and she had read Emily's tea leaves, predicting a long, happy marriage for her. So much for that. Since the day, almost a month ago now, that the telegram arrived, Heather had gone about her work with her large red face averted, her jocular observations on life unnaturally silenced.

As she heaved herself hugely out of bed and padded over to the blue and white china washbasin, Emily replayed yet again the moment that she discovered Valentine had died. It was yet another blazing afternoon. She had spent it gardening, collecting her first crop of strawberries and raspberries and a trugful of pink velvety roses for the bedroom. She had then retired to the cool of their tiny drawing room, trying to get interested in the novel a friend had sent to her. It was a romance, a genre which Emily was known to enjoy, but of a cheap, vulgar kind and she was feeling a tiny bit affronted that her literary tastes had been underestimated. The crunch of a bicycle's tyres up the path and the clatter of the door knocker seemed a welcome distraction. But when she saw the boy standing there on the step, his face sweating, his eyes not meeting hers, she knew what was in the telegram. The sentence that circumscribed the rest of her life was curt. REGRET TO INFORM YOU THAT 2ND LIEUTENANT V. SIDDONS KILLED IN ACTION, NR. PASSCHENDAELE, AUGUST 1917. She had shut the door without a word and wandered through the silent house, running her hand over its meticulously polished surfaces and brightly papered walls as if it were some mute but animate friend.

She was certainly shocked. It was not as if she had even been expecting it. She knew about the battle of third Ypres of course – she didn't read the newspapers herself and the casualty lists depressed her, but her father's letters kept her up to date with the progress of the monumental British assault and the differing official views about its success. Secretly she found his long-winded accounts of military manoeuvres tedious and skimmed his letters for snippets of family news. And perhaps because Valentine had been at war almost all the time he had known her, the chances of him dying seemed more remote. He always came back. Always more bitter, more cynical than before, always treating her efforts to jolly him up with slight boredom or disdain, as if she was in some way responsible for his being at war. Really! Of course she had supported his decision to join up. That was what every young man of her acquaintance had done, many of them much swifter than Valentine. Look at her brother George, who had been decorated after being invalided out, a small piece of silk covering the stump left where his foot was blown off by shrapnel as he led his men over the top on the second day of the Somme. Anyway, even if he had not enlisted, Valentine would have been conscripted by now. The war was not her fault. She knew it was awful, but he didn't seem to realise that she was having a terrible time too.

It was just so unfair. Emily finished washing and stood self-pityingly before the ancient spotted mirror that hung in their bedroom studying her shape. The increasingly bulbous belly was balanced improbably above slender legs and her breasts, normally rather small, were swollen and pointed, covered with blue veins. If only it were not for the pregnancy she could have returned to her normal life, almost as if nothing had happened. She was only twenty-one. Her complexion was still flawless and glowing with health, her corn-coloured hair bright and smooth and her appetite for fun entirely undiminished. To have been widowed so young was tragic, of course – at this point she cast the mirror a bashful upward glance from eyes brimming with feeling – yet she could learn to live again.

But with a baby? Her heart sank. She could be stuck out here in this cottage for ever, receiving the odd visit from friends, hearing accounts of their parties and holidays and clothes-buying trips up to London and their teas at Fortnum's, while she scraped by on an allowance from her father and some tiny royalties from Valentine's poetry. It didn't bear thinking about. Wearily she donned the black dress she had laid out the night before, splashed a lot of lavender water on her neck and wrists, picked out her prettiest necklace – a pearl and ruby cross with matching earrings – and went downstairs to prepare.

★ ★ ★

'Mrs Siddons.'

The curate, his voice hushed and comforting, took her arm at the door. Had it been an ordinary funeral, she thought with relief, she would have had to meet her husband's coffin at the church gate and followed it and the curate up the aisle. But today there was no coffin and no corpse, just a service of remembrance which seemed altogether less funereal. The tiny, bare church was filled with villagers, she saw with surprise. Valentine's parents were in the front row on the other side from her own parents, like some grotesque parody of the wedding they had attended just two years before. Stiff and dignified, she walked through the shafts of autumn sunlight slanting in through the high narrow windows and took her place for the service.

It had been her father's idea. Even though Valentine had received a military burial abroad, he deserved some remembrance in his own country, Dean Torrence had argued. And it proved just as awful as Emily had feared. Her brother read one of Valentine's poems, booming it out in his public school voice regardless of stress and scansion as though it were a safety announcement. The curate, who had stepped in when Lower Binding's vicar had gone off to fight, gave a long, soporific address about the nature of heroism and self-denial, illustrated rather oddly with references to Jacob wrestling with the angel. Swiftly Emily found her thoughts floating off again to her future until the sermon's abrupt ending had the congregation stumbling uncertainly to their feet for the final hymn.

The villagers did not say a lot. It was not in their nature and none of them would have presumed to accompany the two families back to the cottage for lunch. But one farmer, whose own son had been killed in the war and who was planning a memorial for the village green, leaned towards her as she passed from the church porch into the net of shadows under the yew trees, pressing her hand kindly.

'Never forget my dear, your husband died a hero,' he said, his voice gruff Oxfordshire. Emily gave him an automatic, graceful smile, but later the words remained with her and although they sounded glib she found them comforting. A hero. That was something. The whole idea of a hero seemed more solid and vibrant than the Valentine she had known in life. She would never have thought him capable of it. But if he was a hero, then she had chief custody of his memory. She was a hero's widow. That was some inheritance, after all.

As she pondered this in the drawing room of the cottage, pouring tea for Valentine's sniffing mother and dying to get out of her hot black dress, their son – for she knew it would be a son – struggled within her, as if signalling his desire to preserve his father's name in the world.

* * *

'They did for that Dutch dancer, Mata Hari, I see.'

Ralph sliced the heads off a line of asparagus with a single stroke of his knife. The news of the spy's execution in Paris had been reported in *The Times*, but while it caused Connie to shudder, Ralph had been fascinated. He had pored over the picture they printed of Mata Hari striking a semi-naked pose, draped like a marble statue in oriental veils. The idea of a woman being shot seemed to excite him.

The four of them were in the dining room at the manor, an enormous dark panelled space hung with Flemish tapestries and decorated with the Emberley family's priceless collection of Japanese porcelain. Deep crimson silk curtains were closed against the October night. Candlelight glanced off the Queen Anne silverware, casting the most flattering possible glow on the faces of Edward and Frances, Ralph's younger brother and his wife. Frances is what I should have been, Connie thought, not for the first time, but no longer with any anguish or dismay.

Tonight her sister-in-law looked more than ever like a seventeenth-century Puritan. She was dressed in the plainest of grey silk – she favoured sombre colours because she thought they drew less attention to her thickset form and carroty hair. Her body was muscular, mannish almost, due to her inordinate love of horse riding. Her teeth were equine yellow and her redhead's complexion was healthy, broken veined and weatherbeaten, untouched by make-up, fixed in a perpetual pinch of disapproval. She was accompanied, even indoors, by a revolting old spaniel, which stood belligerent guard beside her as she trawled her fingers through its greasy fur. Apart from Connie, nobody else seemed to think anything of it. An unhygienic attachment to dogs was something of a family trait.

Frances, a childhood friend of Ralph and Edward, lived with her husband on the far edge of the estate in a house which with its flinty exterior and freezing rooms uncannily resembled its mistress. Now she was just a guest at the manor, but one day Frances would occupy it as of right because she had what Ralph could only long for: a son – or rather a gratuitous spawn of sons – four altogether and two daughters, the heir with his mother's orange hair and unutterably charmless manner.

The knowledge that her child would inherit the Emberley title was rarely spoken of but always with them and it gave Frances a horribly proprietorial approach to the manor. She had an infuriating habit of inspecting Connie's drapes and screens like condemned men, poking their folds and fabrics with a grimace or sorrowfully shaking her head. She had barely been able to restrain herself when Connie had brought up from London a haul of painted furniture and fabrics from Roger Fry's Omega workshops. She had taken particular exception to a huge wall panel of nude, dancing men and a table with striped blue and yellow legs, the top decorated with purple moons and indigo clouds. She touched it as though it bore some moral contagion.

'To me I'm afraid it really looks no more than a very ordinary kitchen table, on which a very naughty child has been playing with his paintbox.'

Connie always kept her cool. 'Well I think it's rather fresh and witty. Very French. What do you think, Edward?' For Edward, habitual exposure to the confrontations between his wife and sister-in-law had not made them any easier to bear. He was a fundamentally shy man, who often appeared to regard Frances with dread and concealed the depth of his admiration for Connie.

'Well I'm not exactly artistic, Connie, so I probably don't understand it, but frankly I wouldn't feel comfortable leaning my elbows on it, if you see what I mean.'

There was nothing modern about the dinner that night though, except for the deficiency of servants. The manor was less than half staffed. Most of the maids had gone off to work in the local munitions factory and the men had joined up. Ralph had supported this. Indeed he had taken it upon himself personally to drive the former grooms and gardeners and footmen to the station as they departed periodically for the front. The sole remaining footman, too old to join up, stood where he had always stood at Ralph's left shoulder, as still and immaculately positioned as an extra piece of cutlery, darting forward with practised ease to refill a glass or pull back his master's chair.

But staff was one thing. He may have given up his servants with good grace, yet for Ralph there were limits. Unlike most of the nation, now stolidly replacing beef and mutton for their dinner with fish, he was refusing to take any account of the national meat shortage. That night a saddle of mutton had been placed before them, its skin glistening crisply with blistered fat.

'Most people might think your predilection for mutton a little strange considering how strongly the Government has been spreading the message, Ralph,' said Frances reprovingly.

'Well most people don't have hundreds of fat sheep roaming their acreage,' he replied curtly. He disliked being criticised on aspects of his own domain, especially by his brother's family. Fortunately Connie returned to the subject which really interested him.

'Do you think Mata Hari deserved to die?'

'Of course she did. She was a spy, wasn't she? And there's something particularly despicable about a female spy.'

'Oh why?'

'Well I know women are the more treacherous sex, but somehow you just don't expect treachery on that scale. And because the unexpected always attracts more attention, it follows that it needs to be made an example of.'

'Why should women be the more treacherous sex?

Individually surely they're no more liable to treachery than men?' Connie's voice was mild, but it seemed to Ralph calculated to annoy. He assumed a tone implying he was dealing with his intellectual inferior.

'Women are more emotional than men, Constance, I'm sure you'd agree with me on that. That's why discipline in all its forms does not come as easily or naturally to them as it would to a man.'

'And now the Labour party wants to give them the vote.' Edward's contribution to the debate, as so often, was thrown in off target and at random, rather as though he wanted to participate but feared taking sides. To his dismay Connie turned to him, searchingly.

'And you think that's wrong, Edward? Why should women not have the vote? Aren't they already proving they can be the equals of men in their war work? Look at factory jobs and arms manufacturing, all those tasks we presumed men alone were capable of, which are now being done perfectly well by women, despite attempts to prevent them. Perhaps making up our minds about political parties is not beyond us either.'

From across the table, Frances inclined her horse face towards Connie with a benevolent smile. Edward flinched. He knew what was coming.

'I'm sure none of us would forget that you've had some experience of the world, Constance my dear, and perhaps that's why you hold such strong views on it. But you can't expect most women to be as worldly wise as you. It's one thing to be a supporter of women's right to serve but quite another to expect females to be fully informed about politics. Most of them would just vote the way their husbands told them to after all, which would surely defeat the object.'

Frances always brought up Connie's acting career when she wanted to score a point. Tonight, however, attempts to patronise Connie seemed to glance off her as easily as candlelight from the sumptuous ormolu and cut glass chandelier. But Edward, who believed Connie must be mortified by such reference to her social origins, attempted to steer the talk to military matters. He asked Ralph, who had just been down to London, about the progress of the latest campaign in Flanders.

'Are we really going to keep on with this offensive? They say the ground is appalling, absolutely the worst kind of waterlogged clay, the men are sinking up to their waists in it. We're not heading for a repeat of the Somme, I hope.'

Ralph rolled the claret round in his glass. His resolve not to discuss politics in polite society had wavered of late. 'Who knows? Haig is very confident. He says the Germans are demoralised and Ypres is the place we're going to win the war. But Lloyd George still needs persuading. I heard when he went out to the front they took all the fit Boche out of the prisoner of war compounds, so he'd think we were facing an army of men at death's door. Didn't change his mind though. Still, if he does object there's precious little he can do because the Conservatives are all in favour of this one and Haig has the support of the King.'

Far from distracting her, this diversion into military speculation only seemed to provoke Connie more.

'But doesn't everything you say about the latest fighting just reinforce what this man Sassoon is saying? Apparently he's written to all the newspapers claiming that the generals and the politicians are in it together to perpetuate the fighting and that the war is increasingly unjust.'

'Yes, and he's since been sent to some sort of asylum, I understand,' said Ralph shortly, without looking at her.

She was not deterred. 'Probably because he's right.'

*   *   *

She's always been bloody difficult, thought Ralph morosely as he whipped off his black tie in his dressing room that night. Always thinking she has a mind of her own. All that provocative, self-conscious modernity. Not helped by those ghastly people he allowed her to associate with in London.

In recent weeks it had got worse, but secretly he was relieved to have her squabbling cheerfully about politics again, considering how sullen and miserable she had been the past year. It must have been the miscarriage, he supposed, but it had left her moping about the estate as pale and listless as an invalid. The absent, funereal expression she had maintained at house parties and dinners was quite unlike her and would have aroused comment except that everyone assumed that she had lost a relative in the war and made allowances for her.

He glanced through the door to the adjoining bedroom where Connie usually slept alone. She sat before her mirror brushing out her long hair and humming. As she lifted each lock, filaments of hair like slender copper wires glinted in the light. She stopped, and he saw that she was smiling at her reflection. She certainly looked all right for her age. Bottom firm as a round apple beneath a tiny waist. Good chest too, still high and full, probably the only advantage of her childlessness. The sight of her, and her aspect before the mirror, reminded him of the first night he met her, when a group of them had paid a visit to her dressing room at that theatre after the show. Although she was still wearing some silly oriental costume he had been dumbstruck by her neat perfection and the way she regarded him through the mirror's reflection with cool, appraising violet eyes. How strangely erotic that was. As if she could see into him. Shrewd, but not at all critical.

Aware of the heat that was rising within him, Ralph turned glumly away and got ready for bed. Damn shame the way it had turned out. His mother went to her grave thinking she had been right about Connie. God knows what kind of life she had been leading in that background. Perhaps she hadn't been clean, and that was what had cheated him of an heir.

He splashed his face in a basin of bracingly cold water and pulled on his pyjamas. He couldn't complain, really. He'd gone into the marriage with his eyes open, knowing what kind of woman she was. She was an actress and needed an audience. She basked in the admiration of men. Without it she wilted like a neglected child. No inner resources, he supposed.

Yet he still loved her. Frances had told him about Connie's passing passions, her little flirtations and infatuations with those arty types she liked to befriend. To judge by the solemn way in which she had cornered him in the library and rattled out her accusations, Frances obviously expected him to be outraged. But as long as it was fairly innocent, a few harmless friendships were of no concern to him. Some people would say he should have paid her that sort of attention, flattered her, expressed affection, asked her opinion on everything, but frankly that wasn't the kind of thing a husband need be bothered with. Let her get that from her hangers-on in London.

He settled himself in his own ornately carved Jacobean four-poster and picked up Gilbert White's *Natural History of Selborne*. He took a keen interest in the natural world and prided himself on knowing about the latest scientific discoveries, keeping up with the findings of overseas expeditions. In another life he would have liked to have been a naturalist. If duty hadn't called him elsewhere. He loved inspecting the game birds bred for shooting on the estate and importing Chinese ducks for the lake. He could have built up a rare plant collection here at the manor, though God knows what those dreadful nephews of his would do with it. His eyelids were just beginning to droop when the door creaked open and Connie appeared. She padded across the carpet with a smile and came to sit on the side of the bed.

'Hello Ralph.'

Beneath her fine white linen nightdress the dark smudges of her nipples instantly reawakened his arousal. He knew better than to be surprised. She was like that. Long deserts of celibacy then a little oasis of sex. She would come into his bed with a purposeful look in her eye. Never stayed the whole night, though. Not any more. Maybe it was the snoring. Still, women were irrational creatures and no attempt to analyse them got very far. It simply wasn't worth the bother. It wasn't like dealing with dogs or horses. It was a scientific fact that they had smaller brains than men and sex hormones which made them act bizarrely. If a woman was barren, the whole effect was presumably intensified. Pondering these grave thoughts, Ralph pulled back the covers to make room for her and shooed his ancient retriever off the end of the bed. Connie helped its reluctant exit with the tip of her foot.

CHAPTER TWENTY

THE LOUNGE BAR of the Fox and Grapes in Tattersall Street was arched with black, tarred beams, its windows and alcoves draped with mock tapestry curtains. Beside the bar, hung with mediaeval style artefacts, a darts match was in progress. Elsa and Simon sat in a corner seat, drinking. They had decided to pause before Simon drove them back to London, though Elsa was watching the amount of gin and tonic disappearing down his throat with a nervous eye.

'I just think they were very strange. What did she mean? A good man. I mean, of course he was a good man.'

Elsa said: 'Tell me again. She said he'd done a terrible thing. Could she just have meant fighting in the war? Maybe they're pacifists, the Wineleeses.'

Outside in the fading light, the pigeon-grey spire of St John's could just be seen above the rooftops, a decaying symbol of certain immutable beliefs. Simon drained his gin, cracking the ice between his teeth.

'Hardly. Not the way he was talking about his father. He was obviously proud of his war record.'

'Perhaps she meant a good poet. She may have thought we were literary revisionists, trying to trash his reputation. If you had dug up some other, slightly inferior stuff . . .'

'Which as it happens we have . . .'

'Well then, perhaps she knows all about that but doesn't want his literary status undermined.'

Elsa looked at her watch. She wondered if she should call Oliver now, from the pub telephone and catch him before he went into High Table, or wait until late, when they were back in London. She liked talking to him when he was in bed, using the phone by his bedside. His voice was always lower and huskier, his conversation even more loving. Suddenly Simon reached across and took her wrist roughly. His eyes were slightly bloodshot, and there was a flash of annoyance in them.

'Look I know you're fretting about getting back to your

bloody boyfriend but we're on to something interesting here. Can't you just listen to what I'm saying?'

The shock of Simon's temper was like a sudden squall of bad weather in an otherwise calm day. Elsa knew she should be offended, and treat him with icy dignity, but as she looked at the passion flare up in him, she warmed to him. She liked him like this, involved, assertive. His usually sallow skin was flushed with excitement. Penitently she said: 'Sorry, Simon. I am listening.'

'Well, I just think the vicar knew much more than he was saying. There have been other people down here, asking questions, for God's sake. Who, and when? I mean we can't just leave it at that. I got the impression that if he was pushed a little more, he'd tell us.'

'Perhaps he wanted paying . . .'

'Oh don't be silly.'

'Well considering Mrs Winelees wouldn't even let you back in the house when you forgot the book, I hardly think it's worth going back, do you?'

'Why don't we wander along to the church? Just have a quick look. No one can stop you going into a church, can they? It's against ecclesiastical law, I think.'

'They don't seem to have many rules in the Church of England,' Elsa said doubtfully.

'It's OK. Let's go.'

Outside the night had an edge of ice. Elsa shivered and pulled her coat on as they walked through the street. As they approached the blackened railings of St John's and made their way up the path there was a clatter of feet and two teenage girls ran out laughing. A few more people, making their way out, looked at them without interest. Inside the church the stillness hung heavy, almost tangible. The air was cold as a blade. Up at the front, beyond the altar, an iron-haired woman was collecting music sheets.

'Can I help you?' she called, briskly.

'We're just looking, really.'

'Well we're locking up here now, I'm afraid.'

'Couldn't we just have a look round?' said Elsa, lamely, giving a touristy swivel at the Victorian pillars and plaques around her.

'I'm sorry, but we're only open this late for choir practice. There's a parish council meeting tonight, and there's absolutely no one to supervise the church. If you want to come back tomorrow...'

'That's all right, Maureen, I'll look after these people.'

The Reverend Winelees had stepped from the shadow of the vestry. He surveyed them briefly, his hands on his hips, then said: 'Come in here, if you would.' To Maureen he said: 'Go on to the meeting, I won't keep you long. I'll lock up.'

Inside the vestry a gas fire added a fluttery warmth to the air. Andrew Winelees sat down heavily behind his desk and steepled his fingers beneath his chin. The last shafts of evening light, penetrating a stained glass window, tattooed his face blood red and azure. He gave a thin smile.

'I suppose I haven't been completely straight with you. But with your sort that's probably the best policy. I suppose there's no point asking whether you have any connection with these other people who have been badgering us about Valentine Siddons?'

'No,' said Simon. 'I don't know anything about that.'

The vicar looked at him with disdain.

'Well I want to make clear that if there's any more trouble I shall refer the whole matter to the police.'

'What are you talking about?' said Elsa.

'I think you know perfectly well. We've had a very nasty experience. That man tried to threaten my wife.'

Simon shuffled his feet in agitation. 'I don't know who these people can be, but I assure you, we've nothing to do with them. We're an independent film company and we're making a film about the battle of Passchendaele. We think we may have found something rather interesting to do with Siddons' poetry, that's all.'

Winelees scrutinised them warily.

'Come on. We may be simple old country folk but we're not that stupid, you know. It's a bit much to expect me to believe that two entirely separate lots of people tip up here asking questions about the same dead poet. You've got nothing out of my wife, so you're trying the more civilised approach with me. What the hell do you expect me to tell you?'

Simon stared at him blankly. His voice was strange, flat. 'What do you want to tell us?'

The vicar looked up at him sharply.

'If I tell you what I know, will you leave us alone?'

Elsa cried: 'Mr Winelees, of course we'll leave you alone. Whatever happened to your wife has nothing to do with us.'

Winelees leaned back in his chair and looked up through the window, as if for inspiration, or authorisation perhaps. After a few moments, he sighed.

'I would like to say that whatever he did, Valentine Siddons was a good man. And I know, because I knew him.'

Simon frowned. 'You knew him? But you weren't born in 1917, surely, I mean your father was—'

'Not 1917,' cut in Winelees quietly. 'I knew him later. He came to stay with us for a while. After the first world war.'

Elsa felt as though she was two steps behind everyone else. 'But he died in the war,' she pointed out.

The vicar did not answer her immediately. Then, in the way that vicars do, he changed the subject. 'You know that poem of his, "Betrayal". I've often wondered about that.'

'The one he wrote the night before he died,' said Elsa, automatically, the lines of the verses running unbidden through her head.

The Revererd Winelees' watery eyes stared absently ahead. 'Technically, yes. Except he didn't die. That night he had gone out to rescue one of his fellow officers, and some time later a pretty smashed-up body was brought back. It had no face left, some limbs missing from what I understand, and the papers and identity tag were missing too. But it had Valentine Siddons' notebook in the pocket. It was marked down as Siddons and buried. Things were busy then, bodies coming in all the time. His commanding officer wrote to his relations. They did their grieving.'

Simon butted in: 'So what are you saying? That it wasn't him?'

'Well I think you already know, don't you. Siddons was pretty shot up out there, of course, shell shocked and everything. He tried to find his way back to the British lines, but in fact he went way off course and got lost. He found himself in a wood and got by for a couple of days there feeding off the rations and water from the bottles of dead soldiers. I understand he sheltered in a local barn. When he finally made his way back to a casualty dressing station, he was delirious and they found this other chap's identity tag in his pocket. It was attached to a small piece of pottery, wrapped in a rag, which he clung to. Wouldn't let anyone take it from him. He was raving, you realise. So they shipped him back to Britain and gave him some treatment, but the mental problems didn't really clear up and he was discharged.'

'So he deserted?'

'Did he? Who can say? He would only say that he thought he was going to die. His nerves were plainly shattered. He says when he surfaced and found he'd been processed as someone else, with papers home to England, he carried on back in a daze. Then when he got home and had his discharge, Valentine Siddons was officially dead and, what's more, a hero. Instead, he was technically a deserter, and faced a firing squad.'

'And he came to your father's house?' said Simon.

'Oh not straight away he didn't. Not until after the war. I haven't any idea where he went immediately. I was just a little lad. Even then I wasn't told who he was, but I remember my mother was very, very gentle with him. He was having nightmares. I'd lie in my bed listening to a terrible howling, followed by wrenching sobs. He was only in his twenties but he seemed much older. And dreadfully sad. He used to go out and paint the hop fields. It was about the only time he could stop his hands trembling. I went with him sometimes.'

Simon stared at Winelees intently, lips parted, not a muscle moving in his face. His voice had sunk to a whisper. 'And then, where did he go then?'

'I'm afraid I can't help you there. A place was found for him apparently, somewhere peaceful. I never saw him again. I did communicate with his wife, some time later, when she sent our family a copy of his poems and prose. But we didn't know whether she was completely in the dark, or not. So it wasn't mentioned, at all. Just a short little thank-you note. Very polite.'

'So he didn't go back to his wife?'

'I don't know. She had a little girl by that time. It would

have been extremely traumatic to have him returned to them alive. A rather unwelcome Lazarus.'

Up in the rafters Elsa could hear the soft shuffle of roosting pigeons like the flocked spirits of the dead.

'But,' the vicar hesitated. 'I thought you knew all this. Isn't this why you're here?'

'Not exactly.' Simon sank into a chair. 'We think we've found some early Siddons poems. We only came here on the off-chance you might know something about them. Because your family was sent the first edition we thought maybe your father discussed poetry with him. Had some sort of special interest.'

'Poetry? No, that wasn't their thing at all. In fact I seem to remember my father telling me that Siddons gave up poetry altogether after the war. Said the poet in him had died. It was painting they talked about. That was their shared passion. That's why he left my father so many of his works – like the one you saw earlier. He gave one to me too in fact, a rather beautiful autumn landscape. That one used to hang in pride of place in our house, but I'm afraid it went into the auction too.'

'When was this auction?'

'Oh a couple of months ago now. For the steeple appeal, you know. General bric-à-brac, books, some *objects d'art*. And the sponsored sack race in the garden. We raised nearly £2,000, which is a good figure in this day and age, with these car boot sales and suchlike virtually every weekend. My painting was bought by the Midland Bank in the high street, which is lucky, because I bank there so whenever I go in I can still see it.'

Elsa was anxious to cut short this pleasant digression. 'Mr Winelees, do you really have no idea where Valentine Siddons is?'

The vicar turned to her aggressively.

'On the contrary. I have a very good idea where he is. I should say he's with his maker. Considering how unwell he seemed when I last saw him, I would be extremely surprised if he was still with us. So if it was your intention to go hounding some poor extremely elderly man, then I'm very pleased to say you're out of luck.'

'No, you don't understand, we . . .'

'I think I understand perfectly,' said the vicar, rising to his feet. 'And I hope you understand that any recurrence of the previous unpleasantness will be taken to the authorities. The only other thing is that if anyone else comes asking questions about what I've told you tonight, I shall deny it all and have absolutely nothing to say. The same, I can assure you, goes for my wife.'

* * *

Elsa flinched at the frigid kiss of the cotton sheets as she drew the bedclothes up around her. Staying overnight in a pub bedroom had seemed their only option an hour ago, after she and Simon had spent the remaining evening in intense discussion of their discovery. Over their lingering meal, Simon had seemed as warm as he had been before Oliver arrived on the scene. After a couple of bottles of wine, neither of them had been in a fit state to drive, so Simon had gone to the Fox and Grapes to enquire about a room. 'They offered us a double,' he laughed boozily when he returned, 'but I thought you'd probably insist on preserving your modesty.'

Something in his tone made Elsa blush. She felt she had missed something, obtusely, like the person who hears the punch line, but doesn't quite catch the joke.

The bells of St John's chimed midnight. Elsa tried to sink beneath the waves of alcohol-induced fatigue, but she could not obliterate the questions still ringing in her head. If Siddons deliberately switched his identity tag with that of another man, what kind of hero did that make him? Where did he go, after the war, and what did he do? Nudging between these questions was another, more urgent suggestion she could hardly bear to contemplate. What about Oliver? Was Siddons' biographer, polisher of his niche in posterity, aware of this? Should his *Valentine Siddons: A Life*, be more accurately entitled *Valentine Siddons: A Lie?*

Suddenly, a movement in the gloom cut through her drowsy thoughts. Elsa stiffened as she detected a figure come through the door and approach the bed. As he rose above her she suppressed a startled shriek.

'Shhh,' said Simon sitting on the bed.

When she discerned his pale face, Elsa's fear was replaced with indignation.

'Simon. For God's sake, what do you want? Don't you know you can bloody well terrify people creeping into their bedrooms at night?'

Simon did not bother to respond. He carried on as if resuming their dinnertime conversation after a short interruption to pay the bill.

'I can't sleep thinking about it. There's really no doubt about it. Of course Siddons meant to desert: why else would he write a poem about betrayal just hours before?'

Elsa sat up and ran her hand through her hair. She was still wearing the creased cotton shirt she'd had on all day. She knew she must look terrible, and felt relieved Simon had not switched on the overhead light as he came in, bathing her in its unflattering neon glare. It was just the sort of thing he would do without noticing.

'We know he wrote a poem, but that doesn't mean anything. Who knows what betrayal was on his mind? There are more kinds of betrayal than straightforward desertion, you know.'

'Oh come on. You're not telling me that for someone stuck out in the front line trenches in 1917, facing one of the bloodiest battles of the war, betrayal has any other meaning than a purely military one. Don't go all Eng. lit. on me.'

'Well don't come into my bedroom past midnight and expect to get a coherent answer out of me,' she responded sharply.

In the shadowy room Simon regarded Elsa. He knew he should have resisted the temptation to come in. She sat, with her knees drawn up beneath her chin, starfish hands stretched in a yawn, her dark tousled hair falling into her face. Even while she tried to make conversation, there was a prickle of defensive apprehension in her brown eyes and he knew he ought to make his apologies and leave. She wasn't used to him like this, she didn't know what to expect. He smelt the familiar sweet perfume she wore coming off her warm body like a crushed flower and wondered how her breasts would look naked. He ached to reach out and unwrap her rumpled shirt and hold her small, soft body against his.

He touched her shoulder briefly. 'I'm sorry, I shouldn't have woken you.'

'No, it's all right.'

With a wrench he forced himself to get up and trudged back to his own cold room. His entire body felt rigid with desire. Another missed chance. Why couldn't he make it work? He lit a cigarette and as the first bitter smoke curled down his throat, wondered how long he would have to wait.

★ ★ ★

Michelle's face brimmed with suppressed irritation and self-importance. 'There's someone waiting for you,' she hissed, as they opened the glass door to Durban Films. 'You might have told me where you were going.'

Before they had time to look round, the short figure of Daniel Eckstein sprang energetically from the sofa. His eyes lit up when he saw Elsa.

'Ah, Miss Meyers. Simon. I'll never get used to the relaxed office hours you keep here. So different from the States, but so much more civilised, I suppose.'

'We're just back from an assignment, actually. A bit of research.'

'Fine. Great. Well, I thought, as I was passing, I'd drop off here and give you the good news myself.' Eckstein paused for dramatic effect. 'We've got a green light on development funding for *Passchendaele*. How about that? We conference-called it late last night. Pluto just acquired part of a studio complex over here and suddenly they're keen for all things Brit, so our chairman said go ahead. Personally, I'm extremely glad. I think you have a great film on your hands. As I was telling Simon here, up until very recently war history was a complete no-no, except of course for native American which is still very hot, but what with the company expanding here, everybody loves your idea. Can't get enough of it. All those uniforms and young English actors with, you know, those beautiful haircuts and upper-class accents, are just the biggest turn-on. Though I'm warning you, the script is going to need a total rewrite. I'm talking about a lot more action adventure – and had you thought of an American lead?

Canadian might do. Our lads were out there too, weren't they? There are doubts about the title I have to say. Passion Dale. As one of our EVPs said, it sounds like some kinda ice-cream. Hopeless Hollywood ignorance, I'm afraid. Me, I love it. War's about passion, after all. Passion, action, love, suffering, history. All that.'

CHAPTER TWENTY-ONE

NORMAN PARDOE WAS bending over his rose bushes when Simon found him, issuing small, audible grunts of effort as he pruned. Unlike his peer group, Norman's latterday involvement with the natural world took the form of a futile, but incessant guerrilla warfare against encroaching herbaceous chaos. Simon leaned against the wall of the house watching him grapple with the fronds of some thorny Hydra. This was the garden where he and his brothers had grown up and he was glad to see the scars of its history still visible beneath a decade and a half of vegetation. The skeleton of a tree house they'd had one summer clung tenaciously to the horse chestnut, the worn ruts of a bike racing track were ribs of mud just visible beneath the anaemic grass. Once this garden must have looked like the battleground it was, filled with the boys' cries and Norman's impotent shouts of rage as he watched them trampling the flowerbeds or removing bark from trees for some obscure red Indian carving game. Norman was not the kind of father to join in children's games. Nor, come to that, did he furnish a more feminine role by providing the playing boys with a comforting counterpoint of cooking smells or efficient first aid when they finally tired of their games.

Norman's face lit up as he saw his son, but he did not allow himself to show pleasure. He withdrew the cigarette parked at the corner of his mouth.

'Oh it's you, is it? Don't give me any warning, will you? Why don't you go inside and make me a cup of tea while I finish this.'

Simon went into the house and reflected with quiet satisfaction that he could have found his way around as a blind man. It was like Sleeping Beauty's castle – nothing had changed for the last twenty years. From habit he roamed around the place, an archaeologist of the recent past. In his former bedroom forlorn piles of books and LPs still stood, like skins of a snake long since shed, awaiting the return of the Tolkien reader or the Rolling Stones fan who had once possessed them. The pogo stick leaned against the wall, the Frisbee nestled on a hippie bedspread, icons of another age. His brother's room too had been preserved intact, a long-abandoned shrine to Tottenham Hotspur, its walls peeling with posters of White Hart Lane's ancient gods. In the kitchen the tea caddy, portraying a scratched but impossibly romantic Princess Elizabeth, stood in the same place on the shelf as it had always stood, its position delineated by a ring of greasy dust, the biscuit tin stationed alongside it with its regulation Rich Teas. The pans for Norman's modest lunch were filed as always on the draining board. Even the traditional National Trust calendar looked identical to its predecessors, though the date had moved on. As Simon placed the cups on the Formica table top and waited for the kettle to boil, he reflected that his current problem too was not exactly a novel one.

It was women again. Why did they so often fail to get the picture? Usually this difficulty afflicted them more when Simon had no interest in them, but Elsa was a different case. She must know how he felt by now. After all, she seemed to understand so much about him. Unlike those women with whom he had previously attempted the spasms of sporadic intimacy they described as a 'relationship', he could talk to her for hours and she didn't give any overt sign of being bored. She didn't look at her nails or gaze vacantly out the window. She didn't interrupt his conversation with a complete *non sequitur* or nag irrelevantly about the state of his career or clothes or car. She didn't sulk about him being too ambitious, or not ambitious enough, or count aloud how many genuine friends he had. She didn't criticise the way he dressed, lived, laughed, or as one girlfriend memorably had, the way he breathed. Elsa was also the first woman he admired who had failed to comment on how miserable he looked. His habitual grimace was in fact due to simple facial architecture rather than perpetual unhappiness, but he was constantly told to cheer up because it 'might never happen'. As it was, it invariably did.

It had come upon him suddenly, this urgent, unresolved

ache that demanded a response. Tolerance for Elsa had developed into affection, but these comfortable feelings had been superseded by something far more difficult to contain. It was a painful, exhilarating want. For all his solitary disposition, Simon was not unconfident, and scarcely considered Elsa's existing lover a serious hurdle. She would soon see him for what he was. The problem for Simon was one of communication. How did you get these things across?

Yet surely she must know. Admittedly he had never tackled the issue head-on. But coming back from Faversham in the car, dissecting excitedly the implications of Andrew Winelees' revelation, a new understanding seemed to have developed between them. That had been compounded by the welcome news that Dan Eckstein had finally pulled it off with his film company masters and it looked like *Passchendaele* the movie was going to get off the starting blocks. And just as he thought everything was going so well and that it was worth abandoning the traditional demarcation between business and pleasure, she chose that moment to start an argument.

The scene kept rerunning in his head like the refrain of a bad song. The calm way she had turned to him, as if it didn't matter where her salary was coming from, almost as soon as Eckstein had been ushered out the door, and said in a voice of frigid nonchalance:

'Simon, I have to tell you I don't want to make this film any more. Under these circumstances it's going to be a travesty. All that stuff about passion and haircuts. All Pluto Films want is some dreadful, sepia-tinted, love story but this is the first world war, for God's sake. To see it their way is an insult to the people who went through it. We should absolutely refuse to amend the scripts.'

Her manner was so irksome Simon had turned on her, an acid tide of irritation rising in him.

'Listen to yourself. You complain about realism, but you're the one who's not being realistic. These are serious film makers. They're spending serious money. Of course they're going to want some say in the script. Of course they want some American characters written in. People who refuse to compromise in this business end up making films on a shoestring which get shown at the Bognor Regis arts festival. For one night. If they're lucky.'

God she was frustrating with that superior look, lips pursed with contempt, sleek hair swinging round her face. Perhaps that was what had pushed him too far.

'The fact is, Elsa the reason you really don't want to make this film any more is because it could embarrass your boyfriend.'

For a moment she looked like she might hit him. But she merely exhaled in a frighteningly controlled manner.

'The fact is, Simon, I want to tell the truth about Valentine Siddons.'

'And how's old Eastway going to react if we make a film which says his precious grandfather's a fake?'

'What the hell is that to do with you?'

At that she had turned away from him and started collecting her things. He let out a growl of frustration. 'Well you don't need to worry. There's no possibility of telling the truth about Siddons. Any attempt to sabotage his reputation is likely to go down like a lead balloon. You heard Eckstein. It's a hero film they're after. A feelgood movie about daring and honour among dashing gentlemen. They don't want desertion and nervous exhaustion. That's more Vietnam than Flanders.'

'Fine,' she snapped. 'Well you can do it without me, then.'

He'd been going anyhow, so had the fractional satisfaction of turning on his heel and leaving the office first. But as he looked back, his infuriated face framed momentarily in the slammed glass door, he had been startled to see tears, either of anger or frustration, blurring her eyes.

* * *

'Just been talking to Gordon next door.' Norman came in and sat down, accepting his cooling tea without comment. 'Wretched time that poor sod has of it.'

'Why?'

'It's that ghastly wife of his, isn't it? Keeps him at it all day with DIY and whatever and now she's even stopping him coming down for a drink with me at the pub.'

Simon thought of Gordon, a contented man in his middle sixties, with a friendly wife, always cooking him fattening meals and adding new faces to the photographs of her grandchildren ranked on the windowsills. An evening with her would seem infinitely preferable to listening to one of Norman's dirges on modern life down at the Green Man. He wondered if Gordon's wife had really issued any such ban. His father warmed to his theme.

'Bloody women. Always meddling. Your brother's wife's the same. He doesn't get to see his team play half as much now that the kids have arrived. Spends his time milling round the shopping centre on Saturday afternoons. Spare us.' He looked over at Simon and smiled, revealing a dental hygienist's nightmare.

'You're more like me, son. You're not going to let women ruin your life. You're not the sort to compromise.'

Simon felt the usual complicit smile freeze on his lips. Without warning, the satisfaction he had always enjoyed, of being singled out as the son who most resembled his father, dried up for ever. Unlike Norman, he didn't actually see women as the enemy. Yet he had still inherited his emotional coat of armour, a chilling chain mail of indifference so useful for repelling their advances. He remembered the stream of women who had passed through this house in his youth, awkwardly sipping their gin and tonics, smiling bravely when the three boys could be persuaded to look up from their television programme – *Batman, Blue Peter, Mission: Impossible* – or break off from their Meccano or Subbuteo, for an introduction.

'Meet Sue, that's Miss Thurman to you, who works down the library. We're popping out for a drink.'

And how even the skinny, fish-faced librarian, with her glasses like dead cod's eyes, would have been welcomed by the boys if she would come and take the weight of Norman from their shoulders. Yet all each passing woman saw was Norman's own impenetrable stare, reprinted threefold on the upturned faces of his sons, like some daunting piece of Cubist art.

He rejected Norman's proffered pack of Benson and Hedges with a frown and watched his father reach for the ashtray – stolen from the Hotel Osborne on the Isle of Wight – with a stained, automatic hand. Suddenly, sitting there in the same old kitchen, in his childhood home, its unchanging nature no longer seemed charming but a curse.

He thought of the infinite choreography of genes, repeating their patterns through the generations, synchronised swimmers in unending plasma seas. In the stillness he could almost feel his own cells dividing and dying. Deep in the red gloaming of his body, a billion tiny sets of instructions curled, mapping out indelibly his behaviour at dinner parties and deciding how courteous he would be towards strangers. Biology is destiny, wasn't that what the glossy magazines liked to say?

But if he was a carbon copy of Norman, he didn't want to be any more. He didn't care if Nature or Nurture was in charge when it came to dealing out the personality problems, Simon was determined to change. Elsa might not know how he felt, and might still prefer the creep from Oxford when he told her, but that was no excuse for not telling her. He realised he'd always taken pride in being cryptic. As cool and complex as poetry. But what was the point in being difficult to decipher? People should say what they meant and say it plainly.

★   ★   ★

When the clatter and rumble from the street beneath Elsa's desk began to swell, signifying that people were leaving their offices and thronging on the way to the tube or bus stop at the end of the day, she realised she had lost all track of time. She had not called Oliver. Indeed she was terrified he might call her before she had decided exactly what she should say to him, how to raise the issue of her discovery, and in just how challenging a tone. Yet she was desperate to talk to someone, so she tried Alison. When she finally tracked her down, at a recording studio in central London, her friend sounded snappish.

'I can't see you today. I'm working like a slave. The company's hit on this wonderful way of saving money by making us record programmes in the middle of the night. I mean we don't finish till past eight tonight so bang goes my social life.'

'Haven't you got a few minutes spare? I've got something

I'd really appreciate talking over with you.'

'What's so urgent?'

'It's not really the sort of thing I can discuss over the phone.'

'Well, I don't know. I'm having a hellish day. We're doing a network production, *Special Counsel*, but the guests are being a real drag. I mean you get these sad cases and just when you try and give them free helpful advice and even pay them, for God's sake, they turn uncooperative. Bloody uncooperative. I could have told them the agoraphobic would pull out.'

'I'll come to you. It won't take long.'

Predictably, Alison's curiosity overcame her fatigue. 'Oh all right. Eight-thirty. But I hope there's alcohol involved. I'll be gasping by then.'

After she had replaced the phone, Elsa continued to ruminate on the day's events. Some time later she saw out of the corner of her eye that Michelle was putting her coat on and collecting her bag. She materialised next to Elsa's desk in an accusing stance, arms folded.

'You've been staring out of that window for an hour.'

'What? Oh yes.'

'Love life, is it?'

'Mmm. Suppose so. Don't let me keep you, Michelle, have a good evening.'

'You don't want to worry, you know.'

'What do you mean?'

'I mean he's dead keen on you. It's perfectly plain.'

'Is it?'

'Simon's not as good at hiding things as he likes to think.'

'Simon?'

'Well of course. I mean, that was who you were thinking about?' She observed Elsa's face. 'Whoops. It wasn't, was it?'

Elsa laughed politely. 'No. Don't be silly. Though I wouldn't say anything about Simon is perfectly plain. Go on. I'll lock up.'

Simon. She shouldn't laugh, but it was funny really. In truth she had noticed him trying to suppress his snarls recently, tamping down the curses with a bitten lip, smiling experimentally, like a stroke victim recovering from paralysis. And although she appreciated that and knew that this emotional artifice was aimed at her, the thing was, she liked him as he was. His blackness was not the kind that drew you into its depths. Instead it had a kind of reflective quality, he made people around him feel more buoyant and bright by comparison.

But she did wish he could try to understand her a little. For a start, he should have realised that her quarrel over the film was not with him. The most amateur of psychologists would realise that the discoveries of the last few days had left her emotions in disarray. She had not even had time to consider what Simon had intended when he came to her bedroom in the pub. Let alone analyse whether she had wanted the same.

★   ★   ★

Streams of blank-faced people made their way out of the studio complex where *Good Relations* was recorded, like survivors of some frightening natural disaster. Alison ran her programme like a Californian encounter group, encouraging guests and audience to 'interface constructively', by which she meant egging on the audience to heckle and abuse the unfortunates who had agreed to bare their problems on her sofa. Then she would enter the ranks of the audience, brandishing her microphone like an electronic club and pick on people there, hectoring and quarrelling aggressively just as she had seen it done on American cable shows.

The programme she had just recorded was next week's 'special' on relationship counselling, a subject on which Alison was spectacularly ill-equipped to pontificate. Though her straightforward manner, which diplomatic people described as 'direct' and others merely labelled 'rude', gave her a semblance of common sense, Alison was about as well qualified as the royal family to advise on the single pair bond.

Elsa thought back to how long she had known Alison and tried to count up how many of her relationships could not be officially classed as disastrous. Her parents, aged and moneyed, had shuffled off to the south of France at an early date, marooning their only daughter in an English boarding school where her continental connections and supposed wealth made her the target of yet further isolation. Alison had overcompensated with a kind of brutal cheer, which in later life doomed her to men who wanted mothering. In fact Alison's parenting skills were sadly deficient. Even her tiny dog, a nervy oriental breed, spent most of its neglected existence beneath her bed, only emerging, like a dropped sheepskin mitten with teeth, to nip the feet of unwary visitors.

In the emptying studio, Alison was thanking the lachrymose selection of people who had volunteered to be counselled on screen. There was a 'serial adulterer', whose haircut alone should have qualified him for special advice, a truculent kleptomaniac and a sufferer from post-traumatic stress disorder, who lingered stupefied in her chair. The secret alcoholic, a querulous woman in her thirties, was arguing loudly about the fee while the guest counsellor himself was downing gin in the hospitality suite.

Alison hailed Elsa with relief and bustled her off to a nearby wine bar.

'Forget counselling. That lot should either be in prison or an asylum.' Then, adopting an attitude of on-screen concern, she pointed her cigarette at Elsa like a finger. 'So what's so urgent, then? Don't tell me you and the dishy doctor have had a row.'

'I need you to keep this confidential.'

Alison looked clownishly sad, as if dismayed that Elsa could ever doubt her discretion.

'No, I mean it.'

'Counsellor's honour.'

Elsa poured the wine and told her friend almost everything about their trip to Kent and the revelations of Andrew Winelees. Gratifyingly, Alison managed to remain silent throughout. Like them, she instantly wanted to know where Siddons had sheltered during the post-war years.

'We don't really know. All we know was that he was in Faversham for a while.'

'Did he see his wife and daughter?'

'We can't tell. Emily never said anything and now Violet's dead too.'

'What did you say her name was again?'

'Violet? She was the daughter, Oliver's mother.'

Alison paused and coached another cigarette from her packet with a satisfied tap. 'Oh well. That solves one problem, then.'

'What do you mean?'

'Those poems you showed me. The ones with the initials VS? Who wrote them?'

'Well Valentine Siddons, we believe.'

'Think, Elsa. Who else had the initials VS? You say the daughter was called Violet. Well obviously she's the author.'

'Pretending to be Valentine?'

'Oh no. In her own right.'

'I don't follow. She wasn't a poet.'

'Well any fool can tell that from the poetry. It has to explain why they're nothing like any Siddons poem you ever read. Why they're exactly like an adolescent girl's love poems. Mystery over, I'm afraid.'

'I don't know . . .'

'Oh come on, Elsa. It's obvious. All girls do it. I mean didn't you ever write embarrassing ramblings about spotty horrors who kissed you on Saturday and ditched you the next day? I know I did. I tell you, some of those poems could have been fresh from my old tearstained pillow. The only difference is, most of us aren't stupid enough to keep them. We burn them before anyone else can get hold of them.'

Elsa tried to recall parts of the poems. A fragment of 'Past' ran through her mind.

> What's past is past and can't be swayed
> You said. But each one makes his own
> And pasts once made can be unmade,
> Forgotten, altered or betrayed.
> Yes, even your dear face could fade.

'It's not really like that, Alison. They're not straightforward love poems. They're so . . . oblique. Sort of secretive.'

'Of course they are. We all wrote in code at that age. I mean, we dreaded anyone finding them. Remember? It would have been so uncool.'

Alison exhaled a triumphant nimbus of smoke. Her explanation seemed dismally plausible. The poems Elsa had believed a great find were not Siddons juvenilia at all, but his daughter's worthless doodlings. And she, the supposed literature graduate, had been too obtuse to tell the difference. Elsa felt her long-suppressed enthusiasm fade, like the patina on a fake antique. Despite complaints from Alison, who was clearly anticipating a lengthy drinking session, she hurried home, impatient to go over the poems again and consider them afresh in the cold light of common sense.

The street where Elsa lived in Shepherd's Bush had never ranked among London's more fashionable addresses. A changing cast of characters, drifting in and out of a nearby pub, reinforced the shiftless, rootless ethos of the whole area. Here there was no chance of tripping over the destitute, as there was in smarter streets in Kensington or Chelsea, because their appeals would have fallen on deaf or foreign ears. Instead the busy concourse was cruised by fat men in tracksuits murmuring into mobile phones, lolling teenagers refuelling on junk food and squalling children navigating the armchairs inexplicably abandoned on the pavement or jumping the legs which extended periodically from beneath rusting cars. Even nocturnally the activity in Elsa's road was undiminished, with music leaking out from opened windows and stray scuffles spilling from pub doors. Normally, the very presence of this clamorous traffic was enough to make Elsa feel safe, but that night when she reached her home and descended the dank steps to the narrow basement entrance, she had a distinct feeling of unease.

There was something empty about the flat. The emptiness bounced back from the front door's hollow slam and resounded in a vacancy within her. Before she even saw it she knew the pause would be there on her answerphone. This time the anonymous exhalations had acquired a kind of confessional hush, a world-weary wordlessness which seemed to know that Elsa would agonise over every second of its non-conversation. The click when it came was as sharp as a trigger.

Automatically Elsa moved towards the kitchen. She was fiercely hungry but she remembered she had done no shopping for days. The fridge held only a carton of tomato juice, half a withered lemon and some bread and milk. She made a Virgin Mary with the tomato juice, cooked a slice of dry toast and flicked on the TV while she ate it. It was the local news, dully narrated by a woman with tawny make-up and bad hair. The usual diet – train stoppages, fire engine shortages and air travel chaos forecast for the coming Easter weekend.

The sight of the supine Heathrow tourists, staking out uncomfortable territory on their little steel benches, reminded Elsa of Oliver's promise to take her away somewhere for Easter. It was to be his surprise, he had told her airily, just pack a small bag with casual clothes. And although she secretly believed being ignorant and ill-prepared for one's destination was the worst possible precursor to a romantic frame of mind, at the time Elsa had greeted the suggestion with childish happiness.

Flicking off the TV she went over to the drawer in her rolltop desk where she had left the folder of poems perched on a pile of scraps, letters from family, photos, bank statements and bills. It took her a moment to register that it was no longer there. Nor was it in any of the drawers below. There weren't many other places in the flat it could be lying, but she riffled swiftly through them all anyway: under the bed, behind the sofa, the bedside table, the bookshelf.

Absurdly, frantically, she ran round the tiny flat, checking the rooms and the windows. She was trembling. Had someone been there, and if so, had they taken anything else? Its doors sealed, its windows fastened, its cupboards firmly shut, the flat stared blankly back at her. She sat down on the sofa to calm herself. She was disorgnised, she told herself. The folder was undoubtedly on her office desk, or even in Simon's car. She considered calling Simon to check, but dismissed the idea instantly. It was far too late now. She realised she knew very little about his private life. She tried to picture what Simon might be doing. She had no idea whether he would be out or in bed, and if in bed, whether he was alone. Disconsolately she pulled her own duvet around her, a bulky but ineffective barrier to the nameless fears that assailed her.

Simon had had a bad night. He didn't like thinking about his father. It depressed him. Norman had been grumbling about the family plans for an Easter Sunday lunch, kindly arranged by Angus's wife. In truth Simon thought she was a saint to invite Norman back year after year, each time a touch more tramp-like, a little more frayed and stained round the edges. Each time he was a little less inhibited about dispensing with everyday courtesies, the frail glue of civilised life. The thought of his father becoming old and incapable was one he usually tried to ignore, but increasingly, words like 'incontinence' and 'dementia' crept horribly into Simon's mind. He gave a mental shudder. Women were best at these things. He sincerely hoped that Norman had not managed to alienate his daughters-in-law entirely by the time he was in need of such female assistance.

After a while, with the sun insistently feeling its way through the curtains, there was no point staying in bed any longer. Stumbling across the room, he drew the curtains and let the dawn surge in. On the table lay his copy of *Between the Lines*. Simon sat down heavily and started flicking through the Siddons poems and the small section of reproduced watercolours. He stared curiously at the pictures. They weren't at all bad. Even if he'd kept up with his painting, Simon doubted he could have done that well. Like him, Siddons evidently preferred landscapes to portraits. There were scenes of the ravaged battlefields as violent in their way as the work of Paul Nash. But there were other, gentler views of the unmistakable English countryside, its contours at once subtle and voluptuous, its colours kind to the eye.

Underneath the photographs in small print it said that the pictures were from the collection of the Winelees family. One in particular he kept coming back to. It was just fields, trees and a house, but there was something curious about it. Sitting there, blinking in the sunlight, excitement began to prick at him. What was it his art teacher had once said? That a good landscape should be as revealing as a face? Simon sat up and shut the book with a decisive snap. A few minutes

later, after a double-strength instant coffee, he was dressed
and ready to go.

★ ★ ★

The Midland Bank in Faversham high street was packed
with jostling mid-morning customers, busier than usual
because of the coming holiday weekend. Behind the
ubiquitous smoky plastic barriers and red queue cordons,
the bank was still a fine Victorian building, its posters about
financial services and high-interest deposit accounts failing
to conceal completely the handsome oak panelling. Simon
was not completely sure what he was going to do if it was
not there, but just one glance was enough to assure him he
was in luck. The picture which Andrew Winelees had sold
hung, unassumingly, above a hatch marked ENQUIRIES. An
unpretentious vista of rolling fields, brown and gold, lit by
the late year's mellow sun. In one corner, pearly smoke
signified stubble burning and across the horizon, in glorious
diagonal, ran the line of slender poplars, their dying leaves
flushed by a faint autumnal ochre. At the base of the
painting, in tiny letters, he could just make out the signature.
It was what he had expected.

CHAPTER TWENTY-TWO

As ELSA'S CAR passed through Hereford, she flicked off the windscreen wipers. The shower passed, watery sunshine splashed the Border hillsides and rain dripped from the trees in tiny aqueous blades. The countryside here was steeped in irrepressible spring green. Elsa chose the B-roads to Hay-on-Wye, dipping over the gentle hills, slipping through fields edged with shadowy woods. It was more isolated this way; hardly any cars passed. And yet she kept looking in her mirror, possessed of an inexplicable sensation of flight. The feeling had been building since she left, early that morning. She could not say from what she was running.

She breasted a tiny grey bridge into the town, parked the car and looked around her. It was a pretty little place, the sloping streets edged with fields of cows, its flint-faced houses suggesting centuries of sober living. Castle Street, John Harvey had said on the phone. Up a steepish hill, opposite the ruined castle. Harvey's bookshop. If you have a problem, ask anyone.

A bell pinged as she entered the shop, but at first it appeared entirely deserted. It was a long, narrow tomb-like room, little more than a tunnel of books, with volumes stacked against the windows creating a crepuscular gloom. Gradually a rustling sound alerted Elsa to one corner, where she saw an old man on his knees, delving between two impossible towers of volumes. He wore braces and wire-rimmed glasses, and pale hair radiated from his head as from an electric current. He gave the impression of a small feral animal fossicking around in a pile of leaves. If he perceived her presence, he gave no sign of it, continuing his hunt until he withdrew a volume and rocked back on his heels to admire it. Elsa clumped her shoes on the floorboards, deliberately to alert him to her presence and he turned conversationally, saying:

'An early Gibbon. I knew I had it. A beautiful edition. You

know what the Duke of Gloucester said when he was presented with this book? "Always scribble, scribble, scribble, eh Mr Gibbon?" So much for great literature. That's all the thanks he got.'

'He's had better reviews since,' Elsa conceded.

'Yes, but the first judgement could have destroyed him, you see. They can be very sensitive, writers.'

The man seemed eccentric, to say the least. Elsa began to wonder whether coming all this way to meet John Harvey had not been a bad idea. But it had the merit of keeping her out of Oliver's way, at least until she decided what to say to him. The truth about Valentine Siddons lay leaden within her. She carried it, heavy as stolen treasure, silent and wary with its weight.

'I'm Elsa Meyers. I take it you're Mr Harvey. We spoke on the phone – about the Passchendaele film and your mother, er Amarine?'

'Miss Meyers, delighted to meet you. Or should I say Ms? I never know with young women these days. You look like a miss to me.'

'Ms, then,' said Elsa.

'Now I thought with a name like Meyers you would be German.'

'I am, half. But the English half is much more visible.'

'Well I'm half French, but you wouldn't guess it. After my mother married she never spoke anything but English again. Her in-laws couldn't abide the idea of a foreigner in the family. Rather sad for her, really.'

He motioned her over to a table at the back of the shop and said, 'Now, I have a few first editions of Siddons. I'm not quite sure what you're looking for but I think we may have something. They don't come cheap, I have to warn you.'

'Oh no. I don't want to buy anything. I just want to talk.'

The disappointment on his face was no less visible for being momentary. 'Oh I see. You didn't make that quite clear on the telephone. Well as long as there are no customers . . .'

Elsa tried a bit harder. 'But I'd be very interested to hear your experience. That could be, er, valuable to our project.'

'Oh well then, that's a different matter.' He opened a

thermos of tea. Elsa sat on a rickety chair as the old man continued unprompted.

'Not that my mother didn't have a good time after leaving my father. That was in the twenties and I was just a boy, of course, but I remember all her Garsington friends came to visit her here. G. F. Robbins, Heybridge, Witheroe. They all came to see us. All except Foxley.'

'Foxley?'

'Yes. He ran a very small circulation magazine called the *Journal*. It folded in 1925 I think, but we sold it here until it did. He and my mother had fallen out.'

'Why?'

He handed her a cup of fine china, cobwebbed with cracks.

'Mother used to get upset over his attitude towards Valentine Siddons. Apparently he went around saying Siddons had been a moral coward – which was a bit rough, considering the chap died a war hero – and making sort of mad threats. He got put away of course, in the end.'

'Put away?'

'Well, sort of long-stay hospital you might call it. Loony bin I call it. There was an acquaintance of his, some kind of patron I think, who leaned on an eminent friend to get a place for him. That was quite easy in those days if a man was . . . well, that way inclined.'

Elsa must have looked puzzled because he leaned towards her with a significant nod. 'Sexually deviant, I mean. It was illegal you see, so it was treated like an illness. They may even have threatened him with prison as an alternative. Anyway, Foxley was never welcome here, but we still saw all the others. They used to talk about the war. My mother was very keen on caring for damaged soldiers, you see. We had one working here for years in fact.'

'Really?'

'Yes. We took him in and he lived in the front bedroom upstairs. He barely went out. Spent every evening writing what he called his life story. The kind of story that must have been repeated a thousand times, I imagine.'

'And what did it say?'

'Oh, I'm afraid I never could be bothered to read it. Huge

great book it is and all in tiny, scrappy handwriting. Funnily enough we had a gentleman in the shop earlier and I let him have a look at it, for a small fee of course. Now he says he wants to buy it. Well, I've no use for it so I said help yourself.'

Elsa cut in: 'But you never knew Siddons personally?'

'Well no. How could I?'

Not for the first time that day, Elsa wondered why she had come. She could feel the conversation straying from the specific subject of Foxley and Siddons, back into the wide No Man's Land of first world war anecdotage. How keen people were to discuss its terrible beauty, its individual sacrifices. Sometimes it seemed almost impossible to prevent all these little tales melting down and merging into one, into the Soldier of the Great War, whose bronzed impassive features gave nothing away on memorials all over the land. How much would she ever know for sure about Valentine Siddons? She felt an immense frustration with the fugue of past events, their momentary glimmer like the glint of fish, drowned by the great, bland, obliterating present. Outside, the shoppers of Hay-on-Wye marched by, treading the past back into oblivion. She made another effort.

'I wonder if you have any photographs I could look at?'

'Well, hold on now. Let me see. There are some but they're upstairs. Stacked away in poor Robert's room. I suppose I could look them out.'

She waited tensely until Harvey returned with a heap of photograph albums, their contents spilling untidily out of the sides.

'Here they are. Quite a lot of them, as you see . . .'

'You said Robert's room. Was he the man who lived with you?'

'That's right. Robert Fleming.'

Elsa felt her heart quicken. 'And he had a wife and child?'

'Oh you knew them, did you? Yes, it was a little girl, I think. Don't ask me why he didn't live with them, the wife had a new chap I suppose, but I do believe he missed her. He went back to his home finally, but it proved rather traumatic for him, poor soul. He came back here in a dreadful state. It was soon after that that he did it. Shot himself. Up in his room one weekend. It was a Sunday.

Mother was at church and he tended to keep himself to himself at weekends. He'd have meals up in his room, which suited us. But that did mean we didn't find him for some hours so we'll never know if we could have saved him. Very young to die. Very sad, really.'

Elsa's mouth was dry. She sipped the stagnant tea automatically.

'I don't suppose I could have a look at his room?' she asked.

Harvey paused. His little eyes behind the thick spectacles were calculating.

'Well I'm not sure. I'm not a museum, you know. I can't have people traipsing round the house in shop hours. And my gentleman is coming back again this afternoon with the cash for the book. I don't take credit cards, as it says clearly on the door.'

Elsa stared at him bewildered. Then he relented. 'Oh I suppose if you hurry. It's the front bedroom, top of the stairs. Excuse me if I don't come up again, but my knees aren't what they were.'

Once in the room she found it immediately, laid out on a small deal table by the window. She stood there looking down at the dark curled leather, its soft calf covering nestling comfortably, weightily in her hands like a body of evidence. Its pages were crammed with his spindly, slanting writing so it took her a moment to make out the first line. 'I have betrayed and I have been betrayed.'

She could not say how long she stood there. She felt entranced, the world around her falling away into silence. Then, at some point, through the tiny window before her she became aware of a dark green car pulling up outside. She recognised its long, gleaming form instantly; its engine thrummed expensively like a gentle reproach. Although she withdrew instinctively from the window, her limbs were paralysed. But instead of being apprehensive as she heard the stump of footsteps up the stairs, she felt tranquillised by her find, slowed and frozen by the glare of insight like a rabbit in a car's headlights.

Oliver looked startled when he entered the room. He masked his fleeting incomprehension with an awkward grin. 'Darling. What a surprise. Are you finished?'

He gave her a kiss on the mouth and she felt the gentle, firm press of his hand on her back. With his other hand he took the book from her.

'That's mine now. The mercenary old devil has just taken £100 off me for it. And he thought it was worthless.'

He steered her downstairs and she stood silently as he thanked John Harvey for his help. If the old man was disappointed at receiving no payment from Elsa, he said nothing. In the street she found herself gliding along by Oliver's side. Without looking at her he said: 'I thought I might find you somewhere around here. I've taken a room at this hotel. Now it can be our Easter break.'

Elsa did not reply. She allowed herself to be swept along by him. It was oddly relaxing to be with someone who knew exactly what he wanted to do. He turned into the arched doorway of a pretty, redbrick hotel and left her in the lobby as he went over to the reception desk. Swinging a plastic key he guided her up to their room.

Thankfully, the room lacked any air of romance. Dark, cumbersome thirties furniture crowded round the twin beds like awkward party guests. The window looked out on to a courtyard where Elsa caught sight of a young, laughing couple, unloading suitcases from a Range Rover. She felt a stab of envy.

Oliver shut the door behind him, sat down on one bed and pulled her down beside him, his face close to hers. She felt the slow, sea-green burn of his eyes. He stroked her hair, as though she were an invalid.

'I know it's confusing and I know what you're thinking, but you've changed my life, Elsa. I don't want to lose you.'

Elsa forced herself to sit up and pulled away from his caress. 'Did you follow me here?' she asked.

'Your kind receptionist mentioned some research trip.'

'Oliver. I've found out some things that are obviously . . . important, and I want to know the rest.'

He continued stroking, stroking, stroking.

'My darling, whatever you've found out, and whatever I tell you, just remember it doesn't matter to us. Please. It's a past misunderstanding, that's all, no more than that. OK?'

Then he told her what he knew.

'I started the whole thing myself, really. By asking questions. That's always fatal. Like a pebble starting an avalanche. Then when I found out something, I stopped asking, but it was too late. Do you remember my friend Justin Emberley?'

Elsa recalled the brash arrogance of the English aristocrat who was trying and failing to penetrate the American aristocracy of Hollywood. How she had instinctively disliked him.

'The first inkling came when I went over to California to talk to him about his Great-Aunt Constance, who as you know was a patron of sorts to Siddons. Despite what he suggested on the phone, Justin seemed to know virtually nothing and I was beginning to curse myself for having paid the airfare, though I must admit sitting by a swimming pool in Bel Air in the name of research is not entirely unpleasant, when he did let out something interesting. Constance, you see, was very beautiful and as an actress she'd had plenty of admirers. Justin remembered there was some suggestion of a slight scandal in the marriage – a messy infidelity or something of the kind. I was intrigued by that, but unfortunately he had no idea further except that the chap might have been an artist, which was meaningless because she knew a huge number of artists and bohemian types. I did of course wonder whether it could have been Siddons, but Justin said the one thing he was certain about was that the scandal ended after the first world war. He knew that because the aggravation of it and the effort of hushing it up was said to have contributed to the heart attack which killed Ralph Emberley. That of course meant his brother Edward, who was Justin's grandfather, inherited the country seat and the title and so, in time, when Justin tires of fooling about in America, he can come back here and inherit £50 million.'

He paused bitterly.

'But what did he tell you about Siddons?'

'Well, nothing directly. The conversation did nothing more than place a question mark in my mind. I came back here and got on with my work and everything went swimmingly for a while until my mother died.'

Oliver rolled over on to his back and stared at the ceiling.

'Do you remember me telling you about my mother's papers in the chest at Lower Binding? I showed you them the day we met. Well, she'd always been so strange, so insistent that I didn't read them until after her death. And I respected her wishes and didn't. But then soon after she died and I was midway through the biography, I went out there one weekend and began to trawl my way through them. There was an awful lot of stuff – letters, notes, a copy of Grandmother's will, investment and tax records and all that sort of thing, but I couldn't find anything to justify mother's peculiar attitude. It wasn't until I was shutting the box up in fact that I saw an extra partition in the lid, and I dare say you can guess what I found slipped in there.'

'The love poems?'

'Yes. Six of them – one marked with her initials, VS. They were hers, you see, Elsa.'

Elsa said nothing.

'But the poems weren't the surprise. It was the envelope they were sealed in. On the outside there was this brief line in my mother's handwriting saying something like "Encounters with my Father". I understood immediately.'

Elsa sat up. 'What did you understand?'

'Surely it's obvious, darling. All that sharp, adolescent anguish. She was commemorating a visit from the father she thought was dead.'

'She was writing about her father?'

'Yes of course. It confirmed what Justin had made me suspect. That Siddons deserted.'

Elsa did not want to stem the explanation that had begun to flood out. 'What did he do? Did he go back to Lower Binding straight away?'

'No. Not for some years. Violet must have been twelve or thirteen. From what I can gather when he did return briefly Emily took him in, but they didn't tell my mother who he was. It would have been a big shock for a young girl. More than that really – a huge trauma. I mean, I don't think we have any idea what desertion actually meant at a time when a whole generation of young men had given up their lives. A whole society was in bereavement. And for an officer to desert, well . . .'

'Not just an officer. A war hero,' added Elsa.

'Yes.' Oliver's voice was wry. His face, in profile, gave nothing away. 'Anyway, she evidently found out, or it was broken to her. And the reality obviously fell some way short of the myth. Valentine Siddons the deserter plainly didn't fit her idea of a father figure. It seems she couldn't – or wouldn't – accept him as he really was. He had to go.'

'And what about you? You were halfway through the book.'

'Exactly.' He turned back to her with gratitude in his eyes. 'I knew you'd understand. There was nothing I could do. It would have meant letting down so many people. I closed my mind to it. It was best to draw a veil over it.'

'Then Alan Evans came along?'

He sighed. 'Alan Evans. I curse the day I heard that name. He was a friend of Justin's, working on some ineffably dull thesis at UCLA. He'd written to me in the past about coming to discuss Valentine Siddons and I'd fobbed him off. Then I suppose my visit must have prompted Justin to reminisce about the Constance Emberley connection, and he thought it might make a nice little adjunct to his thesis. "War Hero's secret lover" sort of thing. Nothing more than that, really. Unfortunately, when he actually came over here you were obliging enough to offer him a job and let him get on with his researches in depth while paying the rent. When I found out about the film, I finally threw in the towel and realised I was going to have to meet him. And what a pain he was, so boring, so American . . .' Here Oliver assumed a west coast accent and rolled his eyes. ' "But surely Dr Eastway, if we go back for a moment to the second stanza of 'The Enchantress' we see that the poem could only have been addressed to Constance . . ." And as it turned out he was also a thief.'

'He stole the poems?'

'Right. Do you remember you said something about how easy it must be to steal from the cottage? Well obviously the same thought occurred to him. But I went one further and lent him the key. Needless to say he went there, opened up the chest, found the poems and disappeared with them. I didn't discover until he turned up for what he mendaciously described as a script meeting and sprang on me that he had irrefutable proof that my grandfather had been a deserter. He'd come to exactly the same conclusions as I had. It wasn't pleasant, I can tell you.'

He was bending back his knuckles rhythmically. It was a nervous habit she'd noticed before. He seemed entirely serene until you noticed this digital masochism, the tiny violence in his lap. 'So what did you do?'

'Well I wasn't sure exactly what he wanted from me. An admission, I suppose, that I knew. An official corroboration to stand up the story. So in best academic fashion I delayed and fudged. Ridiculed the poems, the theory, the method, and the conclusion. And privately panicked. But then the next thing I knew, I got a call from you saying he'd vanished into thin air.'

'So why didn't you just let it drop? Why did you stay involved in the film and agree to meet me?'

He gave her a rueful smile and rubbed the fine stubble peppering his chin. 'You regret that, do you? Well, it was a fine judgement. But Evans had told me that you had bought into the orthodox Siddons story very heavily and I thought with a film behind me too, it would be so much harder to challenge the official version. And then when I met you my decision was totally justified.'

Despite herself, Elsa's heart jumped. 'Why?'

'You were so . . . admiring, so unquestioning.'

Bitterly she said: 'So you decided to seduce me?'

'It wasn't as simple as that. Not at first. But things got more difficult. Do you remember that night we met in Dino's?'

'Mmmn.'

'I'd just been to see my publishers. They'd heard on the grapevine about another Siddons biography coming out. I guessed before they could tell me that it was Evans' work of course, billed – rather crudely I have to say – as telling "the real story of Valentine Siddons". Obviously the man's no historian. The blurb, if I remember rightly, was promising fresh documentary evidence to support a sensational new theory about one of the first world war's finest poets. It was quite awful. My lot were threatening to pulp my work.'

At this point he put his head in his hands and massaged

his brow. He looked old, the folds of his face drawn down with the little hooks of gravity. Instinctively, Elsa squeezed his shoulder. He looked up gratefully.

'Then, amazingly, that same night, came my salvation. You took me back to your flat and showed me the poems. I recognised them immediately. I couldn't believe it. I knew as long as you had the poems, and I had you, I'd be safe.'

'Because I was just a foolish little girl who would keep quiet and believe anything you said.'

Oliver turned away from her and looked out at the blank hills beyond, blurred by a soft drizzle. He resumed a soothing, reasonable tone, as though he was conducting a tutorial.

'Not foolish, Elsa, no. You just weren't as enquiring as Evans. You were totally on the wrong track in believing they were Siddons' poems. Astonishingly you seemed quite unable to realise they were written by a young woman. And besides,' he reached a hand towards her but she did not respond so he let it drop on the bed, 'other complications arose with you.'

She shifted away from him. 'Did you hear from Evans again?'

'Rather amusingly, considering he'd made himself so elusive, he materialised out of nowhere once the wretched poems disappeared. He realised you were the girl who got into his flat and having somehow heard about our . . . association . . . he thought I'd put you up to it. He was livid. So he tried to burgle your office to get them back. That obviously didn't work and after he'd done everything he could think of to find out more about my grandfather, including going down to Kent to pester some old friends of his, he turned up in Oxford and threatened me. I gave nothing away, he stormed off and as far as I know, he's now back in America. And fortunately, without any of his much-vaunted documentary evidence, it looks like the book he's trying to flog is dead in the water. Which reminds me.' He got up and placed the leather book containing Siddons' life story inside his suitcase, then locked it.

Elsa watched him from across the room. 'Did you know about that too, then?'

'Not at all. That's all thanks to you, darling. As soon as I heard you were coming here, I guessed it would be something to do with the Harvey bookshop. Clever of you to find out about it. Anyway, I nipped down the motorway and it turned out to be more useful than I could possibly have imagined. Reading my grandfather's life story has filled in all those annoying little gaps. With just the poems to go on, the whole picture was still hopelessly distant and unattainable. It was like a broken mosaic, with some events left irreversibly blank. Now I suppose I know the whole truth.'

CHAPTER TWENTY-THREE

VALENTINE HAD KEPT quiet on his way back to England. Had anyone asked his identity he might have broken down, but as it was he was processed quite simply. Not knowing where to go, he found his way to Garsington and for a while was sheltered there. The secret proved surprisingly easy to keep. The very small circle who knew of it did not interrogate him. Those that did not know were not told. It was not like now, Oliver said grimly, when secrets are so hard to keep, with the press and other people truffling over events as though the exposure of hypocrisy was the only moral imperative left to us since the death of God.

Elsa fixed her eyes blankly on the damask curtains shuffling in an edgy spring breeze. 'And what about Constance Emberley, then?'

'That's strange. He seemed to blame her for everything. Obviously there had been some kind of relationship or affair because Ronald Foxley tried to blackmail the Viscount over it after the war. Wrote to the press and circulated nasty rumours in their social circles. If he'd known Siddons was still alive it would have been even worse. He had to be dispensed with. Constance had him sent off somewhere, some institution for veterans with neurasthenia, though he didn't noticeably have the entrance requirements. But he was homosexual, and a liability, and he had made some powerful enemies.'

'But if it's true, what you say, why did Valentine end up down here?'

Oliver turned towards her.

'Funnily enough that's the only part of the story he doesn't really explain. He continually says Constance "betrayed" him. Ottoline thought him difficult and possessive. It seems he was asked to leave Garsington. Luckily for him Amarine Harvey was loyal and offered him a quiet place. Though she did suggest he used Fleming's name.'

'And did Constance betray him?'

'God knows. She moved down to London after Ralph died and got very involved in literary and theatrical circles there. She hankered after a return to acting and rather wanted to get into films, according to Justin, but she was past it of course. A bit pathetic, really. In later life she had a rather peripatetic existence from what I can gather, staying in all sorts of grand hotels in Paris, Rome, Monaco, Geneva. She ended up taking a place in the south of France. But whether she tired of Valentine, or took up with someone else, or found the class difference between them too great, I don't know.'

'Perhaps it was the age gap.'

Oliver eyed her keenly. 'Would that matter? Who can say? That's one thing we'll never know. Either way I'll feel dreadful about destroying this book. Academics hold it a cardinal sin to cremate a primary text, you know. God, what a mess. I'm so glad I can tell you. It means everything that you understand.'

With a sigh of relief he moved towards her and suddenly his mouth was on hers, with bruising, pleading kisses. Elsa found herself opening up to him instinctively, as smooth and dispassionate as an automatic door.

'Good girl.'

He rose and she felt the hardness of him over her. He took her face in his hands but his embrace, which had once seemed to Elsa so wonderfully secure, now felt for the first time like something else. Like a prison, perhaps. But it was a benign prison and one whose walls she would barely notice. His eyes searched hers, his voice low and warm.

'It's not too much to ask that you keep this secret, is it, Elsa? I love you. I want us to have a child together. We couldn't let the past destroy us, could we?'

She longed to agree. But he was right. Secrets were hard to keep. She felt the corrupting weight of the confidence that had been passed to her, heavy with the grief and anxiety of the years in which it had been carried close, like a deadly growth, in the hearts of the women who concealed it. Suddenly she yearned for someone on whom history did not hang so heavily, someone bound by hopes for the future, rather than the ties of the past. She felt the tears slipping down her cheek.

'What about the poems? Aren't you worried what I could do with them?'

'You haven't got them, I'm afraid. I collected them from your flat yesterday and destroyed them.'

She gasped. 'I could still tell people about it.'

'Your word against mine? I'd discredit you, darling. In every way I could. Don't doubt me, I know what's for the best.'

He shook his head and smiled. 'But it won't come to that. I'm telling you, Elsa, it's past now. A closed chapter.'

'Oh Oliver.' She was almost talking to herself. 'The past is never gone, though. It's there all the time, isn't it?'

*   *   *

Elsa lay stiffly, cramped in the corner of the bed from where she had shunned the rites of reconciliation. Beside her, icy inches apart, Oliver had slipped into an estranged sleep. Her skin rigid with tension, Elsa watched the clock's arthritic ticking as the edges of the day darkened and light began to seep from the sky. If she did not leave now, it meant spending the night in this place.

It took a few moments to slip noiselessly from the bed and gather up her discarded clothes. As she turned the door handle she looked back at him and his face, finally relaxed, caught at her heart.

She walked quickly down the narrow cobbles that led to Hay-on-Wye's market-place, breathing in great gulps of the sweet dusk air, pungent with the fragrance of the nearby fields after rain. Don't let him wake up until I've gone, she whispered to herself, don't let him find me. The smell of cooking from a restaurant door assaulted her and she realised she was beginning to feel light-headed with hunger. But there was no time to stop and eat.

She was still far from her car when she heard the slap of the footsteps running behind her. She quickened her step, but the approaching pound of feet was already overtaking her. Quietly she felt something die within her, as though she was already a prisoner. She turned with resignation.

CHAPTER TWENTY-THREE

'Elsa, thank goodness I've found you.'

It was Simon. His eyes glowed with relief.

'Look, I was worried about you. You left in such a rage. And Michelle said you were probably coming here. I got the train but the second I reached the bookshop and found you were gone, I realised there was practically no chance I'd find you. I've been roaming round this place all day. I was just about to catch the last train back.'

Emotion, or surprise, rendered her momentarily speechless.

'Elsa, I know you're angry with me.' He stepped forward and put a hand on her arm. 'But I have to explain something . . .'

'Is it about the film?'

'Huh? Oh, partly. If you're not happy about this film, then we won't do it. We're partners, right, after all?'

He pushed his tangled hair out of his eyes and stood there, panting. He looked so young and earnest. Elsa had forgotten their row entirely.

'It's not that I'm not happy about the film,' she said. 'I just want it to be . . . truthful. True to the facts, I mean. Whatever they are. There's just so much more to say now. But look, can we leave this place? I might as well tell you what I've found out.'

Telling Simon was a relief. They walked out towards the outskirts of the town, to where the last houses met the encroaching fields. Articulating her conversation with Oliver as a narrative seemed to lend it some finality. Never had Elsa so relished the past tense. When she finished, the story hung heavily in the air between them.

'Now Oliver's destroyed the poems, there's nothing to prove Siddons came back at all.'

'Not necessarily,' Simon said pensively. 'If you drive us back to London, I've got something to show you.'

CHAPTER TWENTY-FOUR

AFTER STOPPING FOR a late dinner in Bristol, they drove east all night. By the time they reached the outskirts of London, the first glimmers of a purposeful dawn were prodding the streets into routine suburban tumult. Milk vans buzzed along like grounded beetles, litter scurried busily down the gutter, paperboys disseminated information through each letter-box's tiny yawn. As the background activity of civilisation rumbled on like white noise, the gurgling digestion of some great sleeping beast, Elsa felt the sadness lifting off her. She ought to be exhausted, but it was invigorating to re-enter the city's embrace, to see the everyday world going by as if it had been there all along.

'Your place or mine?'

Simon had never used the cliché before, but as it slipped from his mouth he was struck by the full force of its daring originality, its aching balance between implied sexual promise and request. He looked across at Elsa to see if she thought the same, but she only said levelly:

'Well your place is further, but I suppose it had better be there if you're going to show me what you've found.'

Simon's flat was at the top of a tall Victorian block in a back street off the Strand. Elsa was about to complain at the aerobic effort required on the five flights of stairs, but instead she gazed around her in surprise. It was not at all what she had expected. It was tidy, of course, but she had envisaged something monkish and austere. Instead the cosy attic rooms were saturated with colour. Battered leather furniture, the colour of burnished conkers, stood on rich red Persian rugs. On a small table strident yellow daffodils burst from a vase and from above them a high garret skylight brought the bright sun blazing into the room. The walls were crammed with photographs, paintings and sketches. Beyond the window the London skyline unrolled, a random roofscape of tiles and aerials where giant cranes stretched with silent, balletic poise. The difference between this place and the gloomy cell she had imagined Simon inhabiting made Elsa wonder what else he could be concealing. As he put on some Mozart and disappeared into the kitchen, she pottered around and then ventured into the bedroom.

To her secret relief, a quick glance revealed none of the accoutrements of female cohabitation. There was however a lone picture hanging significantly above the bed and Elsa could not resist a look. It was a freckle-faced young woman on a beach, dark hair escaping from a headscarf, grin fixed bravely into the teeth of an English seaside wind. She looked not exactly beautiful, but happy. The kind of person you might well want to know. As she studied it, Elsa felt Simon approach behind her.

'Who's that?'

'My mother. Cornwall, 1963. I painted it from a photograph. I don't really remember her.' They stood for a moment in awkward silence, then he said: 'Come and eat.'

In the tiny kitchen he had prepared a plate of bacon, eggs, hash browns and French toast. Elsa, whose previous image of Simon might have had him gnawing ascetically on a hunk of dry bread, was amazed to find he could cook with some panache. They sat and drank strong Italian coffee, *The Marriage of Figaro* floating exuberantly round them. As Elsa looked at Simon's face, lost in the music's joyful geometry, she realised she understood the schoolgirlish devotion of his admirers. His grey eyes caught her contemplation.

'Simon . . .'

'What?'

'Oh nothing. It sounds terrible, really. I was going to say there's another side to you. From what I usually see. But probably it was just me being blinkered.'

'Oh I do have another side. Several in fact,' he smiled drily. 'I'm virtually cubic, you'll find.' Jumping up he added: 'But before we get on to my hidden depths, let me show you what I've found.'

He brought over *Between the Lines* and turned to the reproduction of the landscape, with its unassuming house and church and the windbreak of trees stretching out of the picture like an arrow into an uncertain future.

'There you are. There's the proof that Valentine Siddons returned. Art never lies.'

'Where? I can't see it.'

'You will if you look carefully. That's the Siddons watercolour that Andrew Winelees sold in the church fête. A signed picture of Lower Binding. The place is quite recognisable, though it isn't identified.'

'So . . .'

'It's a picture of poplars you see . . .' His words were tumbling over each other.

'I don't see . . .'

'Nor would most people. Nor did I, at first. But as soon as I saw that picture reproduced in the anthology there was something about it that nagged at me. Then I realised that Valentine Siddons could never have painted The Poplars.'

'Why?'

'Because remember, those poplars were not planted until after the war. They were put there in his memory, in memory of the men who died in Flanders. The only way Valentine Siddons could have seen them was if he returned to his home after the war.'

* * *

They decided to take a walk while they discussed the future of their film. It was the start of the Easter weekend and the vacational heart of London lay unnaturally still. A man swept a litter of fallen blossom with tetchy haste as though tidying the aftermath of irresponsible partying. Outside the National Gallery newspaper stands were proclaiming another blow in Britain's latest bureaucratic wrangle with Europe. Two of the tabloids said it was war.

'Bang goes our chance of a grant from the European Film Foundation,' said Simon.

'Listen, I'm not saying we shouldn't accept the offer from Pluto Films,' said Elsa slowly. 'I just think if we do, we have to tell the truth. We'll have to reshape the film entirely, looking at Valentine Siddons from a totally new angle.'

'The desertion, you mean?'

'Not just that. I mean we can't ignore it, of course, but I'd like to rework it. To tell the daughter's story.'

There was a long pause. Then Simon said noncommittally: 'Eckstein warned me we'd run into problems doing a period film. They say you always get these little difficulties with detail.'

'So you'll talk to him?'

He sighed. 'OK. If you're sure that's what you want and it doesn't cause you any . . . personal problems.'

'And if it does?'

'Don't worry about any of that.'

Down by the Embankment they stopped to gaze into the Thames as it slid alongside them, rust coloured and blue veined like an upturned tongue, its surface pitted by a stiff breeze. Seabirds ducked and burrowed in the moving water, engaged in an endless and apparently fruitless search. Simon leaned on the stone balustrade like a loner in an all-night bar and glared at the oily depths as if they might part and reveal to him the way to make a decisive move. He simply couldn't wait any longer. In the chill air he felt the edges of his skin tingle, marking out the ineradicable boundaries of himself. He thought of all the reasons that relationships were bound to fail. Affections were shifting, transitory things. Betrayal was commonplace. Rejection hurt. Misunderstanding, sexual boredom, ennui. The choppy waves brought into his mind Matthew Arnold's 'unplumbed, salt, estranging sea'. The space preventing the true union of lovers, dooming them to eternal spiritual isolation. But what made poets a reliable authority on relationships? You might as well listen to Alison Joliffe. Or his father.

'How's Norman?'

He started. It was as though she could read his mind. She gazed at him and her eyes, which he saw at close range were flecked with streaks of gold, crinkled enchantingly at the edges. Instinctively he reached across and brushed the strands of windswept hair from her face. Then, in one small step, which was also a giant leap for their business partnership, he drew her shoulders to him and kissed her. She did not object. In fact, he had to admit to himself when he analysed the moment later, she definitely responded. A confetti of raindrops scattered across them and she shifted closer, as if seeking sanctuary in his sinewy frame. He clasped her tighter, feeling the forces of sexual chemistry working their long-awaited reaction with explosive warmth.

Eventually she pulled away and surveyed his face. 'It's nice to see you smile. You should try it more often.'

'That's your male romantic archetype for you. They're not supposed to smile. Not according to English literature, I understand.'

'Don't believe everything you read.' She pressed closer against him. 'Why don't we go back to your flat?'

Again he hesitated. But this time it was an exuberant deliberation, a deliciously delayed gratification. 'Well, I don't think it's a very good idea.'

It was a new-found pleasure to tease her. Her dark eyes widened. She was as startled as a cat. 'Why?'

He kissed her again. 'Because you're meeting your father for lunch.'

She flinched as though physically struck. 'My father?'

'He's over from Germany apparently on some job. He rang the office. Said he'd been trying to get hold of you for ages but every time he rang your home the answerphone was on. He seems to have some objection to talking on them. Perhaps he thought you were avoiding him. Anyway, he left a message with me. Thank God I remembered.'

'What does he want?'

'Funnily enough I didn't ask. Does your own father need a reason to see you?'

She paused, then said slowly: 'I don't know if I'll go.'

'Of course you must go.'

'Would you come too?'

'Sure. But only if you agree to meet Norman some time.'

'Oh but I want to get to know him. Is he anything like you?'

'We used to be alike,' Simon reflected, taking her arm as they turned to go. 'But not any more.'

All Fourth Estate books are available at your local bookshop or newsagent, or can be ordered direct from the publisher.

Indicate the number of copies required and quote the author and title.

Send cheque/eurocheque/postal order (Sterling only), made payable to Book Service by Post, to:

Fourth Estate Books
Book Service By Post
PO Box 29, Douglas
I-O-M, IM99 1BQ.

Or phone: 01624 675137

Or fax: 01624 670923

Or e-mail: bookshop@enterprise.net

Alternatively pay by Access, Visa or Mastercard

Card number: ☐☐☐☐☐☐☐☐☐☐☐☐☐☐☐☐

Expiry date   ....

Signature   ....

Post and packing is free in the UK. Overseas customers please allow £1.00 per book for post and packing.

Name   ....

Address   ....

....

....

Please allow 28 days for delivery. Please tick the box if you do not wish to receive any additional information. ☐

Prices and availability subject to change without notice.